OMNIVM
LVX
CIVIVM
MDCCCLII
MDCCC
LXXVIII
BOSTON
PUBLIC
LIBRARY

A TUPOLEV TOO FAR

BOOKS BY BRIAN ALDISS

Remembrance Day 1993
Dracula Unbound 1991
Forgotten Life 1989
Trillion Year Spree 1986
Seasons in Flight 1986
Helliconia Winter 1985
Helliconia Summer 1983
Helliconia Spring 1982
An Island Called Moreau 1981
Life in the West 1980
A Rude Awakening 1978
Enemies of the System 1978
Last Orders 1977
The Malacia Tapestry 1977
The Eighty-Minute Hour 1974
Frankenstein Unbound 1973
A Soldier Erect 1971
The Hand-Reared Boy 1970
Barefoot in the Head 1970
Report on Probability A 1969
Cryptozoic 1968
The Dark Light Years 1964
Greybeard 1964
The Long Afternoon of Earth 1962
Galaxies Like Grains of Sand 1960
Starship 1959
No Time Like Tomorrow 1959

BRIAN ALDISS

A TUPOLEV TOO FAR

AND OTHER STORIES

St. Martin's Press
New York

A Tupolev Too Far first appeared in *Other Edens 3*, 1989; *Ratbird* first appeared in *New Worlds 2*; *FOAM* first appeared in *New Worlds 1*, 1991; *Summertime was Nearly Over* first appeared in *The Ultimate Frankenstein*, 1990; *Better Morphosis* first appeared in *Magazine of Fantasy & Science Fiction*, June 1991; *Three Degrees Over* first appeared in *Dark Fantasies*, 1989; *A Life of Matter and Death* first appeared in *Interzone*, June 1990; *A Day in the Life of a Galactic Empire* first appeared in *Zenith*, 1989; *Confluence* first appeared in *Punch*, 1967; *Confluence Revisited* first appeared in *Other Edens 2*, 1988; *North of the Abyss* first appeared in *Magazine of Fantasy & Science Fiction*, October 1989; *Alphabet of Ameliorating Hope* first appeared in *New Pathways*, 1992.

ISBN 0-312-10565-7

First published in Great Britain by HarperCollins*Publishers*.

First U.S. Edition: February 1994
10 9 8 7 6 5 4 3 2 1

SHORT STORIES

When someone in the audience asked how
I saw my short stories, I offered them
Antarctica. The ice shelf grinding
Forward with the century
Carrying freights of fossil Bronze Age snow
Until a thousand flaws united.
Then with huge mammalian groans
The burdened stone thing calved.

You know (I told my listeners, hoping
They might), those icebergs there are frequently
Over a hundred kilometres long –
As big as Monte Carlo. Solemnly
They drift beyond the Weddell Sea
Like Matterhorns breasting the South Atlantic.
Riding out gales shaved by the wind and warmth
Heading north for Rio and Capricorn.

But as they're sighting the Malvinas
They suffer the environment.
These old cathedrals of the cold
Have shrunk. They'd go into your gin
And tonic. So they're lost to human ken
But for some months they have a real existence
And scientists keep tabs on them.
They're mad and lovely while they last.

That's how (I told the audience)
I see my stories. They formed part of me.
Those who sight them in those desolate
Latitudes of publishing sometimes
Are awed. They praise a colour
Or an unexpected shape.
They seldom hear the groans of birth.
A year, a year, and they are gone.

The audience clapped uncertainly
Then asked if I kept office hours.

Brian Aldiss
OXFORD, 1993

CONTENTS

A TUPOLEV TOO FAR

I KNOW you want fiction for this anthology, but perhaps for once you would consider a true story. I offer a thought in extenuation for what is to follow: that this story is so fantastic and unbelievable it might as well be science fiction.

Well, it would be SF except for the fact that there is no scientific explanation for the bizarre central occurrence – or none beyond the way bizarre events occur with regularity, as vouched for by Charles Fort, Arthur Koestler, Carl Jung, Jesus Christ and other historic figures.

Unfortunately, the story is not only bizarre but raunchy. It is the sort of tale men tell each other late at night, in a bar in Helsinki or somewhere similar. It has no moral and precious little morality.

Sex and lust come into it. And murder and incest and brigandage of the worst sort. There are some insights to be gleaned regarding the differing natures of men and women, if that is any consolation.

Another thing I have to add. This is not my story. I heard it from a friend. One of those friends you know off and on throughout life. He always enjoyed talking about the bad times.

We'll call him Ron Wallace. And this is what he told me.

This helping of agony took place in 1989, which had turned out to be a better year for Ron than he expected – and for much of Europe. He had been unemployed for a while. Now he had a good job with a West Country firm who made safes and security equipment employing the latest electronic devices. Ron was their overseas salesman. The Russians approached his company, who were sending Ron out to Moscow as a result. The managing director, who was a good guy, briefed Ron before he left, and he set off on the flight from Penge Airport in good fettle. His wife Stephanie saw him off.

Ron flew Royal Russian Airlines. Which, after TransAm, is regarded as the world's best airline. Plenty of leg room, little engine noise, pretty hostesses.

It was a brief flight. On the way, he picked up an in-flight magazine which had an illustrated article on the Russian Commonwealth and on modern Moscow in particular. There were photographs of Czar Nicholas III with the Czarina opening the grand new Governance of Nations building, designed by Richard Rogers, on White Square, and of the redecorated Metro in St Petersburg. Ron dozed off while leafing through such commonplaces and was woken by a terrific bang.

The aircraft was passing through a ferocious storm, or so it seemed. Lightning flashed outside and the airliner began to fall. It shook violently as it fell.

Ron sat tight. He remembered his grandfather's account of the terrible firestorm which had partially destroyed Berlin in July 1914. His grandfather had been working in Berlin at the time and always talked about the experience. The old man claimed that was the first occasion on which all Europe had united in a major rescue operation; it had changed history, he claimed.

These thoughts and less pleasant ones ran through Ron's mind as the plane fell earthwards.

'I'll never screw Steff again – or any other woman,' he said aloud. To his mind, that was the biggest bugbear regarding death: no screwing.

For an instant the plane was bathed in unnatural light. Then all became calm, as if nothing had happened.

The plane pulled from its dive. Cabin staff in their white uniforms moved down the aisles, soothing the passengers and bringing them drinks.

Everyone started talking to each other. But only for a few minutes. After which, a silence fell over them; they became uncannily quiet as they tried to digest their narrow escape from disaster.

Twenty minutes later, they landed at Sheremeteivo Airport.

Ron was surprised to find how drab and small everything was. He was surprised, too, to see how many men were in uniform – unfamiliar uniforms, too, with mysterious red stars on their caps. He had no idea what the stars stood for, unless for Mars, on which planet the Russians had just landed.

Of course, Ron had got down as much whisky as he could, following the alarming incident on the plane. His perceptions were possibly a little awry. All the same, he could not help noticing that most of the planes on the ground belonged to an airline called Aeroflot, of which he had never heard. There were no Royal Russian Airline planes to be seen.

When, at the luggage carousel, he asked a fellow passenger about Aeroflot, the man replied, 'You ask too many questions round here, you find yourself in the gulag.'

Ron began to feel rather cold and shaky. Something had happened. He did not know what.

The whole airport, the reception area, the customs area, gave no sign of the high-tech sheen for which Russia was renowned. He felt a sense of disorientation, which was calmed slightly when he was met by his Russian contact, Vassili Rugorsky, who made him welcome.

As they passed out through the foyer of the building, Ron observed a large framed portrait dominating the exits where he might have expected to see a picture of the graceful young Czar. Instead, the portrait showed a thick-set, almost neckless man with glittering eyes, a mottled complexion and an unpleasant expression.

'Who's that?' he asked.

Vassili looked curiously at Ron, as if expecting him to be joking.

'Comrade Leonid Brezhnev, of course,' he said.

Ron dared ask nothing more, but his sense of unease deepened. Who was Brezhnev?

He was shown to a black car. Soon they were driving through the city. Ron could hardly believe what he saw. Moscow was always billed as one of Europe's great pleasure cities, with smart people, and a vivid nightlife staged amid elegant buildings – fruit of Russia's great renaissance in the early 1940s, when the Czarina Elizabeta Ship Canal had linked Baltic with Black Sea. Here Parisian panache thrived among Parisian-type boulevards. Or so the legend had it. As they wound through a dreary suburb, he saw lines of dowdy people queueing at shops hardly worthy of the name. The buildings themselves were grey and grubby.

Red flags and banners flew everywhere. He could not understand. It was as if the whole place had been hit by revolution.

But the men he dealt with were agreeable enough. Ron prided himself on his powers of negotiation; his opposite numbers were cautious but amiable. He gathered to his mild astonishment that they regarded British technology to be in advance of their own.

'Of course, the KGB have all latest Western equipment,' one man said jokingly as the contracts were signed. Ron did not like to ask what KGB stood for; he was clearly expected to know. It was all peculiar. He wondered if the electric storm he had flown through had affected his mind in some way.

It was on his second day that the contracts were signed. The first day was given over to discussion, when Ron often felt that the Russians were pumping him. At one point, when he had occasion to mention the Czarina Elizabeta Ship Canal, they all looked blank.

Even more disconcertingly, the Russians asked him how he liked being in the Soviet Union, and similar remarks. Ron belonged to an electronics union himself, but had never heard of a Soviet Union. He could almost fancy he had arrived in the wrong country.

Nevertheless, the contracts were signed on the second day, on terms favourable to Ron's company. They were witnessed in the ministry at three in the afternoon, following which the parties involved got down to some serious drinking. As well as Russian champagne there were vodka, wine and a good Georgian brandy. Ron was an experienced drinker. He arrived back at the Hotel Moskva, contract in briefcase, just after 6.30, still more or less in control of his wits.

I'm trying to tell you this story as Ron Wallace told it to me. When he came to describe the Hotel Moskva I had to interrupt him. I've stayed in that hotel a couple of times. Once I took the Camberwell–Moscow Trans-Continent Express on a package tour which included three nights in that very hotel. It was the pleasantest place in which I have ever stayed, light and airy, and full of elegant people. In fact, a few too many of the Russian aristocracy for my simple tastes.

It was not the dowdiness and gloom of the hotel about which Ron chiefly complained, or the uninteresting food but the lack of beautiful women. Ron was always rather a ladies' man.

An old-fashioned band was playing old-fashioned music in the hotel restaurant. It was a period piece, like the hotel itself. He could not credit it. The dining room was cavernous, with stained-glass windows at one end, and a faded style of furnishing. The band lurched from Beatles' hits to the 'Destiny' waltz. The place, he said, was a cross between the Café Royal in the 1920s and Salisbury Cathedral in the 1420s.

As Ron told his tale, I kept thinking about the concept of alternative worlds. Although the idea is at first fantastic, there is, after all, a well-attested theory which says that whatever is imagined moves nearer to reality. Edmund Husserl, in his pioneering work on phenomenology, *Investigations in Logic,* shows how little the psychological nature of historical processes are understood. Turning points in history – generatives, in Husserl's term – occur in greater or lesser modes related to quantal thought impulses which are themselves subject to random factors. The logical structures on which such points depend exist independently of their psychological correlates, so that we can expect subjective experiences to generate a multiplicity of effects, each of which bears equivalent objective reality; thus, whether or not signatures are appended to a treaty, for example, is dependent on various epistemological assumptions of transient nature, while the results of signing or non-signing may be multiplex generatives, giving rise to a spectrum of alternative objectivities, varying from slight to immense, affecting the lives of many people over considerable areas of space and time. I know this to be so because I read it in a book.

So it seemed clear to me – though not to Ron, who is no intellectual and consequently does not believe in variant subjective realities – that the electric storm which hit the Tupolev had been a Husserl's generative, causing Ron to switch objectivities, and materialize in a parallel version of objectivity along the spectrum, where history had at some point taken a decided turn for the worse.

Feeling a little weary, Ron decided not to go up to his room immediately, but to eat and then retreat to bed, in preparation for his early flight home the following morning.

Diners were few. They could scarcely be distinguished from the diners in a provincial Pan-European town, Belgrade, say, or Boheimkirchen, or Bergen. There was none of the glitter he had expected. And the service was terribly slow.

The maître d' had shown Ron to a small table, rather distant from the nearest light globe. From this vantage point, he looked the clientele over while awaiting his soup.

At the table nearest to him, two orientals sat drinking champagne. Their mood was subdued. He judged them to be Korean. Ron spared hardly a glance for the man. As he told me, 'I could hardly take my eyes off the woman. Mainly I saw her in half-profile. A real beauty, clear-cut features, hawkish nose, dark eyes, red lips . . . Terrific.'

When she smiled at her partner and raised her glass to her lips she was a vision of seduction. Ron dropped his napkin on the floor in order to take a look at her legs. She was wearing a long black evening dress.

He said his one thought was, 'If only her husband would get lost . . . '

His desires turned naturally to sex. But he had sworn an oath to his wife, Steff, on the subject of fidelity. As he was averting his eyes from the Korean couple, the woman turned to look at him. Even across the space between their tables, the stare was strong and disturbing. Ron could not tell what was in that stare. It made him curious, while at the same time repelling him.

He took a paperback book of crossword puzzles from his briefcase and tried to study a puzzle he had already started, but could not concentrate.

A memory came back to him of his first love. Then, how innocent had been her gaze. He could recall it perfectly. It had been a gaze of love and trust; all the sweetness of youth, of innocence, was in it. It could not be recovered. No one would ever look at him in that fashion again.

The Korean couple had decided something between them. The Korean man rose from the table, laid down his napkin, and came across to Ron.

'My God,' Ron thought, 'the little bugger's going to tell me not to ogle his wife . . . '

The Korean was short and sturdy. Perhaps he was in his mid-thirties. His face was solemn, his eyes dark, his whole body held rigidly, and it was a rigid bow he made to Ron Wallace.

'You are English?' he asked, speaking in English with a heavy accent. 'We saw you dining here last night and made enquiries. I am on official duties in the Soviet Union, a diplomat from the Democratic People's Republic of North Korea.' He gave his name.

'What do you want? I'm having dinner.'

'Meals are a source of fear to me. I can never rid my mind of one dinner in particular when I was a child of five. Someone from political motives poisoned my father. A servant was held responsible, but we never found out who was paying the servant. The servant did not tell, despite severe torture. My father rose from his place, screamed like a wounded horse, spun about, and fell head first into a dish – well, in our dialect it's *pruang hai*, I suppose a sort of kedgeree, though with little green chillies. He struggled a moment, sending rice all over us frightened children. Then he was still, and naturally the meal was ruined.'

Ron Wallace took a sip of mineral water. Although the Korean was white and trembling, Ron would not ask him to sit down.

The Korean continued. 'I should explain that there were four of us children. Three of us were triplets, and there was a younger sibling. My mother was demoralized by my father's death. I have to confess she was of the bourgeois class. Never a very stable personality, for she was an actress, she suffered illusions. One starry night, she jumped from a tall window through the glass roof of the conservatory to the ground. A theory was that she had seen the stars reflected in the glass and thought the conservatory was the Yalu river. This was never proved.

'We children were handed over into the care of an uncle and aunt who ran a rather poor pig and sorghum farm in the mountainous area of our land. My uncle was a bully, given to drink and criminality. He committed sexual atrocities on us poor defenceless children, and even on his farm animals. You can imagine how we suffered.'

He looked fixedly at Ron, but Ron made no reply. Ron was aware of the avid gaze of the Korean's partner, back at the table, smiling yet not smiling in his direction.

'Our one consolation was the school to which we were sent. It was a long walk away, down the mountain, a cruel trial for us in winter months when the snow was deep. But the school was run by a remarkable Englishman, a Mr Holmberg. I have been told that Holmberg is not an English name. I cannot explain how that came about. In the world struggle, there are many anomalies.

'Mr Holmberg had many skills and was unfailingly kind. He taught us something of the world. He also explained to us the mysteries of sex, and kindly drew pictures of the female sexual organs on the blackboard, with the fallopian tubes in red, despite a shortage of chalk.

'The day came when the ninth birthday approached for us three poor orphans. There we sat in the little classroom, stinking of sorghum and pigs, and this wonderful Englishman presented us with a marvellous gift, a kite he had made himself. It was such a kite as Koreans made in dynastic times to carry the spirits of the dead, very strong, very large and well decorated. It was, for us, the first gift we had received since our father was poisoned. You can imagine our delight.'

He paused.

'Where's my bloody boeuf stroganoff?' asked Ron, looking round for a waitress.

Greatly though he desired something to eat, he desired much more the absence of this little man who stood by his table, telling his awful life story unbidden. Ron had never heard of the Democratic People's Republic of North Korea, and did not much want to. It was another department of the terrible world into which he had fallen.

He tried to think of pleasant English things – Ovaltine, Bob Monkhouse, cream teas, Southend, the National Anthem, Agatha Christie, the *Sun*, Saxby's pork pies – but they were drowned out by the Korean's doomed narrative.

'We had a problem. We feared that our cruel uncle would steal the kite from us. We resolved to fly it on the way home from school, to enjoy that pleasure at least once. Halfway up the mountain was a good eminence, with a view of the distant ocean and a strong up-draught. The three of us hung on to the string and up went the grand kite, sailing into the sky. How we cheered. Just for a moment, we had no cares.

'Our little brother begged to be allowed to hold the kite. As we handed him the string, we heard the sound of shots being fired farther up the mountain. Our anxieties were easily awoken. In those lawless times, bandits were everywhere. Alas, one can pay for one moment's carelessness with a lifetime's regret. We turned to find that the kite was carrying away our little brother. His hand was caught in the loop in the string and up he was going. He cried. We cried. We waved.

'Helpless, we watched him about to be dashed against the rocks. Fortunately, he cleared them as the kite gained height. It drifted towards the north-east, and the ocean and the south-eastern coast of the Soviet Union. That was the last we saw of him. It is not impossible that even now he lives, and speaks and thinks in the Russian language.'

The Korean bowed his head for a moment, while Ron tried to attract the attention of a distant waitress, who had lapsed into immobility, as if also overcome by the tragic tale.

'We were upset by this incident. We had lost our valued gift, and a rather annoying little brother as well. We fell to punching each other, each claiming the other two were to blame. Then we went home, up the rest of the mountain track.

'My uncle was in his favourite apple tree, quiet for once and not swearing at us. He hung head down, a rope round his ankles securing him to one of the branches of the tree. His hands were tied and he was fiercely gagged. His face was so red that we burst out laughing.

'Since he was still alive, we had a splendid time spinning him round. He could not cry out but he looked pretty funny. Then we got rakes and spades from the shed and battered him to death.

'Our aunt had been thrown in the pond. Many and dreadful were the atrocities committed on her body. We dragged her from the water but, so near to death was she, we put her back where we had found her.

'The house had been looted by the bandits whose firing we had heard. Those were lawless days before our great leader, Kim Il Sung, took over control of our destinies. We were happy to have the place to ourselves, especially since my uncle's two huge sons had been shot, bayoneted and beheaded by the bandits.

'Unfortunately, the bandits returned in the night, since it had begun to rain. They came for shelter. They found us asleep, tied the three of us up, put us in a foul dung cart, and promised to sell us for slaves to a foreign power in the market of Yuman-dong. Next morning, down the mountain we bumped. More rain fell. The monsoon came on in full force. We were crossing a wooden bridge over a river when a great rush of water struck the bridge.

'The bandits were thrown into confusion or drowned. We were better off in the cart, which floated, and we managed to get free.

'We ran to Yuman-dong for safety, since we had another uncle there. He took us in with protestations of affection, and his elder daughter fed us. Unfortunately, the town was the headquarters of the brigands, as we soon discovered. My uncle was the biggest brigand. The three of us children were made to work at the degrading business of carting night soil from the village and spreading it on the fields. You can imagine our humiliation.'

The Korean shook his head sadly and searched Ron's face for signs of compassion.

'Where's my bloody food?' Ron asked.

'But fortune was as ever on our side. It was then that our great leader, Kim Il Sung, became President of our people's republic. My uncle was awarded the post of local commissar, since in his career of bandit he had harassed rich oppressor landlords such as my late uncle and aunt up in the mountain. Much celebration followed this event and everyone in the village remained totally drunk for twenty-one days, including the dogs. Three died. Maybe four. It was during this period of joy that a dog bit off the left ear of one of my brothers.

'Those were happy times. Under my uncle we marched from farm to farm along the valley, beating up the farmers, threatening and exhorting the workers. There was nothing we would not do for the Cause. Unfortunately, much misery was to follow.'

'Don't tell me – let me guess,' murmured Ron Wallace.

'But you cannot guess what befell us triplets. It was discovered after many years that the brother who had lost an ear was a capitalist running dog and had been associating secretly with the enemies of the state, who varied from time to time. Sometimes the enemies were Chinese, sometimes Russians. My brother had associated with all of them. I felt bound to denounce him myself, and his wife. A terrible vendetta of blood then started – '

In desperation, Ron stood up, waving his book of crossword puzzles.

'Sorry,' he said. 'I have to finish this page. It is a secret code. I am employed by MI5.'

'I appreciate your feelings,' said the Korean, standing rigid. 'We must all exercise our duties. However, I tell you something of my history for a reason. The remarkable Englishman, Mr Holmberg, who taught me at school, stays ever in my mind as an example of decency, morality, fairness and liberalism. It is no less than the truth to say that I have modelled my life on him.

'Unfortunately, however, during the revolutionary times of the Flying Horse movement, it was necessary to have Mr Holmberg shot. A tribunal convicted him of being a foreigner in wartime. To me befell the honour of carrying out the execution with my own hands. I have a small souvenir for his family back in England which I wish you to carry home to present to them. Please come to my table and I shall give it to you, concealed in a copy of *Pravda*.'

Ron Wallace hesitated only for a moment. All he wanted was his dinner. But if he went over to this madman's table, he would be able to snatch a closer look at his companion. He rose.

At the Korean table sat the remarkable person with the bright-red lips and shoulder-length black hair. The full-length gown swept to the floor. Diamonds sparkled at the smooth neck. A cigarette in a holder sent a trail of smoke ceilingwards from a bejewelled right hand. A look of black intensity was fixed on Ron. He bowed.

'I'm pleased to meet your wife,' he said to the North Korean.

'My brother.' The Korean corrected him. 'My sole surviving brother. Here is the souvenir for the Holmberg family – in fact for the small daughter of the son of the man I knew, who was convicted of the crime against the state. Her address is enclosed. Please take it, deliver it faithfully.'

Ron had been expecting to receive the head of the late Mr Holmberg, but it was a smaller object which the Korean passed over, easily rolled inside a copy of *Pravda*. He bowed again, shook hands with the Korean, smiled at his brother, who gave him a winning smile in return, and returned to his table. A waitress was delivering a boeuf stroganoff to his place.

'Thank you,' he said. 'Bring me another bottle of wine and a bottle of mineral water.'

'Immediately,' she said. But she paused for a second before leaving the table.

Setting the newspaper between his stomach and the table, Ron unrolled it. Inside lay a wooden doll with plaits, a savage grin painted on its wooden face. It wore traditional dress of red and white. Tied round its neck was a label on which was written the name Doreen Holmberg and an address in Surrey. He rolled it up in the paper again and shut it in his briefcase.

He began to eat without appetite the dish the waitress had brought, forking mouthfuls slowly between his lips, staring over the bleak reaches of the restaurant permeated by the strains of 'Yesterday', and avoiding any glance towards the Korean table. He sighed. It would be a relief to get home to his wife, although he had some problems there.

The waitress returned with the two bottles of wine and mineral water on a tray. She could be sighted first behind a carved wooden screen which partly hid the entrance to the kitchens. Then she was observed behind a large aspidistra. Then she hove into full view, walking towards Ron's table, a thin middle-aged woman with straggling dyed hair.

He had been too preoccupied with the Koreans to pay the waitress any attention. As he scrutinized her in the way he scrutinized anything female, he saw that her gaze was fixed on him, not with the usual weary indifference characteristic of a waitress towards diners, but in a curious and not unfriendly fashion. He straightened slightly in his chair.

She set the bottles down on the table. Was there something suggestive in the way she fingered the neck of the wine bottle before uncorking it? She poured him a glass of the wine and a glass of the mineral water in slow motion. He caught a whiff of her underarm odour as she came near. Her hip brushed against his arm.

'You're imagining things,' he said to himself.

He raised the wine glass to his lips and looked at her.

'Enjoy it please,' she said in English, and turned away.

She was tired and in her late thirties, he judged. Not much of a bottom. Not really an attractive proposition. Besides, a waitress in a Russian hotel restaurant . . .

However, after a few more mouthfuls of the stroganoff, he summoned her across the room on the pretext of ordering a bread roll. She came readily enough, but he saw in the language of her angular body an independence of mind not yet eroded of all geniality. A spark of intent lit in his brain. He knew that spark. It could so easily be fanned into flame.

She did look worn. Her face was weathered, the flesh lifeless and dry, with strong lines moving downwards on either side of thin lips. Nothing to recommend her. Yet the expression on her face, the light-grey eyes – somehow, he liked what he saw. Out of that ugly dress, those hideous shoes, she would be more attractive. His imagination ran ahead of him. He felt an erection stirring in his trousers.

Her breasts were not very noticeable as she bent to place the bread by Ron's side. No doubt she ate scraps in the kitchen off people's plates. A fatty diet. No doubt she had taken orders all her life. It was a matter of speculation as to what her private life could be.

He asked her if she ever did crosswords.

The shake of her head was contemptuous. Again the whiff of body odour. Possibly she did not understand what he said. She smiled a little. Her teeth were irregular, but it was an appealing smile.

Watching her hips, her legs, her ugly shoes, as she retreated, he told himself to relax and to think of something that a candle did in a low place, in six letters.

But a long dull evening stretched before him. He hated his own company.

Over the sweet, he extracted a few words from the waitress. She spoke a little German, a little English. She had worked in this hotel for five years. No, she cared nothing about the work. The lipstick she wore was not expertly applied. But there was no doubt that in some measure she was interested in him.

When she brought him a cup of bitter coffee, he said, 'Will you come up to my room?'

The waitress shook her head, almost regretfully, as if she had anticipated the question. It did not surprise her; probably she had often been asked the same question by drunken clients.

Her glance went to where the impassive maître d'hotel stood, guardian of his underlings' Soviet morality. No doubt he had awful powers over them. She left Ron's table, to disappear into the kitchens.

Ron looked down at his puzzle.

When she came to pour him a second cup of coffee, he suggested that they went back to her place.

The waitress gave him a long hard look, weighing him up. The look disconcerted him, inasmuch as he felt himself judged. He saw himself sitting there, secure and decently dressed, possessor of foreign currency, about to return to the strange capitalist world from which he had come. Not bad-looking. And yet – yet another man out of thousands, with a vacant evening before him, just wanting a bit of fun.

'There is difficulties,' she said.

The words told him he was halfway to his desire.

Elation ran through him, not unmixed with a tinge of apprehension. Again, the stirrings of an erection. He told her she was wonderful. He would do anything. He smiled. She frowned. She made a small gesture with her hand: Be quiet. Or, Be patient.

As if she already had her regrets, she left the table hastily, clutching the coffee pot to her chest. Ron observed that she said something to an older waitress as they passed on the way to the kitchens.

Now he had to wait. He tried to think of an uncomplicated curative plant in six letters.

The waitress had disappeared. Perhaps he had, after all, been mistaken. When his impatience got the better of him, he rose to his feet. She appeared and came over. He had a sterling note ready – of a modest denomination, so as not to offend her.

'Where and when?'

Their faces were close. Her foreignness excited him, nor was he repelled by her body odour. She barely responded, barely moved her lips.

'Rear door by the wood hut. Midnight.'

'I'll be there.'

'Will you?'

He nodded a curt good night to the North Koreans, and retreated with his case to the bar. He sat alone, apart from a group of what he guessed were Swedes, getting heavily drunk in one corner. He had three hours to wait.

Idly, he picked up a newspaper printed in English and started to glance through it. It bewildered him utterly. For a while he entertained the thought that his company was playing an elaborate joke on him.

According to the newspaper, there was no Liberal government in power in Britain. Nor was there any mention of Bernard Mattingly. The Prime Minister, it was said, was a Mrs Thatcher, head of a Conservative government. This piece of information disturbed him more than anything he had encountered so far. It seemed that the

President of the United States was not Alan Stevenson but someone called Ronald Reagan.

In a medical column, he read that the whole world was being ravaged by a sexually transmitted disease called AIDS. Ron had never heard of it. Yet the column claimed that thousands of people were dying of it, in Africa, Europe and the United States. No cure had been found.

Just as disturbingly, an editorial on disarmament moves appeared to be saying that there had been two wars involving the whole world during the twentieth century.

Ron knew this could not have happened. There was no way in which Albania and Italy or England and Germany – to take two instances – could possibly attempt to destroy each other. What it all meant he did not know.

With a sudden uneasy inspiration, he checked on the date of the newspaper. It read September 1989 clearly enough. The idea had entered his head that he had been caught in a time warp and was back in the early years of the twentieth century, before the days of the reforming Czars. Such was not the case.

He hid the newspaper under the table and clutched his head.

He was going mad. The sooner he got home the better.

After an hour, the Korean couple entered the bar. They ignored him and sat with their backs to him.

He thought of his wife. Their marriage had been a good one. Both had ruined it by their infidelity. Both nourished hurt feelings and a desire to get their own back. One of them was always an infidelity ahead of the other. Yet Steff had remained with him, had put up with all his drunkenness and bullying and failures. Now they had a little place of their own, heavily mortgaged, it was true, and were trying to build a better relationship. Ron had vowed never to hit her again.

The best advice he could give himself was to forget about that slut of a waitress and enjoy a good night's sleep in his comfortless single room. He had to catch the early flight from Moscow's Sheremeteivo Airport, to be in time for an important meeting with Bob Butler, his boss, tomorrow afternoon in Slough. He might get promoted. Steff would be pleased about that. She would also ask if he had been fucking other women.

He could lie his way out of this one, particularly if the promotion to sales manager came through.

Besides, this creature might give him some insight into what was happening. Perhaps she could tell him who Brezhnev was and what KGB stood for.

By this time, Ron – not an imaginative man – began to realize he had somehow got on an alternative possibility track. The shabby city that surrounded him felt heavy with sin – no, with sinfulness. It was as if some terrible crime had been committed which everyone had conspired not to discuss. And this secret had weighed the population down, so that the cheerful Moscow of his own time had sunk down into the earth from human view.

God knows what weird versions of clap the waitress might be carrying round with her. He had no idea what he was getting into.

Still, the thought of a woman's company in this miserable place was greatly attractive.

He tried to look at it all as a great stunt, a caper. How his pals would laugh when he told them. If he ever got back to them.

He smoked cigarettes and eked out a beer. The Swedes grew louder.

Came 11.30, Ron put on his coat, grabbed his case, and went out into the streets. Everywhere seemed dark and depressing. It was as if he had somehow crossed a border between day and night, between yin and yang, between positive and negative.

As he walked along by the Moskva he observed there was none of the cheerful riverside restaurants, no floating pleasure-boats, which he had heard were the centre of the city's nightlife. No music, no wine, no women. The river flowed dark between high concrete banks, unloved, neglected, isolated from the life of Moscow, rushing on its secretive dark way. What if I am stuck here alone for ever, he asked himself. Isn't there a science of Chaos, and haven't I fallen into it?

It was impossible to know whether the waitress was an escape from or an embodiment of the unreason into which he had fallen.

He turned on his heel and made his way warily down a back alley to the rear of the hotel. A rat scampered, but there were no humans about. He came to an area of broken pavements covered with litter, which he waded through in the dark, cursing as he trod in something soft and deep. He could not see. From a small barred window came an orange fragment of light. Spreading a hand out before him, he arrived against a barrier. Searching carefully with his fingers, he found he was touching wood. Most probably this was the hut the waitress had designated.

Feeling his way, staggering and tripping, he finally reassured himself that he was waiting in the right place. He located the back door of the hotel, tried it, found it locked.

He stood in the dark, cold and uneasy. No stars shone overhead.

Following the sound of tumblers turning in a lock, the hotel door opened. A man emerged and walked off briskly into the night. The door was locked again from the inside; he heard the sound of a bolt being shot. The Russians had a mania for secrecy. So did Ron. He understood.

Several staff emerged from the door in pairs or alone. Worried in case his waitress missed him, Ron stood out from the sheltering hut. Nobody looked in his direction.

A lorry with one headlight jolted along the alley and wheezed to a halt. Two men got out. As Ron shrank back, he saw that one of the men was old and bent, moving painfully as he climbed from the cab. They both began to sort among the rubbish outside the hotel, occasionally throwing something into the back of their vehicle.

The door of the building opened again. Ron's waitress came out. It was ten minutes past midnight. She paused to get her night vision and then walked over to him. He pressed himself against her, feeling her hard body. Neither of them spoke.

With a gesture of caution to Ron, she went over and talked to the men by the lorry. The old man gave a wheezing laugh. There was a brief conversation, during which all three lit cigarettes the waitress distributed. Ron waited impatiently until she returned to his side.

'What's going on?' he asked.

She did not reply, puffing at her cigarette.

After a while, the men were finished with the rubbish. The

younger one gave a whistle. The waitress returned the whistle and went forward. Ron followed as she climbed into the back of the lorry. He had misgivings but he went. They settled themselves down among the trash as the lorry started forward with a lurch.

Once through the maze of back streets, they were driving along a wide thoroughfare lit by sodium street lamps. Ron and the waitress stared at each other, their faces made anonymous in the orange glow. Her face was a mask, centuries old, her hair hung streakily over her temples. He felt in her a life of hard work, without pride. The perception warmed him towards her and he put an arm round her shoulders. He had always loved the downtrodden more than the proud and beautiful. It accorded with his poor image of himself.

She was slow to return his gesture of affection. Languidly, she moved a leg against his. He stared down the vanishing street, as once more they turned into a dark quarter. The excitement of the adventure on which he was now embarked dulled his apprehension, although he wondered about her relationship with the two lorry men, speculating whether they would beat him up and rob him at journey's end. He clutched his briefcase between his knees; it was metal and would be a useful weapon in a fight.

Here at least he was on familiar ground. Ron was no stranger to fights over women, and was used to giving a good account of himself. Whatever else had gone wrong with the universe, some constants remained: the art of getting the leg over, the swift knee in a rival's goolies. He sang a familiar little song in her ear:

'With moonlight and romance
If you don't seize the chance
To get it on the sly
Your archetype will be awry
As time goes by.'

The waitress gave every appearance of not knowing the words, and silenced him with a hand over his mouth. They bumped on in silence and discomfort for a while.

'How far to go?'

'Ein kilometre.' Holding up one finger.

He tried to observe the route in case he had to walk back. Where would he turn for help in case of trouble? He did not want to end up in the Moskva. He had a mad pal in Leeds who had been beaten up and thrown into the canal.

The depressing suburbs through which they passed, where hardly a light showed, were without visible feature. Flat, closed, bleak, Asiatic façades. At one point, on a corner, they passed a fight, where half a dozen men were hitting each other with what might have been pick-helves.

The rumpus vanished into the night. Moscow slept like an ill-fed gourmet, full of undigested secrets. The lorry stopped abruptly, sending its passengers sliding among the filth. Ron climbed out fast, ready for trouble, the waitress following. They stood on a broken road surface. Immediately, the lorry bucked and moved off.

They were isolated in an area of desolation. It was possible to make out an immense pile of splintered wood, crowned by a bulldozer, where some rough-looking men sat by the machine, perhaps guarding it, warming themselves round a wood fire. To Ron's other hand, where a solitary lamp shone, a row of small concrete houses stood, ending in a shuttered box of a shop which advertised beer. Further away, black against the night sky, silhouettes of tall apartment blocks could be seen. It was towards these blocks that the waitress now led Ron.

The heap of wood and beams was more extensive than he had thought. There were figures standing in it at intervals. It seemed to him that a complete old-fashioned village had been bulldozed to make way for Moscow's sprawl. Homes had been reduced to matchwood.

Someone called out to them, but the waitress made no answer. She led down a side lane, where the way underfoot was unpaved.

To encourage Ron, she pointed ahead to a looming block of jagged outline.

They skirted a low wall and reached the building. She went to a side door, knocked and waited. Ron stood there, staring about him, clutching his case and feeling that he needed a drink.

After a long delay, the door was unbolted, unlocked and dragged open. They went in, and the waitress passed a small package from her coat to a dumpy matron in black. Without changing her expression, the dumpy woman locked and bolted the door behind them and retreated into a small fortified office.

The smell of the place hit Ron as soon as he stepped into the passage. It reminded him of his term in jail. This institution was similar to prison. The smell was a compound of underprivilege, mixing disinfectant, polish, urine, dirt, fatty foods and general staleness, bred by too many people being confined in an old building.

The waitress led him past noticeboards, battered lockers and a broken armchair to another corridor, and on to a stairwell. The odours became sharper. They ascended the stairs.

The steps were of pre-cast concrete, the rail of cold metal, and the staircase cared nothing for human frailty. It was carpeted only as far as the first floor. As the waitress ascended beside him, Ron saw the weariness in her step. 'Some night this is going to be,' he told himself. He placed a hand encouragingly in the small of her back. She grimaced a smile without turning her head.

Smells of laundry, damp sheets, overworked heating appliances came and went. On the upper floors, he listened to a low stratum of noise issuing from behind locked doors. Despite the late hour, several women were wandering about the corridors. None took any notice of Ron and the waitress.

In a side passage the waitress pulled a large key from her coat pocket, unlocked a door, and motioned Ron to go in. As he entered, he saw how scratched and bruised the panels of the door were, almost as if it had been attacked by animals.

The same sense of something under duress was apparent in her room. The furnishings crowded together as if for protection. Every surface was fingered and stained, their overused appearance reinforced by the dim luminance of a forty-watt bulb shining overhead. The murkiest corner was filled by a cupboard on which stood a tin basin; this was the washing alcove. Close by was a one-ring electric stove, much rusted. The greater part of the room was occupied by a bed, covered by a patchwork peasant quilt which provided the one note of colour in the room. A crucifix hung by a chain from one of the bedposts. Beside the bed, encroaching on it for lack of space, was a cupboard on top of which cardboard boxes were piled. The only other furniture – there was scarcely room for more – consisted of a table standing under a narrow and grimy window letting in the dark of the night.

The waitress locked her door and bolted it before crossing to the window and dragging a heavy curtain over it. By the window and under the bed were piled old cigarette cartons, all foreign, from Germany, France, England, China and the States. He knew instinctively they were empty – probably saved from the hotel refuse bins. Perhaps she liked the foreign names, Philip Morris and the rest. Well. He was up to his neck in the unknown now, and no mistake. Still. Nothing was ever going to be a greater shock than his first day at the orphanage, when he was four.

He was beginning to enjoy the adventure. He said to himself, 'Now then, Ronnie, if you can't fight your way out of trouble, you'd better fuck your way out.'

He set his case down and pulled off his coat. She hung the coat with hers on a hook behind the door, then went to the cupboard and brought out an unlabelled bottle with two small glasses. She poured clear liquid and passed him a glass. He sniffed. Vodka.

They toasted each other and drank.

He offered her an English cigarette, then handed her the pack. As they lit up, she gave him a smile, looking rather timid. Turning abruptly as if to hide weakness, she recorked her bottle and put it back in the cupboard. That was all he was getting in the way of alcohol.

'An instinctive liking,' he said. 'I mean, this is how it should be, eh? Friends on sight, right?' They sat side by side on the bed, puffing at their cigarettes; he laid a hand on her meagre thigh.

Two cheap reproductions hung on the walls facing them, one of birch forests lost in mist, one of a woman looking out of a deep-set window into a well-lit street. He pointed to it, saying he liked it.

'Frank-land,' she said. 'Franzosisch.'

She threw down her vodka, rose, pulled out a stained and tattered nightdress from under her bolster. It was or had been blue. She smoothed the wrinkles with one hand, while looking at him interrogatively.

'You won't need that,' he said, and laughed.

She paused, then threw the garment down on the end of the bed.

Suddenly, in her hesitation, he saw that she considered saying no to him and throwing him out. He dropped his gaze. The decision was hers. He never forced a woman.

Thoughts of Steff came back to him. He remembered the bitterness they went through after his trip a few weeks ago to Lyons in France. Steff had discovered that he had gone with a prostitute. A row had followed, which rumbled on for days. She had poured out hatred, had made the house almost unlivable. In the first throes of her fury, she had coshed him with a frying pan when he was asleep on the sofa. He had become terrified of her and of what she might do next. Finally, he swore that he would never go with other women again.

Yet here he was, settling in with this strange creature with the disgusting nightdress. The little whore in Lyons had been pernickety clean, a beauty in every way. Steff was always clean, always having a shower, washing her hair. This poor bitch had no shower. Her hair looked as if it had never seen shampoo.

Stubbing out her cigarette, the waitress paused by the light, then switched it off. The room was plunged into darkness. She had made up her mind to let him stay. He heard the sounds of her getting undressed, and began to do the same.

As his eyes accustomed themselves to the dark, he saw her clearly by the corridor light shining under the bottom of the door. She pulled off soiled undergarments and threw them on the table. Fanning out, the light shone most strongly on her feet. They were grey and heavily veined, the toes splayed, their nails curved and long like bird claws. He saw they were filthy. They disappeared from view as she threw herself naked on the bed and pulled the quilt over herself.

An icy draught blew under the door. Ron put his clothes neatly on the table, trying to avoid her dirty undergarments, and climbed under the quilt beside her. She lifted her arms and wrapped them round his neck.

A rank odour assailed him, ancient and indecent. It caught in his throat. He almost gagged. It wafted from her, from all parts. She was settling back, opening her legs. He could scarcely breathe.

He sat up. 'You'll have to wash yourself,' he said. 'I can't bear it.'

He climbed off the bed again, fanning the air, rather than have her climb over him.

'You not like?' she asked.

When he did not reply, she got up and went on her grey feet over to the basin. Her toenails clicked on the floor covering. She poured water in the basin and commenced washing. He pulled open her cupboard, to drink from her vodka bottle, tipping the stuff down his throat. The waitress made no comment.

She rinsed her armpits and her sexual quarters with a dripping rag, drying herself on a square of towel.

'And the feet,' he ordered, pointing.

Meekly, she washed her feet, dragging each up in turn to reach nearer the basin.

This is Ron's story, not mine. But I had to ask myself if there wasn't, in this sordid lie he was telling me, something I deeply envied. I mean, not just the tacky woman, the foul room, the filthy fantasy world of 'Brezhnev's Russia', whatever that meant, but the whole desperate situation, something that took a man up wholly. This wish to be consumed. The whole romantic and absurd involvement. A hell. Oh yes, a hell all right.

And yet – we work away to build our security, to get a little roof and pay the rates. Still there's that thing unappeased. Don't we all secretly long, in our safe Britain, to take a Tupolev too far, to some godforsaken somewhere, where everything's to play for . . . ?

I only ask it.

At length she came back to the bed, standing looking at Ron in the deep gloom, as if asking his permission to re-enter.

At this point in the proceedings, he was again tempted to call the whole thing off. As he struggled with his feelings, to his reluctance to pass by any willing woman was added his kind of perpetual good humour with the other sex, quite different from his aggressive manner with men, which urged him not to disappoint this unlucky creature who had so far exhibited nothing but good will.

The waitress had started all this by encouraging him at the dinner table. He did not know if there was danger involved in this escapade but, if so, then she probably had more to lose than he. Men might not be allowed in this – lodging house, or whatever it was. He would hardly be sent to the gulag if he was caught, but no one could say what might happen to the waitress. He supposed that at the least she might lose her job; which would bring with it a whole train of difficulties in Brezhnev's Russia.

I should explain where I was when my friend Ron was telling me this story, just to give you a little background.

We met by accident on Paddington Station. We had not seen each other for about a year. I had come up on the train from Bournemouth to consult my parent company in Islington, and was crossing the forecourt when someone called my name.

There was Ron Wallace, grinning. He looked much as usual in a rather shabby grey suit with a cream shirt and a floppy tie – the picture, you might say, of an unprofessional professional man working for some down-at-heel outfit.

We were pleased to see each other, and went into the station bar for a pint or two of beer and a chat. I asked him where he was off to. This is what he said: 'I'm off to Glastonbury to see a wise old man who will tell me where my life's going. With any luck.'

It was an answer I liked. Of course, I had some knowledge of how his life had been, and the hard times he had seen. I asked after his wife, Stephanie, and it was then that he started telling me this story I repeat to you. Just don't let it go any further.

So there he was stuck in this poky little room with the waitress. Torn between compassion, lust, boredom and exasperation. The way one always is, really.

He lay in the bed. She stood naked before him in the half-light, looking helpless.

'You ought to look after yourself better,' he said, raising the quilt to let her in.

A sickly smell still pursued him. Concluding it came from the bed itself, he ignored it. She laid her head beside him on the patterned bolster. She smoothed dull hair back to gaze at him through the dim curdled light.

He stroked her cheek. When she buried her face suddenly in his chest, in a gesture of dependence, he caught the aroma of greasy kitchens, but he snuggled against her, feeling her still damp body. The waitress sniffed at him and sighed, rubbing against his thighs, perhaps excited by talc and deodorant scents, stigmata of the prosperous capitalist class. Prosperous! If only she knew! Ron and Steff had all manner of debts.

She opened her legs. As Ron groped in her moist pubic hair, he thought – a flash of humour – that he had his hand on the one thing that made life in the Soviet Union endurable. The Soviet Union and elsewhere . . . He penetrated her and she went almost immediately into orgasm, clutching him fiercely, bringing out a cry from the back of her throat. He thrust into her with savage glee.

Only afterwards, as they lay against each other, she clutching his limp penis, did her story start. She began to tell it in a low voice. He was idle, not really listening, comfortable with her against him, half-wanting a cigarette.

What she was saying became more important. She sat up, clutching a corner of the quilt over her naked breasts, addressing him fiercely. Her supply of English and German words was running out. He gathered this was something about her childhood. Yet maybe it wasn't. A horse was dying. It had to be shot. Or it had been shot. This was somewhere on a farm. The name Vladimir was repeated, but he was not sure if she referred to the town or a man. He tried to question her, to make things clear, but she was intent on pouring out her misery.

Now it was about an infant – 'eine kleine kind', and the waitress was acting out her drama, dropping the quilt to gesticulate. The baby had been seized and banged against a wall – this demonstrated by a violent banging of her own head against the wall behind her. He could not understand if she was talking about herself or about a baby of hers. But the pain came through.

The waitress was sobbing and crying aloud, waving her arms, frequently calling the word 'smert', which he knew meant 'death'. Her body shook with the grief of it all.

It reached a melancholy conclusion. The story, incomprehensible and disturbing, ended with her coming alone to Moscow to work.

'To work here in this place. Arbeit. Nur Arbeit. Work alone. Abschliessen.'

'There, there.' He comforted her as he once used to comfort Steff's and his only child, wrapping her in his arms, rocking her. He was shaken by the agony of her outburst, angry with himself for failing to understand.

Of course there was no misunderstanding her misery. He felt it in his stomach, having known misery himself. Even in the pretty comfortable world he had left – to which he hoped to return on the morrow – personal tragedy was no rarity; some people always held the wrong cards. But he had fallen by accident into a shadow world, the world labelled 'Brezhnev's Russia' or 'Soviet Union', a world racked by terrible world wars and diseases. It was safe to say that whatever woes the poor waitress suffered, she represented millions who laboured under similar burdens.

He gave her a cigarette. A simple human gesture. He could think of nothing else to do.

She cried a little in a resigned fashion and wiped her tears on the quilt. Then she began to make love to him in a tender and provocative way. For a while paradise existed in the squalid room.

Ron Wallace woke. A full bladder had roused him. The waitress lay beside him, asleep and breathing softly. In the dim light, her face was young, even childlike.

Disengaging his arm from under her neck, Ron sat up and looked at his watch. Next moment, he was out of bed. The time was 5.50 A.M. A suspicion of daylight showed round the curtains, and his flight was due to leave at 9.30. His check-in time at Sheremeteivo Airport was 8.00 A.M. He had two hours in which to get to the airport, and no idea of where he was.

He listened at the door. All was quiet in the building. He had to return to the hotel and collect his suitcase. And first he had to have a pee.

His impulse was to awaken the waitress. Capable though she had shown herself to be, she might be less reliable this morning. She would find herself in a difficult situation to which perhaps she had given no thought on the previous evening; the entertaining of foreigners in one's apartment was surely a crime in Brezhnev's Russia.

Since she did not stir, he decided to leave her sleeping. Keeping his gaze on her face, he dressed fast and quietly. He stood for a moment looking down at her, then unstrapped his watch from his wrist and laid it by the bedside as a parting present.

As noiselessly as possible, he slipped into his coat and unbolted and unlocked the door. In the corridor, he closed the door behind him. Thought of the tragic life he left behind came to him; damn it, that was none of his business. It was urgent that he got to a toilet. There must be one on this floor.

All the doors were locked. He ran from one to another in increasing agony. There seemed to be no toilet. He was sweating. He must piss outside, fast.

He went quickly down the stairs, alert for other people. He heard voices but saw no one.

His penis tingled. 'Oh God,' he thought, 'have I caught a dose off that bitch? I must have been mad. How can I tell Steff? She'll leave me this time. Steff, I love you, I'm sorry, I'm a right bastard, I know it.'

He rushed to the front door, which had a narrow fanlight above it, admitting wan signs of dawn. The door was double-locked, with a mortice lock and a large padlocked bar across it. Next to the door stood a cramped concierge's office, firmly closed. Everyone had been locked in for the night.

He ran about the ground floor rather haphazardly, gasping, and came on the side door by which, he believed, he had entered the previous evening. That too was securely locked. He gasped a prayer. At any moment his bladder would burst.

At this point in Ron's story, I broke into heartless laughter.

He stared at me halfway between anger and amusement.

'It's no fun, going off your head for want of a piss,' he said.

I controlled my laughter. Ron is not a guy you like to offend. What amused me was the thought of a man who had been inside for GBH and done a stretch for breaking and entering in a situation where he was attempting breaking and exiting.

After trying and failing to kick in a panel on the side door, Ron ran about almost at random looking for a way of escape.

Two steps at the end of the main corridor led down to another locked door, a boiler room in all probability. Next to the door was a broom cupboard and an alcove containing a mop, a brass tap and a drain.

With a groan of relief, Ron unzipped his trousers and pissed violently into the drain. The relief almost made him faint.

By now it must be almost half-past six.

As the urine drained from his body, he heard a door open along the corridor and a woman coughing. Her footsteps led away from where he stood. He heard her mount the stairs. Other doors were opening, female voices sounded, a snatch of song floated down; the noise level in the building was rising.

At last he was finished. He zipped his trousers, wondering what he should do to escape.

Two men were coming towards him. Although he saw them only in silhouette along the dark corridor, he recognized that they were old. They walked slowly, slack-kneed, and one jangled a bunch of keys. Ron sank back into the alcove.

The men passed within eighteen inches of him, talking to each other, not noticing him in the gloom. They unlocked the boiler-room door and went in.

Immediately they were gone, Ron came out of his hiding place and hurried back to the main door. As he went, he tried each handle in the corridor in turn. All were locked.

At the front door, he was looking up at the narrow fanlight, wondering if it would open, when he heard faint sounds from the concierge's nook. Impelled by urgency, he pushed the office door open and looked in.

A plump old woman with her hair in a bun was just leaving the main room to enter a cubbyhole which served as a kitchen. She began to rattle a coffee pot.

In the room lay three men, sleeping in ungainly attitudes. Two were huddled on a sturdy table pushed against the far wall, the third lay under the table, his head resting peacefully on a pair of boots. A cluster of empty bottles and full ashtrays suggested that they had had a good night of it.

The room, in considerable disarray, had five sides. It served regularly as a bedroom as well as an office; against the left-hand wall a bed stood under a shelf bulging with files. Timetables and keys hung from the walls.

The loud and laboured breathing of the men reinforced the stuffy atmosphere. Where two of the walls came to a point was a window which the old woman had evidently opened to let air into the room.

Without hesitation, Ron crossed over to the window. In doing so, he kicked one of the empty vodka bottles. It rattled against its companions. He did not look round to see if the woman had caught sight of him.

One pane of the window had been repaired with brown paper. Taking little care not to injure himself, he forced himself through the opening feet first. The ground was further down than he had expected. He landed on concrete with a painful bump. Above him, an angry old woman stuck her head out and yelled at him. Ron got up and ran round the corner. At least he was free of that damned prison, where women were locked in every night.

Then came the thought.

'My bloody briefcase!'

He had left it standing by the waitress's bed.

Cursing furiously, he marched round the outside of the fortress. It was built of grey stone. All of its windows were barred.

A pile of rubbish, including the burnt-out carcass of a vehicle, stood against one wall. Even if he climbed up that way, it led only to a barred window. He prowled about, searching for the window of the boiler room, assuming there was one; he might be able to bribe the two old men to let him in that way.

He was frantic, and mad to know how the time was slipping away – what a fool to leave his watch with that bitch. He had to catch his plane, otherwise there would be trouble with his company and with Steff, not to mention all the difficulties with the airline – whatever it was called now . . . Aeroflot. And he could not leave without the briefcase. In it were his precious contracts.

Struggling to deal with his anxiety levels, he kept from his mind the more dreadful and nebulous fear: that the airliner would deliver him not to his lovely Steff and the England he knew but to some other England ruled over not by Queen Margaret and PM Bernard Mattingly but by – whoever the lady was as mentioned in the newspaper – he had forgotten her name. He would perish if he was trapped for ever in a dreadful shadow world where history had taken a wrong turn.

Despite his frenzy, he remembered something else. The damned doll the North Korean had given him. He was convinced it was packed with heroin or some other illegal substance. He had not believed the Korean's unlikely story about Mr Holmberg for one moment, and had intended to throw away the doll as soon as he was outside the hotel. Sexual pursuit had made him forget.

Ron became really frightened.

Running round the building, isolated on its wasteland, he could find no low boiler-room window. He stood back, frustrated, when a stocky female figure in a black coat emerged from the building and walked off rapidly in the direction of the gigantic piles of broken wood Ron recalled from the previous night.

She had emerged from a side door. He ran to it, only to find it already locked. But even as he stood against it cursing, he heard the key turn from within, and it opened again. As another woman emerged, Ron dashed in. When an old man standing inside, key in hand, moved to stop him, Ron pushed him brutally in the chest. Other women were pressing to leave the building for the day's work, stern of face, burly of shoulder. He ran into the main corridor and hastened upstairs.

But which floor?

Which bloody floor?

He had seen from outside there were five floors.

Which floor was the waitress on?

Not the ground or first floors. Not the top . . .

Christ!

The scene was changed from a few minutes earlier. Everyone was now up and about, and women in states of undress were wandering the corridors. They yelled at him and tried to grab him. In a few minutes, they would get themselves organized. Then he would be arrested.

He tried the second floor. He ran down the side passage. First door on right. He remembered that. As soon as he faced the door, he remembered the markings on the waitress's door, the savage scratches as if an animal had been there. This was not it.

He ran up to the third floor, causing more disturbance, and to the side passage. God, this nightmare! He was furious with himself. Now he faced the door with the deep scratch marks, and hammered on it. The door opened.

Ron took a swift look back. No one saw him, though he heard sounds of pursuit. He went in.

The waitress stood there, half-dressed, hand up to mouth in an attitude of misgiving.

One reason for that misgiving was clear. On the bed – that bed! – on top of the quilt and the dirty blue nightdress, the contents of Ron's briefcase had been spread, a dirty shirt, a pair of socks, a pair of underpants, some aspirins, the crossword book, the Korean doll, a copy of the *Daily Express* from a week ago, the precious contracts, and other belongings. The case lay with a screwdriver beside it. She had managed to prise the lock open.

'Get dressed,' he said. 'Schnell. I need you to get me out of here.'

'And to get me back to that sodding hotel,' he thought.

The waitress tried to make some apology. She had not expected him back. She thought the case was a present. He barked at her. She hurried to put on yesterday's dress and fit her grey feet into her heavy working shoes, whimpering as she did so.

He hardly looked to see what he was doing as he pushed everything into the briefcase, shouting to her to move. She was now his guarantee. She could get him out of the lodging house. She knew the way back to the Hotel Moskva.

'Schnell,' he growled, deliberately scaring her as he forced the case shut.

She offered him his watch back but he shook his head.

'Let's go. Fast. Vite. Schnell.'

'OK, OK,' she said.

Together they hurried down the corridor and down the stone stairs, Ron with a firm grasp on her arm. Several women gathered. They called to the waitress, but when she snapped back at them they stood aside and let her pass. A younger woman began to laugh. Others took it up. Soon there was general laughter. This was not the first time a woman had had a lodger for the night. Probably, Ron reflected, this was not the first time the waitress had had a lodger for the night.

The old man unlocked the side door and they were out with a stream of other workers into the chill air. Great was his relief. He had a chance with Steff yet.

'The hotel,' he said. 'Schnell. I must catch that bloody plane.'

Ron Wallace caught the bloody plane. He rang his office from Penge. The managing director had had to go up to Halifax, so happily he was not wanted till the following morning. The day was his. He was able to go back to Steff, preparing as he went to be innocent. After all, she meant far more to him than any of these stray bitches. He would serve another stretch for Steff. He told himself he had learnt a lesson. He would never go with another woman.

Sitting on the coach going home, he was relieved to find everything was as normal. The *Daily Express* he picked up at the airport carried a photograph of Bernard Mattingly, Britain's popular Prime Minister, opening the first stretch of a new motorway that would run between London and Birmingham. He searched for a reference to Russia. A small paragraph announced that Russia had a record wheat surplus, which they were shipping to the Third World. And the Pope had returned to Rome from his tour of Siberia.

Everything was normal. He thought again of the strange electric storm which had bathed his plane on the flight out. Perhaps that had all been subjective, a major ischaemic event in the brain stem. He had been working too hard recently.

Nothing had happened. He had imagined that whole dark world, Brezhnev, the waitress and all.

Steff was amiable and credulous and listened to all he had to say about the boredom of Moscow. While he was showering, she even went to unpack his things for him.

He stepped naked from the shower. She had opened the briefcase. She was holding up for his inspection a dirty blue nightdress.

RATBIRD

> . . . To warn and warn: that one night, never more
> To light and warm us, down will sink the lurid sun
> Beneath the sea, and none
> Shall see us more upon this passionate shore.

THE DISINTEGRATION of the old world? Easy. I'll manage it. Everything will end not with a bang but a whisper – a whisper of last words. Words. So it began. So it will end. When I grow up.

Here I lie on this crimson equatorial shore, far from where the great electronic city dissolves itself under its own photochemical smogs.

Here I lie, about to tell you the legend of the *Other Side*. Also about to go on a journey of self-discovery which must bring me back to my beginnings. As sure as I have tusks, this is ontology on the hoof.

So to begin with what's overhead. The sun disputes its rights to rule in the sky above. Every day it loses the struggle, every morning it begins the dispute over again. Brave, never-disheartened sun!

I lie under the great sea almond tree which sprouts from the sand, looking up into its branches where light and shade dispute their rival territories. This is called beauty. Light and shade cohabit like life and death, the one more vivid for the dread presence of the other.

In my hand I clutch –

. . . But the great grave ocean comes climbing up the beach. There's another eternal dispute. The ocean changes its colours as it sweeps towards where I lie. Horizon purple, mid-sea blue, shore-sea green, lastly golden. Undeterred by however many failures, the waves again attempt to wet my feet. Brave remorseless sea!

(What should a legend contain? Should it be of happiness or of sorrow? Or should it permit them to be in – that word again – dispute?)

– What I clutch in my hand is a fruit of the sea almond. It's not large, it's of a suitable nut shape, it's covered with a fine but coarse fibre like pubic hair. In fact, the nut resembles a girl's pudendum. Else why clutch it? Is that not where all stories lie, in the dumb dell of the pudendum? The generative power of the story lies with the organ of generation – and veneration.

Let me assure you, for it's all part of the legend, at the miracle of my birth I came forth when summoned by my father. He tapped. I emerged. A star burned on my forehead. I'm unique. You believe you are unique? But no, I am unique. In their careless journeys across the worlds, the gods create myriads of everything, of almond trees, of waves, of days, of people. But there's only one Dishayloo, with no navel and a star on his forehead.

So my journey and tale are about to commence. Knowing as much, my friends, who sit or stand with me under the tree, stare out to sea in silence. They think about destiny, oysters or sex. I have on my t-shirt saying 'Perestroika Hots Fax'.

A distant land. That's what's needed. I've met old men who never went to sea. They speak like spiders and don't know it. They have lost something and don't know what they have lost. Like all young men I must make a journey. The dispute between light and shade must be carried elsewhere, waves must be surmounted, pudenda must open with smiles of welcome, fate must be challenged. Before the world disappears.

We all must change our lives.

So I rise and go along the blazing beach to the jetty, to see Old Man Monsoon. They call him Monsoon. His real name has been forgotten in these parts, funny old garbled Christian that he is. He can predict the exact hour the rains will come. And many more things.

Once Monsoon was called Krishna. Once he visited the *Other Side*, as I will relate.

He saw me coming and stood up in his boat. He's a good story-teller. He says, What is the human race (looking obliquely at my tusks as he speaks) but a fantastic tale? Told, he might add, with a welter of cliché and a weight of subordinate clauses, while we await a punchline.

The friends accompany me to the jetty. At first in a bunch, then stringing out, some hastening, some loitering, though the distance is short. So with life.

Monsoon and I shake hands. He wears nothing but a pair of shorts. He is burnt almost black. His withered skin mummifies him, though those old Golconda eyes are golden-black still. People say of Monsoon that he has a fortune buried in a burnt-out refrigerator on one of the many little islands standing knee-deep in the sea. I don't believe that. Well, I do, but only in the way you can believe and not believe simultaneously. Like Rolex watches from a different time zone.

He shows yellow teeth between grey lips and says in a voice from which all colour has faded, 'Isn't there enough trouble in the world without youngsters like you joining in?'

Grey lips, yellow teeth, yet a colourless voice . . . Well, let us not linger over these human paradoxes.

I make up something by way of reply. 'I've lost my shadow, Monsoon, and must find it if I have to go to the end of the Earth. Perhaps you can foretell when the end of the Earth will be?'

He points to the puddle of dark at my feet, giggling, raising an eyebrow to my friends for support.

'That's not *my* shadow,' I tell him. 'I borrowed this one off a pal who wants it back by nightfall. He has to wear it at his mother's wedding.'

When I have climbed into the boat, Monsoon starts the engine with one tug of the starter rope. It's like hauling at a dog's lead. The hound wakes, growls, shakes itself, and with a show of haste begins to pull us towards the four corners of the great morning.

The craft creaks and murmurs to itself, in dispute with the waters beneath its hull. And the sweet playful sound of the waves against old board. The ocean, some idiot said, is God's smile.

Monsoon picks up my thought and distorts it. 'You smile like a little god, Dishayloo, with that star on your brow. Why always so happy?'

I gaze back at my friends ashore. They shrink as they wave. Everything grows smaller. Hasten, hasten, Dishayloo, before the globe itself shrinks to nothing!

'The smile's so as not to infect others with sorrow. It's therapy – a big hospitable hospital. Antidote to the misery virus. Did you ever hear tell of the great white philosopher Bertrand Russell?'

The Golconda eyes are on the horizon to which our boat is hounding us, but Monsoon's never at a loss for an answer. 'Yes, yes, of course. He was a friend of mine. He and I used to sail together to the Spice Islands to trade in vitamin pills and conch shells. I made a loss but Bertra Muscle became a rupee millionaire. These days, he lives in Singapore in a palace of unimaginable concrete and grandeur.'

Now the friends form no more than a frieze, spread thin along the shore, like bread on a lake of butter. Soon, soon, the dazzle has erased them. My memory does the same. Sorry, one and all, but the legend has begun.

Talk's still needed, of course, so I say, 'This was a different man, pappy. The guy I mean said . . . '

But those words too were forgotten.

' . . . Why should I recall what he said? Are we no better than snails, to carry round with us a whole house of past circumstance?'

My hands were trailing in the water. Prose was not my main concern. Monsoon picked up on that.

'Pah. "House of past circumstance . . . " What are you, a poet or something? Something or nothing? The Lord Jesus had a better idea. He knew nothing dies. Even when he snuffed it on Mount Cavalry, he knew he would live again.'

'Easy trick if you're the son of God.'

The Golconda gold eyes flared at me. 'He was a bloke in a million. Go anywhere, do anything.'

'"Have mission, will travel."' All the time the dear water like progress under the prow.

'Born in India, I believe, sailed in Noah's boat because there was no room at the Indus.' His face had taken on the expression of imbecile beatitude the religious sometimes adopt. 'Jesus was poor, like me. He couldn't pay Noah one cent for the trip. Noah was a hard man. He gave him a broom and told him to go and sweep the animal turds off the deck.'

'What happened?'

'Jesus swept.'

Cloud castles stood separately on the horizon, bulbous, like idols awaiting worship.

Something above moving over a smooth sea prompted Monsoon to chatter. I scarcely listened as he continued his thumbnail portrait of Jesus.

'He wasn't exactly a winner but he was honest and decent in every way. Or so the scriptures tell us. And a good hand with a parable.'

The little boat was in the lap of the ocean. The shoreline behind was indistinct; it could have been anything – like a parable. Ahead, two small humps of islands lay stunned with light. I began to feel the charge of distance, its persuasive power.

Perhaps the islands were like humpbacked whales. But the world's old. Everything has already been compared with everything else.

The old man said, 'You'll soon have left us. We'll be no more in your mind, and will die a little because of it. So I'll tell you a story – a parable, perhaps – suitable for your life journey.'

And he began the tale of the ratbird.

Monsoon spoke in more than one voice. I abridge the tale here, there being only so many hours in a day. Also I've removed his further references to Jesus, diluting it. Same tale, different teller, only coconut milk added.

There was this white man – well, two white men if you include Herbert – this white man Monsoon knew as a boy, before he was Monsoon. This white man – well, he and Herbert – arrived at this port in Borneo where Boy Monsoon lived in a thatched hut with Balbindor.

Like many whites, Frederic Sigmoid was crazed by the mere

notion of jungle. He believed jungles were somewhere you went for revelation. In his vain way, he placed the same faith in jungles that earlier whites had put in cathedrals or steam ships. But Frederic Sigmoid – Doctor Sigmoid – was rich. He could afford to be crazy.

Back in Europe, Sigmoid had cured people by his own process, following the teaching of a mystic called Ouspensky and adding a series of physical pressures called reflexology. Now here he was in Simanggang with his mosquito nets, journals, chronometers, compasses, barometer, medicine cabinet, guns and one offspring, out to cure himself or discover a New Way of Thought, whichever would cause most trouble in a world already tormented by too much belief. Seek and ye shall find. Find and ye shall probably regret.

With Sigmoid was his pale son, Herbert. Monsoon and his adoptive father, Balbindor, were hired to escort the two Sigmoids into the interior of Borneo. Into the largely unexplored Hose Range, and an area called the Bukit Tengah, where lived a number of rare and uncollected species, including the ratbird, happy until this juncture in their uncollected state. Animal and insect: all congratulated themselves on failing to make some Cambridge encyclopaedia.

Balbindor was a coastal Malay of the Iban tribe. However, he had been into the interior once before, in the service of two Dutch explorers who, in the manner of all Dutch explorers, had died strange deaths: though not before they had communicated to civilization a mysterious message, 'Wallace and Darwin did not know it, but there are alternatives.' Balbindor, four foot six high, brought the word hot-foot back to the coast.

Sigmoid was keener on alternatives than his son Herbert. Confidence men always have an eye for extra exits. Thirteen days into rainforest, led by Balbindor and sonlet, and the doctor remained more determined than his offspring. The night before they reached the tributary of the Baleh river they sought, Balbindor overheard a significant exchange between father and son.

Herbert complained of heat and hardship, declaring that what he longed for most in the world was a marble bathroom with warm scented water and soft towels. To which his father rejoined that Herbert was a gross materialist. Going further, Sigmoid retreated into one of his annoying fits of purity, declaring, 'To achieve godliness, my boy, you must give up all possessions . . . '

Herbert replied bitterly, 'I'm your one possession you'll never give up.'

Had this been a scene in a movie, it would have been followed by pistol shots and, no doubt, the entry of a deadly snake into the Sigmoid tent. However, the story is now Balbindor's. He shall tell it in his own excruciating words. And Balbindor, never having seen any movie, with the solitary exception of *The Sound of Music* (to which he gave three stars), lacked a sense of drama. Father and son, he reported, kissed each other as usual and went to sleep in their separate bivouacs.

If my story, then I tell. Not some other guy. Many error in all story belong other guy. I Iban man, real name no Balbindor. I no see *Sound Music* ever. Only see trailer one time, maybe two. Julie Andrews good lady, I marry. My kid I take on no call Monsoon. Monsoon late name. Kid, he come from India. I take on. I no call Monsoon, I call Krishna. My son they die logging camp all same place three time. Too much drink. I very sad, adopt Krishna. He my son, good boy. Special golden eye. I like, OK.

This Doctor Sigmoid and he son Herbert very trouble on journey. We go on Baleh river, boat swim good. All time, Herbert he complain. White men no sweat pure, too many clothe. No take off clothe. Then boat swim up tributary Puteh, no swim good. Water he go way under boat. Mud he come, stop boat.

We hide boat, go on feet in jungle. Very much complain Herbert and father he both. They no understand jungle. They no eat insect. Insect eat them.

Jungle many tree, many many tree. Some tree good, some tree bad, some tree never mind. I tell number tree. Tamarind tree, he fruit bitter, quench throat thirst. Help every day. Sigmoid no like, fear poison. I no speak him. All same jungle olive, good tree. We drink pitcher plant, all same like monkey.

Monkey they good guide. Krishna and me we do like monkey. I understand jungle. Wake early, when first light in jungle. Deer trail fresh, maybe catch deer along blowpipe. Monkey wake early, eat, sing, along branches. Sigmoids no like wake early. Day cool. I like wake early, make Sigmoids rise up. Go quiet. Creep along, maybe catch kill snake for pot.

Many ant in Hose Range, big, little, many colour. All go different way. I speak ant, ant speak me. Go this way, go that. Every leaf he fall, he mean a something. I understand. I plenty savvy in jungle.

One week, two week, three week, we walk in jungle, sometime up, sometime down. For Sigmoids, very hard to go. Both smell bad. Too much breath. No control. Dutch men control of breath good. Herbert he very scare. No like jungle, all same long time. No good man, swear me. I understand. Herbert he no think I understand.

Three week, get very near area Bukit Tengah. Now all path go up, need more care. Many cliff, many rock. One fall, maybe finish. Waterfall, he pour bad water. I know smell bad water nose belong me. Krishna and two bearer and I, we no drink bad water. Come from *Other Side*. I tell Sigmoids no drink water come *Other Side*. They no care, no understand, they drink bad waterfall water plenty. Take on bad spirit. Understand. I shout much, Krishna he cry all same long time. Herbert he shout me, try hit little Krishna.

I tell Herbert, 'You drink water belong *Other Side*. Now you got bad spirit. You no get back Europe. You finish man.'

Herbert no savvy. He plenty sick. I see him bad spirit. It suck him soul. Now I plenty scare.

Every day more slow. *Other Side* he come near. Bearer man they two, they no like go more far. I hear what they speak together. I savvy what Orang Asli speak, I tell Dr Sigmoid. He swear. No please me. Both Sigmoids have fever. Black in face, very strange. Smell bad more.

Big storm come over from *Other Side*, maybe hope drive us away. Thunder he flatten ears, lightning he blind eyes, rain he lash flesh, wind he freeze skin. We hide away under raintree, very fear. Night it come, big wizard, I no understand. Too black. In night bearer they go, I no hear. Two bearer they run off. Steal supply. I very sad I no hear. In morning dawnlight I say to doctor sorry. Bearer they scare, go back wife. Doctor he swear again. I say, no good swear. Who hear swear with good nature? Best leave alone, keep silent. He no like. Make bad face.

Day after storm, we come *Other Side*. I see how monkey they no go *Other Side*. Different monkey on *Other Side*, speak different language. Different tree, grow other different leaf. Fruit they different, no wise eat. Insect different.

Also one more bad thing. I see men belong *Other Side* in jungle. They move like ghost but I see. Krishna he see, he point. Plenty eye in jungle belong *Other Side*. No like. *Other Side* men they much difference. How they think different, no good.

I see, I understand, Krishna he understand. I no make Sigmoids understand.

'Geology,' I explain Sigmoids. I speak they language good. 'He change. Different earth begin now since many many old time. All thing different, different time. Different inside time. Womb bring forth different thing. Bad go there, no go. Only look one day.'

'Balls,' he say.

I sick with him doctor. I make speak, 'I keep my ball belong me. You go, and Herbert. I no go one more pace. Krishna, he no go one more pace.'

Herbert he bring out gun. I very fear. I know him mad with bad spirit. I say him, 'Two piece Dutch man they come here. Pretty soon they finish. Why you no sense? Come back home along me, Krishna.'

He get more mad.

I was really disgusted with this idiot native Balbindor or whatever his name was. Here we were. At great expense to ourselves, Father and I had finally arrived on the very threshold of Bukit Tengah, the Middle Mountain, and this difficult little man and his black kid were refusing to proceed.

It just was not rational. But you don't expect rationality from such people. These natives are riddled with superstition.

Also, I blamed him for the way the bearers had deserted us. We had quite an argument. I was trembling violently from head to foot. Most unpleasant.

I want to say this, too, about the whole incident. Balbindor treated

Father and me all along as complete fools. We could grasp that he was trying to tell us we had arrived at some sort of geological shift, much like the Wallace Discontinuity east of Bali, where two tectonic plates meet and flora and fauna are different on the two opposed sides. We knew that better than he did, having researched the matter in books before the expedition, but saw no reason to be superstitious about it.

We had also observed that there were those on the other side of the divide who were watching us. Father and I were going to go in there whether or not Balbindor and his son accompanied us. We saw the necessity to make an immediate impression on the new tribe, since we would be dealing with them soon enough.

That was why I shot Balbindor on the spot. It was mainly to make a good impression on the new tribe.

Little Krishna ran off into the jungle. Perhaps the little idiot thought I was going to shoot him as well. I suppose I might have done. I was pretty steamed up.

'Put your revolver away, you fool,' Father said. That was all the thanks I got from him. When has he ever been grateful?

We had no idea what to do with Balbindor's corpse. Eventually we dragged it to the waterfall and flung it in. We slept by the waterfall that night and next morning at our leisure crossed the divide into the *Other Side* (the silly name had stuck).

For two days we travelled through dense alien jungle. We were aware that there were men among the thickets following us, but it was the monkeys who caused us most trouble. They were no bigger than leaf monkeys, but had black caps and a line of black fur about the eyes, giving them an oddly human look. Father trapped one with the old Malayan gourd trick, and discovered it to have only four toes on each foot and four fingers on each hand. We came at last to a clearing brought about by a massive outcrop of rock. Here we rested, both of us being overcome by fevers. We could see the barbaric scenery about us, the tumbled mass of vegetation, with every tree weighted down by chains of epiphytes and climbers. Above them loomed densely clad peaks of mountains, often as not shrouded by swift-moving cloud.

These clouds took on startling devilish shapes, progressing towards us. It may have been the fever which caused this uncomfortable illusion.

Days must have passed in illness. I cannot say how strange it was, how peculiarly dead I felt, when I awoke to find myself at a distance from my father. Dreadful sensations of isolation overcame me. Moreover, I was walking about. My feet seemed not to touch the ground.

I discovered that I could not get near my father. Whenever I seemed to advance towards him, my steps deviated in some way. It was as if I suffered from an optical illusion so strong that it consumed my other senses. I could do no more than prowl about him.

Father was sitting cross-legged by the remains of a fire on which he had roasted the leg of a small deer. Its remains lay by him. He was talking to a small wizened man with long hair and a curved bone through his cheeks which made him appear tusked. The face of this man was painted white. For some reason, I felt terrified of him, yet what chiefly seemed to scare me was a minor eccentricity of garb: the man wore nothing but an elaborate scarf or band or belt of fabric about his middle. No attempt had been made to cover his genitals, which were painted white like his face.

Prowling in a circular fashion seemed all I was capable of, so I continuously circled the spot. Although I called to my father, he took no notice, appearing totally absorbed in his conversation with the white-faced man. I now noted that the latter had on each hand only three fingers and a thumb, and only four toes on each foot, in the manner of the monkeys we had come across in another existence.

I was filled with such great uneasiness and hatred that I chattered and jibbered and made myself horrible.

Again and again I attempted to advance towards my father. Only now did I realize that I loved this man to whose power I had been subject all my life. Yet he would not – or perhaps could not – take the slightest notice of me. I set up a great screaming to attract his attention. Still he would not hear.

Father, Father, I called to you all my life! Perhaps you never ever heard, so wrapped up were you in your own dreams and ambitions. Now for this last time, I beg you to attend to your poor Herbert.

I know you have your own story. Allow me mine, for pity's sake!

It would be true to say without exaggeration that throughout my mature life, in my quest to transform humanity, I had been in search of Mr White Face, as I thought of him. (He refused to tell his name. That would have given me power over him.) I have a firm belief in transcendental power, unlike poor Herbert.

White Face materialized out of thin air when I was drinking at a pool. There on my hands and knees, by gosh! I looked up – he was standing nearby, large as life. Naked except for the band round his belly; yet something about him marked him immediately as a singular character. (A flair for judging character is one of my more useful talents.)

A remarkable feature of White Face's physiognomy was a pair of small tusks (six inches long) piercing the cheeks. My knowledge of anatomy suggested they were rooted in the maxilla. They gave my new acquaintance a somewhat belligerent aspect, you may be sure!

Already he has told me much. We have spent two whole days from sun-up till sun-down in rapt conversation. His thought processes are entirely different from mine. Yet we have much in common. He is the wise man of his people as I, in Europe, am of mine. Grubby little man he may be – he shits in my presence without embarrassment – yet in his thought I perceive he is fastidious. I can probably adapt some of his ideas.

Much that he says about divisions in the human psyche is reflected in pale form in the Hindu sacred books of the Upanishads (which is hardly surprising, since White Face claims that all the world's knowledge of itself emanated from the '*Other Side*' during the ice age before last, when Other Siders went out like missionaries over the globe, reaching as far as Hindustan).

What I do find difficult to swallow – we argued long about this – is some strange belief of his that the world is immaterial and that humanity (if I have it correctly) is no more than a kind of metaphysical construct projected by nature and relying on *words* rather than *flesh* for its continued existence. Perhaps I've misunderstood the old boy. I'm still slightly feverish. Or he's mad as a hatter.

Only knowledge is precious, he says. And knowledge is perpetually being lost. The world from which I come is in crisis. It is losing its instinctual knowledge. Instinctual knowledge is leaking away under the impact of continual urbanization. That I believe. It is not in conflict with my own doctrines. He thinks our world will shortly die.

Then the *Other Side* will recolonize the world with new plants and animals – and understanding. (His kind of understanding, of course.) He wants to convince me to become his disciple, to go forth and encourage the world-death to come swiftly. By the third day of our discussion, I begin more and more to comprehend how desirable it is that the civilization to which I belong should be utterly destroyed. Yet still I hesitate. We drink some of his potent *boka* and rest from intellectual debate.

I ask, How are things so different here?

For answer, he shows me a ratbird.

Some distance from the rock on which we sat in conference – conferring about the future of the world, if that doesn't sound too pompous – an angsana stood, a large tropical tree, its branches full of birds to which I paid no attention. Birds have never been one of my major interests, I need hardly say.

Mr White Face began a kind of twittering whistle, a finger planted in each corner of his lips. Almost immediately, the birds in the angsana responded by flying out in a flock, showing what I took to be anxiety by sinking to the ground and then rapidly rising again. Each time they sank down, they clustered closely, finally expelling one of their number, who fluttered to the ground and began – as if under compulsion – to walk, or rather scuttle, towards us; whereupon the other birds fled into the shelter of their tree.

As the bird came nearer, White Face changed his tune. The bird crawled between us and lay down at our feet in an unbirdlike manner.

I saw that its anatomy was unbirdlike. Its two pink legs ended in four toes, all pointing forward with only a suggestion of balancing heel. Wings and body were covered in grey fur. And the face was that of a rodent. In some ways it resembled a flying fox, common throughout Malaysia; in some ways it resembled a rat, but its easy flight and way of walking proclaimed it a bird.

And now that I looked again at Mr White Face, I saw that beneath his paint his face had some of the configurations of a rat, with sharp little jaws and pointed nose, not at all like the inhabitants of Sarawak, a blunt-faced company, with which I was acquainted.

Obeying his instruction, I proffered my hand, open palm upwards, towards the animal. The ratbird climbed on and began to preen its fur unconcernedly.

Nobody will blame me if I say that in the circumstances I became very uneasy. It seemed to me that in Mr White Face I had stumbled upon an evolutionary path paralleling – rivalling – our accepted one; that this path sprang from a small ground mammal (possibly tusked) very different from the arboreal tarsier-like creature from which *Homo sapiens* has developed. I was face to face with . . . *Homo rodens* . . . Over millions of years, its physical and mental processes had continued in its own course, parallel to but alien from ours. Indeed, perhaps inimical to ours, in view of the hostility of such long standing between man and rat.

Rising to my feet, I flicked the ratbird into the air. Instead of flying off, it settled at my feet.

I found I was unable to walk about. My legs would not move. Some magic had trapped me. At this unhappy moment, I recalled that mysterious sentence, 'Wallace and Darwin did not know it, but there are alternatives.' The alternative had been revealed to me; with magnificent hardihood, I had ventured into the *Other Side*; was I to suffer the fate of the two Dutch explorers?

Mr White Face continued to sit cross-legged, gazing up at me, his tusked countenance quite inscrutable. I saw the world through glass. It was unmoving. I felt extremely provoked. Perhaps the argumentative Balbindor had been correct in saying I should not have drunk from the waterfall springing from the *Other Side*. It had left me in White Face's power.

And I was uncomfortably aware of the spirit of Herbert. After the foolish lad had died of his fevers – unable to pull through illness like me with my superior physique – his spirit had been powerless to escape. It circled me now, yowling and screaming in a noxious way. I tried to ignore it. But how to escape my predicament?

I stared down at the white face of the ratman. Then, from my days as a chemist, I remembered a formula for bleach. Perhaps the magic of science would overcome this detestable witchcraft (or whatever it was that held me in thrall).

As loudly as I could, I recited the formula by which bleach is produced when chlorine reacts with sodium hydroxide solution: '$C1^2(g) + 2NaOH(aq) \rightarrow NaC1(aq) + NaC10(aq) + H^2o(1)$'.

Even as I chanted, I felt power return to my muscles. The great tousled world about me began to stir with life again. I was free. Thanks to bleach and a Western education – and of course an excellent memory.

I kicked at the ratbird, which fluttered off.

'I don't care for your kind of hospitality,' I told White Face.

'Well, you have passed my test,' he said. 'You are no weakling and your words are strong. To each of us there are two compartments which form our inner workings. One part is blind, one part sees. Most of our ordinary lives are governed by the part that sees, which is capable of performing ordinary tasks. That part is like a living thing which emerges from an egg. But there is the other part, which is blind and never emerges from the egg. It knows only what is unknown. It acts in time of trouble. You understand?'

'You perhaps speak in parable form of two divisions of the brain. If so, then I believe I understand you.' (I did not think it politic to express my reservations.)

He gave a short dry laugh, exposing sharp teeth. 'Oh, we like to believe we understand! Suppose we have never understood one single thing of the world about us and inside us? Suppose we have lived in utter darkness and only believed that darkness was light?'

'All things may be supposed. So what then?'

He said, 'Then on the day that light dawns, it will be to you as if a sudden incomprehensible darkness descends.'

After this horrifying statement he made a beckoning gesture and began running.

Since he made swiftly towards the forest, I had not much option but to follow. But his words had chilled me. Suppose indeed that we were hedged in by limitations of comprehension we could not comprehend? The ratbird had already shaken many of my convictions regarding life on earth and how it had evolved.

Mr White Face's mode of progression through the forest was at odds with my previous guide, Balbindor, and his method of procedure; but then, the trees, the very trees we passed through, were different. Their bark, if bark it was, possessed a highly reflective surface, so that to move forward was to be accompanied by a multitudinous army of distortions of oneself. (In this hallucinatory company, it was impossible not to feel ill at ease. Jumpy, in a word.)

I did not understand how it was possible to find one's way in such a jungle. White Face was presumably trusting to his second compartment, 'the part that never hatched', to see him along his course.

In which case, the blind thing was unexpectedly reliable. After two days of arduous travel, we came to a dark-flowing river. On the far side of it stood a village of longhouses, much like the ones we had left back on the coast, except that these were entered by round doors instead of the normal rectangular ones.

Uncomfortable as I was in White Face's company, there was comfort in the sense of arrival. I was possessed of a lively curiosity to investigate this kampong of the *Other Side* – that lively curiosity which has carried me so successfully through life.

One factor still contributed to my unease. The ghost of my son pursued me yet, his translucent image being reflected from the trunk of every tree, so that it sometimes appeared ahead of me as well as on every side. Herbert waved and screamed in the dreariest manner imaginable (uncanny, yet nevertheless lightly reminiscent of his behaviour throughout his life).

'We shall cross the river,' White Face announced, putting two skinny fingers into the corners of his mouth and whistling to announce our presence.

'Will Herbert cross with us?' I asked, I trust without revealing my nervousness.

He dismissed the very idea. 'Ghosts cannot cross moving water. Only if they are ghosts of men with wooden legs.'

After White Face had signalled to some men on the opposite bank, a narrow dugout canoe was paddled across to collect us. By the time we landed at a rickety jetty, a number of inhabitants had gathered, standing cautiously back to observe us with their heads thrust forward as if they were short-sighted.

All of them had tusks. Some tusks were large and curled, or adorned with leaves. I could not fail to see that all, men, women and children, wore nothing in the tropical heat but a band – in the case of the women this was quite ornate – around their middles, leaving everything else uncovered. The breasts of the women were small, and no more developed than those of the men. (The women also had tusks, so that I wondered if they were used for offence or defence. Presumably the missionary position in coitus would have its dangers. One might be stabbed *in medias res.*)

They were in general a strange lot, with sharp beaky faces quite unlike the Malays to whom I was accustomed. In their movements was something restless. A kind of rictus was common. I saw that here was opportunity for anthropological study which, when reported abroad, could but add to my fame. I wanted to look in a mouth to see where those tusks were anchored.

White Face addressed some of the men in a fast-flowing and high-pitched language. They made respectful way for him as he led me through the village to a longhouse standing apart from the others.

'This is my home and you are welcome,' he said. 'Here you may rest and recover from your fever. The spirit of your son will not harm you.'

To my dismay, I found that the bleach formula had left my mind and would not be recalled. Did this mean I was still under his spell? So it was with reluctance that I climbed the ramp leading into the longhouse with its two great tusks over the circular entrance.

Inside, I was barely able to stand upright at the highest point, for I was head and shoulders taller than my sinister host; and it did not escape my notice that the roof at its highest point was infested with cobwebs, in the corners of which sat large square spiders. Also, when he gestured to me to sit down on the mats which covered the floor, I could not but observe two fairly fresh (tuskless) skulls above the door by which we had entered. Catching my glance, Mr White Face asked, 'Do you speak Dutch?'

'Do they – now?' I asked, with sarcasm.

But he had a response. 'On the night of the full moon they do speak. I cannot silence them. You shall hear them by and by, and become familiar with the eloquence of death.'

We then engaged in philosophical discourse, while a servant woman, cringing as she served us, brought a dark drink like tea in earthenware bowls which fitted neatly between Mr White Face's tusks.

After two hours of conversation, during which he questioned me closely concerning Ouspensky, he apologized that his wife (he used a different word) was not present. It appeared that she was about to deliver a son.

I congratulated him.

'I have twelve sons already,' he said. 'Though this one is special, as you may see. A miraculous son who will further our most powerful ambitions, a wizard of words. So it is written . . . Now let us discuss how the end, closure and abridgement of your world may be brought about, since we are in agreement that such an objective is desirable.'

Although I was less ready than before to agree that such an objective was desirable, I nevertheless found myself entering into his plans. (The dark drink had its effect.) The plans were – to me at least – elaborate and confusing. But the horrifying gist of his argument was that *Homo sapiens* might be extinguished by *pantun*. I understood that *pantun* was a form of Malayan poetry, and could not grasp how this might annihilate anything; but, as he continued, I began to see – or I thought in that dazed state I saw – that he believed all human perceptions to be governed by words and, indeed, distorted and ultimately betrayed by words. Betrayed was the word he used. This, he said, was the weakness of *Homo sapiens*: words had weakened the contract with nature that guaranteed mankind's existence. (All our spiritual ills were evidence of this deteriorating state of affairs.)

There were ways by which all *Homo sapiens* could be reduced – abridged – into a story, a kind of poem. Those who live by the word die by the word. So he said. We could end as a line of *pantun.*

I cannot reduce this plan of his into clear words. It was not delivered to me in clear words, but in some sort of squeaky *Other Side* music with which he aided my understanding. All I can say is that there in that creepy hut, I came to believe it was perfectly easy to turn the whole story of the world I knew into a world of story.

As we were getting into the how of it – and drinking more of that dark liquid – the servant hurried in with an apology and squeaked something. White Face rose.

'Come with me,' he said. 'My wife (he used the different word) is about to bring forth the thirteenth son.'

'Will she mind my presence?'

'Not at all. Indeed, your presence is essential. Without your presence, you can have no absence, isn't that so?' (Whatever that meant. If that is truly what he said.)

In we went, into curtained-off quarters at the far end of the longhouse. All misty with scented things burning and jangling instruments being played by two long-tusked men.

His wife lay on the floor on a mat, attended by the servant girl. Her stomach did not appear extended. She was entirely naked, no embroidered band round her middle. For the first time, I saw – with what sense of shock I cannot explain – *that she had no navel.* Nor was this some kind of unique aberration. The servant girl – perhaps in honour of the occasion – was also nude and without the customary middle band. She also had no navel. I was struck as by an obscenity, and unprepared for what followed. (Tusks I could take; lack of navel implied a different universe of being.)

'Now the birth begins,' said Mr White Face, as his wife lifted one leg, 'and you will find all will go according to plan. The story of your species will become a kind of Möbius strip, but at least you will have had a role in it, Dr Sigmoid.'

He had never used my name previously. I knew myself in his

power; as never before I felt myself powerless, a thin be-navelled creature without understanding. I had believed these strange people of the *Other Side* to be distant descendants of a kind of rodent ancestor. But that was a scientific illusion built on evolutionary terminology. The truth was different, more difficult, less palatable. As the woman lifted her leg, an egg emerged from her womb.

An egg not of shell like a bird's: leathery rather, like a turtle's. An egg! A veritable egg, ostrich-sized.

A terrible rushing noise beset me. The longhouse flew away. I was surrounded by bright sunlight, yet in total darkness, as foretold. Even worse – far worse – I was not I. The terror of wonderment, real understanding, had changed all. Only the egg remained.

With a sense of destiny, I leaned forward and tapped upon it with an invisible finger. It split.

At the miracle of my birth, I came forth when my father summoned me. A star was set upon my forehead. I am unique. The gods that make their careless journeys across the world, playing with science or magic as they will, create thousands of everything, of sea almonds, of waves, of days – of words. Yet there is only one Dishayloo. No navel, and a star in the middle of his forehead.

Born to shine in a world of story.

FOAM

'There's nothing for it when you reach the Point of No Return – except to come back.'

E. James Carvell

MANY Central and Eastern European churches had been dismantled. The deconstruction of Chartres Cathedral was proceeding smartly, unhindered by Operation Total Tartary.

On the previous day, a guide had taken me round Budapest Anthropological Museum. I had wanted to see the *danse macabre* preserved there, once part of the stonework of the cathedral at Nogykanizsa. Although the panel was in poor condition, it showed clearly the dead driving the living to the grave.

The dead were represented by skeletons, frisky and grinning. The line of the living began with prelates in grand clothes, the Pope leading. Merchants came next, men and women, then a prostitute; a beggar brought up the rear, these allegorical figures representing the inescapable gradations of decay.

As I was making notes, measuring, and sketching in my black notebook, the guide was shuffling about behind me, impatient to leave. I had special permission to be in the gallery. Jangling her keys more like a jailer than an attendant, she went to gaze out of a narrow window at what could be seen of the prosperous modern city, returning to peer over my shoulder and sniff.

'A disgusting object,' she remarked, gesticulating with an open hand towards the frieze, which stood severed and out of context on a display bench in front of me.

'"What is beauty, saith my sufferings then?"' I quoted abstractedly. To me the *danse macabre* was a work of art, skilfully executed; nothing more than that. I admired the way in which the leading

Death gestured gallantly towards an open grave, his head bizarrely decked with flags. The unknown artist, I felt sure, had been to Lubeck, where similar postures were depicted. The helpful guide-book, in Hungarian and German, told me that this sportive Death was saying, 'In this doleful jeste of Life, I shew the state of Manne, and how he is called at uncertayne tymes by Me to forget all that he hath and lose All.'

For a while, silence prevailed, except for the footsteps of the guide, walking to the end of the gallery and walking back, sighing in her progress, jingling her keys. We were alone in the gallery. I was sketching the Death playing on a stickado or wooden psalter and goading along a high-bosomed duchess, when the guide again shuffled close.

'Much here is owed to Holbein engraving,' said the guide, to show off her knowledge. She was a small bent woman whose nose was disfigured by a permanent cold. She regarded the work with a contempt perhaps habitual to her. 'Theme of *danse macabre* is much popular in Middle Ages. In Nogykanizsa, half population is wipe out by plague only one years after building the cathedral. Now we know much better, praise be.'

I was fed up with her misery and her disapproval. I wanted only to study the frieze. It would buttress a line of thought I was pursuing.

'In what way do we know better?'

It is unwise ever to argue with a guide. She gave me a long discourse regarding the horrors of the Middle Ages, concluding by saying, 'Then was much misery in Budapest. Now everyone many money. Now we finish with Christianity and Communism, world much better place. People more enlightenment, eh?'

'You believe that?' I asked her. 'You really think people are more enlightened? On what grounds, may I ask? What about the war?'

She shot me a demonic look, emphasized by a smile of outrageous malice. 'We kill off all Russians. Then world better place. Forget all about bad thing.'

The grand steam baths under the Gellert Hotel were full of naked bodies, male and female. Many of the bathers had not merely the posture but the bulk of wallowing hippopotami. Fortunately the steam clothed us in a little decency.

Tiring of the crowd, I climbed from the reeking water. It was time I got to work. Churches long sealed with all their histories in them were to be opened to me this day. By a better guide.

Everyone was taking it easy. Headlines in the English-language paper that morning: STAVROPOL AIRPORT BATTLE: First Use Tactical Nukes: Crimea Blazes. The war had escalated. Everyone agreed you had to bring in the nukes eventually. Hungary was neutral. It supplied Swedish-made arms to all sides, impartially.

The Soviet War marked the recovery of Hungary as a Central European power. It was a godsend. Little I cared. I was researching churches and, in my early forties, too old for conscription.

Wrapped in a white towelling robe I was making my way back towards my room when I encountered a tall bearded man clad only in a towel. He was heading towards the baths I had just left. We looked at each other. I recognized those haggard lineaments, those eroded temples. They belonged to a distant acquaintance, one Montagu Clements.

He recognized me immediately. As we shook hands I felt some embarrassment; he had been sacked from his post in the English Literature and Language Department of the University of East Anglia the previous year. I had not heard of him since.

'What are you doing in Budapest?' I asked.

'Private matter, old chum.' I remembered the dated way he had of addressing people – though he had been sacked for more serious matters. 'I'm here consulting a clever chap called Mircea Antonescu. Something rather strange has happened to me. Do you mind if I tell you? Perhaps you'd like to buy us a drink . . . '

We went up to my room, from the windows of which was a fine view of the Danube with Pest on the other side. I slipped into my jogging gear and handed him a sweater to wear.

'Fits me to a T. I suppose I couldn't keep it, could I?'

I did not like to say no. As I poured two generous Smirnoffs on the rocks from the mini-bar, he started on his problems. '"Music, when soft voices die, Vibrates in the memory . . . " So says the poet

Shelley. But supposing there's no memory in which the soft voices can vibrate . . . '

He paused to raise his glass and take a deep slug of the vodka. 'I'm forty-one, old chum. So I believe. Last month, I found myself in an unknown place. No idea how I got there. Turned out I was here – in Budapest. Budapest! Never been here before in my natural. No idea how I arrived here from London.'

'You're staying here?' I remembered that Clements was a scrounger. Perhaps he was going to touch me for the air fare home. I gave him a hard look. Knowing something about his past, I was determined not to be caught easily.

'I'm attending the Antonescu Clinic. Mircea Antonescu – very clever chap, as I say. At the cutting edge of psycho-technology. Romanian, of course. I'm not staying in the Gellert. Too expensive for someone like me. I rent a cheaper place in Pest. Bit of a flophouse actually.' He laughed. 'You see, this is it, the crunch, the bottom line, as they say – I've lost ten years of my memory. Just lost them. Wiped. The last ten years, gone.'

He shone a look of absolute innocence on me. At which I uttered some condolences.

'The last thing I remember, I was thirty. Ten, almost eleven years, have passed and I have no notion as to what I was doing in all that time.'

All this he related in an old accustomed calm way. Perhaps he concealed his pain. 'How terrible for you,' I said.

'FOAM. That's what they call it. Free of All Memory. A kind of liberty in a way, I suppose. Nothing a chap can't get used to.'

It was fascinating. Other people's sorrows on the whole weigh lightly on our shoulders: a merciful provision. 'What does it feel like?'

I always remember Clements's answer. 'An ocean, old chum. A wide wide ocean with a small island here and there. No continent. The continent has gone.'

I had seen him now and again during those ten years, before his sacking. I suggested that perhaps I could help him fill in gaps in his memory. He appeared moderately grateful. He said there was no one else he knew in Budapest. When I asked him if he had been involved in an accident, he shook his head.

'They don't know. I don't know. A car crash? No bones broken, old boy. Lucky to be alive, you might say. I have no memory of anything that happened to me in the last ten years.'

Unthinkingly, I asked, 'Isn't your wife here with you?'

Whereupon Clements struck his narrow forehead. 'Oh God, don't say I was married!'

He drank the vodka, he kept the sweater. The next day, as suggested, I went round with him to the Antonescu Clinic he had mentioned. The idea was that an expert would question me in order to construct a few more of those small islands in the middle of Clements's ocean of forgetfulness.

The clinic was situated in a little nameless square off Fo Street, wedged in next to the Ministry of Light Industry. Behind its neo-classical façade was a desperate little huddle of rooms partitioned into offices and not at all smart. In one windowless room I was introduced to a Dr Maté Jozsef. Speaking in jerky English round a thin cigar, Maté informed me we could get to work immediately. It would be best procedure if I began to answer a series of questions in a room from which Clements was excluded.

'You understand, Dr Burnell. Using proprietary method here. Dealing with brain injury cases. Exclusive . . . Special to us. Produces the good result. Satisfied customers . . .' His thick furry voice almost precluded the use of finite verbs.

Knowing little about medical practice, I consented to do as he demanded. Maté showed me up two flights of stairs to a windowless room where a uniformed nurse awaited us. I was unfamiliar with the equipment in the room, although I knew an operating table and anaesthetic apparatus when I saw them. It was at that point I began to grow nervous. Nostovision equipment was also in the room; I recognized the neat plastic skull cap.

Coughing, Maté stubbed his cigar out before starting to fiddle with the equipment. The nurse attempted to help. I stood with my back to the partition wall, watching.

'Wartime . . . Many difficulties . . . Many problems . . . For

Hungarians is many trouble . . . ' He was muttering as he elbowed the nurse away from a malfunctioning VDU. 'Because of great inflation rate . . . High taxes . . . Too many gipsy in town. All time . . . The Germans of course . . . The Poles . . . How we get all work done in the time? . . . Too much busy . . . '

'If you're very busy, I could come another day,' I suggested.

He squinted at me and lit another cigar. 'I am expert in all science, so many people take advantage of me. Even when I am small boy, I must carrying to school my small brother. Three kilometre to the gymnasium . . . Now is shortage of material, I must do all. This damned war . . . Many upheaval . . . Spies and traitor . . . Everywhere same . . . Today toilet blockage and how to get repair? You cannot be nervous?'

'I have an appointment, Dr Maté. If later would be more convenient . . . '

'Is no problem. Don't worry . . . I treat many English. Get this nurse to move, I explain all.'

Maté sought to reassure me. They had developed a method of inserting memories into the brains of amnesiacs, but first those memories had to be recorded with full sensory data on to microchip, and then projected by laser into the brain. That at least was the gist of what I gathered from a long complex explanation. While I listened, the nurse gave me an injection in the biceps of my left arm. They would need, Maté said, to append electrodes to my cranium in order to obtain full sensory data matching my answers to his questions.

'I don't really know Montagu Clements well,' I protested. But of course I could not simply refuse to co-operate, could not walk out, could not leave poor Clements without doing my best for him.

Indeed, my eyelids felt heavy. It was luxury to stretch out, to groan, to relax . . . and to fall into the deepest slumber of my life . . .

The cathedral in which we walked was almost lightless. My extended senses told me that it was vast. I asked Dr Maté what we were doing there. His answer was incoherent. I did not press him. He seemed to be smoking a cigar; a little red glow formed occasionally as he inhaled, but I could smell no smoke.

In order to keep my spirits up – I admit I was apprehensive – I talked to him as we progressed step by step. 'I suppose you read Kafka, you understand the complexities with which he found himself faced at every turn. As a psychologist, you must understand that there are people like Kafka for whom existence is an entanglement, a permanent state of war, while for others – why, at the other extreme they sail through life, seemingly unopposed. These differences are accounted for by minute biochemical changes in the brain. Neither state is more or less truthful than the other. For some truth lies in mystery, for others in clarity. Prayer is a great clarifier – or was. My belief is that old Christian churches served as clarifying machines. They helped you to think straight in "this doleful jeste of life".'

I went on in this fashion for some while. Dr Maté laughed quite heartily, his voice echoing in the darkness.

'You're such good company,' he said. 'Is there anything I can do for you in return?'

'More oxygen,' I said. 'It's so hot in here. As a church architect, I have visited, I believe, all the cathedrals in Europe – Chartres, Burgos, Canterbury, Cologne, Saragossa, Milano, Ely, Zagreb, Gozo, Rheims – ' I continued to name them for some while as we tramped down the nave. 'But this is the first time I have ever entered a hot and stuffy cathedral.'

'There are new ways. Neural pathways. Technology is not solely about ways of conducting war. It brings blessings. Not least the new abilities by which we may see human existence anew – relativistically, that is, each person imprisoned in his own umwelt, his own conceptual universe.' He let out a roar of laughter. 'Your friend Kafka – I'd have lobotomized him, speaking personally – he said that it was not only Budapest but the whole world that was tragic. He said, "All protective walls are smashed by the iron fist of technology." Complaining, of course – the fucker always complained. But it's the electronic fist of technology which is smashing the walls between human and human. I exclude the Muslims, of course. Down they go, like the Berlin Wall, if you remember that far back. In the future, we shall all be able to share common memories, understandings. All will be common property. Private thought will be a thing of the past. It's simply a matter of micro-technology.'

I started laughing. I had not realized what good company Hungarians could be.

'In that connection, I might mention that Jesus Christ was evidently pretty au fait with micro-technology. All that resurrection of the body stuff. Depends on advanced technology, much of it developed during that lucky little war against Saddam Hussein in the Gulf. Strictly Frankenstein stuff. Robbing body bags. Dead one day, up and running – back into the conflict – the next.'

Maté was genuinely puzzled. We halted under a memorial statue to Frederick the Great. He had heard of Frankenstein. It was the other great Christian myth which puzzled him. This was the first time I had ever encountered anyone walking into a cathedral who had never heard of Jesus Christ. Explaining about Jesus proved more difficult than I expected. The heat and darkness confused me. I knew Jesus was related to John the Baptist and the Virgin Mary, but could not quite remember how. Was Christ his surname or his Christian name?

My father had been a Christian. All the same, it was difficult to recall the legend exactly. I was better on 'Frankenstein'. But I ended by clarifying Jesus's role in the scheme of things by quoting, as far as I could remember, from a hymn, 'He came down on earth from Heaven, he died to save us all.'

Although I couldn't actually see Maté's sneer, I felt it in the darkness. 'Where was this Jesus when Belsen and Auschwitz and Dresden and Hiroshima happened? Having a smoke out the back?'

Somehow, I felt it was rather sacrilegious to mention Jesus's name aloud where we were. The cathedral was constructed in the form of a T, the horizontal limb being much longer than the vertical, stretching away into the endless dark. Oh, the weight of masonry, felt somehow as pressing on the vertebrae. And, like fossil vertebrae, great columns reared up on every side, engineered to support vast weight, as if this whole edifice was situated many miles under the earth's crust, the mass of which must somehow be borne.

So I say. So I understand it. Yet those stone vertebrae – in defiance of the dull facts of physics – writhed like the chordata, climbing lizard-tailed into the deeper darknesses of the vaulting. It was the cathedral to end all cathedrals.

Maté and I now stood at the junction of the cathedral's great T. The vertical limb of this overpowering architectural masterpiece sloped downwards. We stopped to stare down that slope, more sensed than seen. Kafka could have felt no more trepidation at that time than I, though I covered my nervousness by giggling at Maté's latest joke. He claimed he had not heard of the Virgin Mary either.

I stood at the top of the slope. With me was another church architect, Sir Kingsley Amis.

'The font is somewhere over there,' he said, gesturing into the darkness. 'But I'd better warn you it's not drinking water. Even if it was, you wouldn't want to drink it, would you?' He gave a throaty laugh.

Both he and I were greatly diminished by Dr Maté, who now made a proclamation, reading from a box. 'We're here now, on the spot you see indicated on your map, adjacent to the pons asinorum. Presently a devil will appear and remove one of you. I am not permitted to say where he will remove you to. We have to keep destinations secret in wartime, but I am authorized to say that it will be somewhere fairly unpleasant. As you know, the war between humanity and the rest is still on. But Geneva rules will apply, except in so far as fire and brimstone will be permitted on a strictly controlled basis. All torture will be attended by an authorized member of the International Red Cross.'

'How long do we have to wait? Is there the chance of a drink before we go?' Sir Kingsley Amis asked.

'Devil should be here shortly. ETA 2001,' Maté said.

'Shortly' was just another of the euphemisms such as surface in wartime. It indicated an eternity, just as bombs are described as deterrents. 'This'll spoil his day' means 'We'll kill him', and 'God' means 'A ton of bricks is about to fall on you'. Myself, I prefer euphemisms.

Phew, I was so tired. Time in the building was lethargic, with every minute stretching, stretching out in companionship with the night towards infinity. Reality wore thin, bringing in illusion. At one point I almost imagined I was sitting typing while a dreadful senseless war was waged in the Gulf. But the gulf of time I was in was much greater. Forget reality; it's one of the universe's dead ends . . .

Interest is hard to sustain, but my feeling was as much of interest as terror. Only those who enjoy life feel terror. I admired all the melancholy grandeur round me, the reptilian sense of claustrophobia. It compared favourably with the slum in which I lived.

At the bottom of the slope before us, a stage became illuminated. You must imagine this as an entirely gradual process, not easily represented in words. A. Pause. Stage. Pause. Became. Pause. Ill. Pause. You. Min. Pause. Ay. Pause. Ted. Trumpets. It was illuminated predominantly in bars of intersecting blue and crimson.

Funebrial music began to play, brass and bass predominating.

The music, so akin to the lighting, was familiar to me, yet only just above audibility, as the lighting hovered just above the visible end of the spectrum.

These low levels of activity were in keeping with the enormous silences of the cathedral structure. They were shattered by the sudden incursion of a resounding bass voice which broke into song. That timbre, that mixture of threat and exultation! Unmistakable even to a layman.

'The devil!' Kingsley Amis and I exclaimed together.

'And in good voice,' said Dr Maté. 'So this is where I have to leave you.'

I was stunned by his indifference. 'What about that sewing machine?' I asked. But he was not to be deflected.

Even while speaking, he was shrinking, either in real terms or because he was being sucked into the distance; darkness made it hard to differentiate. However, I had little time to waste on Maté. Attention turned naturally to the devil. Though he had yet to appear on the dim-lit stage, I knew he was going to come for Kingsley Amis.

'I'd better make myself scarce too,' I said. 'Don't want to get in your way.'

'Hang on,' he said. 'You never know. He might be after you. Depends on whether or not he's a literary critic.'

When the devil arrived on stage, he was out of scale, far too large – ridiculously far too large, I might say, meaning no disrespect. It was hard to discern anything of him in the confused dark. He was black and gleaming, his outline as smooth as a dolphin's even down to the hint of rubber. He stepped forward and advanced slowly up the ramp, still singing in that voice which shook the rafters.

This struck me as being, all told, unlikely. It was that very feeling that all was unlikely, that anything likely was over and done with like last year's cricket match, which was most frightening. I trembled. Trembling didn't help one bit.

I turned to Kingsley Amis. He was no longer there. I was alone. The devil was coming for me.

In terror, I peered along the great wide lateral arms of the cathedral.

'Anyone there?' I called. 'Help! Help! Taxi!'

To the left was only stygian darkness, too syrupy for me to think of penetrating, the black from which ignorance is made. As I looked towards the right, however, along the other widespread arm of the building, something materialized there like a stain: light towards the dead dull end of the electromagnetic spectrum.

All this I took in feverishly, for the devil, still singing, was approaching me still. Perhaps I should apologize for my fears. As a rationalist, I had but to snap my rational fingers, it might be argued, and the devil would fade away in a puff of smoke. To which I might say that, rationalist or not, I had spent too many years in my capacity as church architect investigating the fossils of a dead faith not to have imbibed something of the old superstitions. But – this was more germane – I had a belief in the Jungian notion of various traits and twists of the human personality becoming dramatized as persons or personages. This enormous devil could well be an embodiment of the dark side of my character; in which case, I was all the less likely to escape him.

Nor did I.

As I took a pace or two to my right, starting to run towards that faint dull promise of escape, a vision distantly revealed itself. Fading into being came a magnificent palladian façade, lit in a colour like blood, with doric columns and blind doorways. Nothing human was to be seen there – no man to whom I might call. If the burrow to my left represented the squalors of the subconscious, here to my right was the chill of the super-ego.

I ran for it. But was hardly into my stride when the singing devil reached me. I screamed. He snatched me up . . .

. . . and bit off my head.

To any of you with decent sensibilities, I must apologize for these horrific images. You may claim they were subjective, private to me, and should remain private, on the grounds that the world has nightmares enough. Perhaps. But what happened to me was that my head was bitten off almost literally.

My memory was wiped.

It's a curious thing suddenly to find oneself walking. Imagine yourself in a cinema. The movie begins. Its opening shot is of some character walking, walking across a featureless landscape. Photography: grainy. The shot immediately holds your interest, perhaps because our ancestors right back to the Ice Age were great walkers. Now imagine that you're not sitting watching in your comfortable stalls seat: you are that character. Only you're not in a movie. You're for real, or what we call real, according to our limited sensory equipment.

Your life has just begun and you're walking across what turns out to be Salisbury Plain. It's cold, there's a hint of rain in the breeze. The place looks ugly. But walking is no trouble. It's everything else that's trouble.

Like how you got where you are. Like what happened. Like what your name is. Like who you are. Even like – where are you going?

Night is closing in. That much you understand.

What do you do? You go on walking.

Over to your right in the distance, half-hidden by a fold of land, is a broken circle of stone monoliths. You kind of recognize it, although no name comes to you. It's the ruin of a Stone Age cathedral, taken out in the war with the Neanderthals, cobalt against the overpraised English countryside.

You continue as dark continues to fall. Your legs keep working, your pace is unvarying. You become slightly afraid of this remorseless body, asking yourself, Is it mine?

Dusk gathers about you like a coat when you climb a fence and reach a road. There is almost no traffic on the road. You try to thumb a lift from the cars as they approach from either direction, sweeping you with their headlights. Past they go, never pausing. Bastards.

The fourteenth car stops. A woman is driving. A man sits beside her. They ask where you want to go, and you say Anywhere. They laugh and say that is where they are going. You climb in. You huddle on the back seat, unable to answer any of their well-meant questions.

They think you are a loony, and drop you in the nearest village. You are inclined to agree with their judgement. You wander hopelessly along the road, then, frightened, back into the village. The village is called Bishops Linctus. By now its streets are deserted. Lights glow inside the pub, the Gun Dog, but, with no money in your pocket, you are afraid to enter. There are countries where you might enter and be looked after in a hospitable way; you do not feel that could happen in England.

A young man in gum boots saunters along the road with a shotgun under his arm. He stares at you hard as he passes. He returns and addresses you. He is guarded but friendly. He seems not to believe you have lost your memory. Nevertheless, he takes you along to his house, which is one of a line of council houses on the edge of the village, just before the plain recommences its reign.

His old mother greets you. She is surprised, saying that Larry never speaks to anyone. He tells her to shut up. You stand there, back to the kitchen wall, while she fries up Larry's favourite meal, which is sausages and mashed fish fingers. You and Larry sit and eat at the table. It is good.

He has a room he calls His Room. It is locked. The old woman interrupts to say it is full of guns. He says to shut up. He tells you he is a farm labourer or sometimes a brickie. At present he is out of work. He lets you doss on the floor of his bedroom. The place is full of gun magazines, and there is a Kalashnikov in Larry's bed. He sleeps with it.

You express your gratitude.

'I like helping people,' Larry replies. He puts out the light.

You lie there on the floor. Despite all your worries, you feel pleasure and comfort in those words of his, 'I like helping people.' And so you sleep.

Only you're not in this movie. This is my movie. I'm for real – or what I call real, according to my limited sensory equipment.

Morning. When I woke, Larry was already up and about. I could hear his mother shouting at him. For a few seconds, I was living with this present situation. Then the edge of the abyss reappeared. I could remember nothing further back than the time I was walking over that miserable plain.

When I got up, the old woman gave me a cup of thin instant coffee. I stood with her against the sink. She had a canary in a cage.

'It's Kevin. We call it Kevin. I think it's a girl. One of the family, aren't you? Keeps me company. Say hello to Kevin. I wash it every Saturday, under the hot tap. It likes that. Don't you, Kevin? You like a nice wash under the hot tap. It's one of the family. Sing for your mummy then. Who's a good Kevin?'

I was watching through the window, as Larry loaded boxes of ammunition into the back of an old battered Land Rover.

His mother caught my glance. 'He's going into Swindon to try and get a job. You stay here with me. He's a dangerous driver, is Larry. We'll go down and see Dr Roberts. She's a sympathetic woman – trained in London, she was – and she'll help you.'

Larry was looking preoccupied. His movements were slow, his gaze abstracted, as if he were composing a poem in his head. Without glancing back at the house, he climbed into the cab of the Land Rover. Nothing happened. I went to the window to watch, obscurely thinking something was wrong. The back of his head could be seen. Motionless. Not trying to start the vehicle. Just sitting there in the driver's seat.

The council houses followed the curve of the road, which wound up a slight incline. Beyond the houses was open agricultural land, the plain. The village lay in the opposite direction. From the last house, three hundred yards distant, a woman emerged, wearing an old blue raincoat and pushing a baby's push-chair. She had a scarf tied over her head and was evidently going into the village to shop.

Larry moved as she drew nearer. The window of the vehicle wound down. A rifle muzzle protruded from it. A shot sounded.

The woman in the blue raincoat fell to her knees, still clinging with one hand to the push-chair.

As three more shots rang out, the push-chair blew apart. The woman's face was covered with shreds of baby as she fell on the road.

Larry's mother had seen at least part of this. She was drying a plate on a tea towel. She dropped the plate, ran from the kitchen, and opened the front door.

'No, no, Larry! Stop it, you fool. Whatever do you think you're doing?'

Larry had descended from the Land Rover after firing the four shots. He moved slowly, with a sleep-walker's lethargy. With that same lethargy, he snugged the butt of the rifle into his shoulder and fired at his mother. She was blown from the porch back into the passage. He fired two more shots into the house. I ran to the bedroom and heaved myself under the bed, fighting blindly with the magazines. I was sure he was after me.

There the police discovered me, four hours later, lying in a pool of my own urine.

So it was that eventually I found myself in a hospital in Swindon close to other victims of Larry Foot. After shooting the woman from the council house and her baby, and his mother, Larry had walked into Bishops Linctus and shot dead the first three people he met, wounding several others. BISHOPS BLOODBATH screamed the tabloid headlines. The quiet little affair roused much more excitement than the Soviet War (in which British troops were involved) then reaching one of its many climaxes outside Tblisi. Why had Larry done it? The explanation given was that he had always been keen on guns. Presumably the same explanation would cover the Soviet War.

Armed police from Bishops Magnum and Salisbury shot Larry

down behind the Shell garage. He had liked to help people, poor Larry. At least he gave a little pleasure to the bloodthirsty readers of the *Sun*.

This incident got me swiftly – in an ambulance – into the realm of professional medical scrutiny. Within a few days, I again had an identity. I was Roy Edward Burnell, a university lecturer and specialist in church architecture. I had written a learned book, *Architrave and Archetype*, a thesis linking human aspiration with human-designed structures, cathedrals in particular.

The chief medico in charge of my case, a Dr Rosemary Kepepwe, entered my hospital room smiling, bringing with her a copy of my book. 'We're getting somewhere, Roy,' she said. 'We'll contact your wife next.'

I smote my forehead. 'My God, don't say I'm married.'

She laughed. 'I'm afraid so. At least you were married. We'll soon have her tracked down – and other people in your past. What is the last thing you remember before the white-out?'

Even to me, her attitude seemed amateurish. When I said something of the sort, Dr Kepepwe explained that most of the original staff of the hospital were serving with British troops in Operation Total Tartary, in Murmansk, Usbekistan, the front in the Caucasus, and the new revolutionary area opening up round Lake Baikal. The disintegration of the Soviet Union had created a tremendous demand for medication.

'My husband was a brain surgeon,' Kepepwe said. 'The best husband a woman could have. David won the Isle of Wight Sea-Fishing Trophy two years in succession. Everyone respected him. We have three children, one of them at Eton and one now working as a waiter in a Little Chef off the M25 at the South Mimms Service Area. But David volunteered to serve with Total Tartary. I had picked up a bit of surgery from him, of course, so here I am.

'You were quite lucky to get here. Salisbury Plain is all mined these days.'

'Lucky me,' I said. But it appeared I did not know how lucky. I had marvelled that it was such a quiet hospital, and ascribed this to efficiency. Not so, Dr Kepepwe explained. I was the only patient in there. All the other wards were empty. Civilian patients had been turned out three days earlier, as the hospital prepared to receive wounded from the Eastern theatre of war.

'Anyhow, I'd better take your details,' Dr Kepepwe said, reluctantly. 'Then I'll bring you a cup of tea. What did you say was the last thing you remembered?'

I told her. I had gone to South America to view some of the ecclesiastical architecture there. I arrived in Buenos Aires and checked into my hotel. I remembered going up in a gilt elevator. And then – white-out. The fear of standing on the edge of a great abyss overtook me.

Dr Kepepwe saw the expression on my face. 'Don't worry – you're not alone, Roy. How does it feel?'

'An ocean. A wide ocean with a small island here and there. No continent. The continent has gone.'

As I spoke the words, some strange thing struggled in my mind. A name almost came back to me, then died.

So I waited. Waited to be restored. To pass the time I had access to the hospital library on VDU, together with TV and video. Also the new media craze, the NV, or nostovision. Laser projectors could beam whole programmes into the mind, where the programmes became like your own lived memories, though they faded in a few days. In view of my deficiencies, I avoided the NV and stuck to the library; but little I read remained in my mind.

What sins, what meannesses, what grave errors I had committed in the previous ten years had been forgiven me. I waited in calm without apprehension.

Dr Kepepwe assured me active steps were being taken to trace those who had been intimate with me during the ten blank years: my parents, my academic colleagues. The confusions of war, the tight security covering the country, made communication difficult.

When she left in the evening, I wandered through the great empty building. In the dark of the long antiseptic corridors, green LEDs glowed, accompanied often by hums or growls. It was like being in the entrails of a glacier.

On the desk in Rosemary Kepepwe's office stood a photograph of her husband David, very black, smiling genially with a large fish on a scale by his side. I wondered about their lives; but there was nothing on which to speculate. She was little more to me than an embodiment of kindness.

Only my slippered footsteps on the stairs, the tiles. I was a ghost among the ghosts of multitudinous lives whose cvs, like mine, had been lost. Who had lived, died, survived? A phrase came back uncomfortably from the white-out, 'the sorry jeste of Life'.

But, I told myself as I took a service elevator up to the roof, I should not think in the past tense. Any day now and the hospital would be filled again with the living – the military living, harpooned by their wounds, poised on the brink of a final white-out. They would survive or not, to accumulate more memories, happy or sad as the case might be.

On the roof, the installations of air-conditioning plants painted black by a city's grime lived and breathed. I stood on the parapet, looking out over the town of Swindon, willing myself to feel less disembodied. The stars shone overhead, remote but always with promise of something better than the brief rush of biological existence. As I drank them in, a roar of engines sounded.

Three B-52 Stratofortresses flew overhead, from the west towards the eastern stars.

I went downstairs again, to my ward, my nest in the glacier. I must wait. Waiting did not require too much fortitude. One day soon, Dr Kepepwe would do the trick – with luck before the war-damaged moved in to supplant me in her attentions.

The days would pass. Help would come.

Indeed, the days did pass.

And then Stephanie arrived.

Stephanie was a vision of delight, tall, fine-boned, aesthetic of countenance, walking easy and free inside a fawn linen suit. Hair tawny, neat, almost shoulder-length. I admired the way she strolled into the ward, doing quite determinedly something not to her taste. With a cautious smile on her face. And this lady had been my wife. I could have forgotten that? I could have forgotten all the times we had enjoyed together, where we'd been, what we'd done? So it seemed. My head had been bitten off.

Like most gusts of pleasure, this one brought its pain. She sat facing me: calm, sympathetic, but at a distance I had no way of negotiating, as I listened dismayed to what she revealed of those islands, that lost continent.

Stephanie and I had married eight years ago, only four weeks after meeting in Los Angeles for the first time. We were divorced five years later. Here indeed, I thought, must lie some of those sins, meannesses and grave errors. She broke this news to me gently, casting her clear gaze towards the window in preference to seeing my hurt. The hospital authorities had tracked her down in California, where she was enjoying success as a fabric designer and living with a famous composer of film music.

'You don't owe me anything,' she said. And, after a pause, 'I don't owe you anything.'

'It's good of you to come and see me. The war and everything, and that jumbo blown out of the skies over the Atlantic . . . '

A small laugh. 'I was interested, of course. You're a bit of medical history.'

'We had no children?'

She shook her head. 'That whole business was the reason for our falling out.'

'Shit,' I said. A long silence fell between us. I could have crossed the Sahara in it. 'Did I ever – I mean, since we split up – did I ever – did we communicate at all?'

'It was final,' she said. 'I didn't want to know. I like my new life in the States. What you did was up to you, wasn't it? But you did send me postcards. Generally of draughty old churches here and there – of the kind you used to drag me into when we were together.'

'You can't beat a good old draughty old church,' I said, smiling.

She did not return the smile. Perhaps the woman lacked humour.

'I brought a couple of your cards along in my purse,' she said. I noted the Americanism as she dipped into her handbag. She pulled out one card and handed it over, extending it between two outstretched fingers – as if amnesia was catching.

'Huh, just one card. I tore the others up, I'm afraid.' That, I thought, was a little unnecessary pain she had no reason to inflict.

The card, crudely coloured, showed a picture of a church labelled as St Stephen's Basilica, although I saw immediately that architecturally it was not a basilica. I turned it over, glanced at the Hungarian stamp, and read the few words I had scribbled to Stephanie, only three weeks earlier.

'Budapest. Brief visit here. Making notes for lectures as usual. Need some florid Hungarian architecture. Trust you're well. Have met strange old friend – just going round to Antonescu's Clinic with him. Love, Roy.'

I flung my arms round Stephanie and kissed her.

I went back to the Gellert. There, not entirely surprisingly, was Montagu Clements, still wearing my sweater.

He raised his hands in mock-surrender. 'Pax. No offence meant, honest, old chum. Since I lost my job I've worked as a decoy for Antonescu, luring on innocent foreigners who come here to take advantage of low Hungarian prices. Economic necessity and all that.'

'You had your hand in the till – now you've had it in my mind. Stealing a memory is like murder, you miserable slob.'

'Yes, and no doubt it will be legislated against when nostovision becomes less than a seven-day wonder. Till then, Antonescu earns a modest dollar from his bootleg memory bullets. They're short of hard currency, the Hungarians. Let me buy you a drink.'

I almost threw myself on him. 'You've poisoned my life, you bastard, you'd probably poison my drink.'

He was very cool. 'Let's not fall out. You have a contempt for me. Think how I might feel about you. I've had to edit ten years of your memories, a lot of which weren't edifying. You should be happy to be rid of them.'

'I see, Clements – The FOAM Theory of History . . . Never learn anything. Just bloody forget. Haven't you ever heard that saying about those who forget history being doomed to repeat it? Why do you think the world's in such a fucking mess?'

He remained unmoved. 'I have no idea, old boy. Nor, I suspect, do you, for all your academic posturing. Without wishing to hurt your feelings, your last ten years were full of crap. But there – everyone's last ten years were full of crap . . . '

We were standing in the baroque foyer of the hotel, which had been built in the great European hotel age during the peaceful years preceding the first World War. I gestured through the doors, through the glass of which traffic could be seen crossing the Szabadsag Bridge. Beyond lay the dense Magyar thoroughfares, the grandiose piles of masonry, where fat profiteers sweated over their calculators.

'I was already on my way to the police, Clements, *old boy*. Don't pretend we're friends. You had me dumped on Salisbury Plain, don't forget.'

Clements turned on one of his innocent smiles. 'Just think, it could have been the Gobi . . . I interceded on your behalf. Be British, old chap – let's compromise. Let's do a deal.'

'What deal?'

He said, 'We could discuss business better in the bar. You want your memory back, eh? Don't go to the police and I'll bring you your memory this afternoon. Agree? Say three-thirty, after I've taken my customary nap. OK?'

So I agreed on it. I agreed, thinking I would go to the police later. Clements turned up at 3.55.

We sat at the upstairs bar with two tall glasses of iced white Eger wine, for which I paid. He produced in the palm of his right hand two slender plastic spools, which I recognized as nostovision bullets, ready to be inserted into the head-laser.

'I had some trouble getting these, old chap. How about fifty dollars each?'

'Maybe you really have lost your memory or you'd know I wouldn't fall for that. Hand them over. Why two bullets?'

He took a reflective sip of his wine. 'Antonescu's at the cutting edge of psycho-technology. We have to know our customers. They're mainly in America and the Arab World. It's a specialized market. We boiled your memory banks down into two categories – the rest we threw away, sorry to say. There's your speciality, church architecture and all that. That spool has a limited but steady sale to academics – a tribute to all the knowledge you had packed away. I suppose you'll be glad to get that back. Surely it's worth fifty dollars to you?'

'Come on, Clements, what's the other bullet?'

'A hundred dollars, old chum? It's all your life and activities with a woman called Stephanie. Very erotic stuff, believe me. Very popular in Saudi Arabia.'

I threw my wine in his face and grabbed the two bullets.

I leave it to you to decide which bullet I played first.

The Soviet War continues. Heavy fighting in the Caucasus despite bad weather conditions. Radio reports said that Alliance forces used chemical and bacteriological weapons in the Kutaisi area. Questioned, American General 'Gus' Stalinbrass said, 'What the heck else do we do? These assholes don't give up easy.'

Last night, four Georgian soldiers crossed the Tblisi lines, found their way through a minefield, and gave themselves up to a British journalist, Dicky Bowden. One of the soldiers was a boy of fourteen.

Bowden said, 'Starved and disaffected troops like these are all that stand between our advance and the Caspian Sea.'

He was confident that the war would be over in a week or two. Say a month. Maximum two months. A year.

SUMMERTIME WAS NEARLY OVER

I AM RESOLVED to leave some brief account of my days while I am still able. It does not escape me that a fair hand has already written some account of my early days; but that account broke off too soon, for I returned from the realms of ice, to which solitudes my soul – if I may be presumed to have one – was attracted.

In due time, I returned to the country about the city of Geneva. Although I had hoped for justice and understanding when my story was known, that was not to be.

Persecution remained my lot. I had to escape to the nearby wilderness of mountain and ice, to live out my days among chamois and eagle, which were being hunted as avidly as I.

Before leaving the city for ever, I came across a philosopher, Jean-Jacques Rousseau, even more noted than the family of my accursed Master. At the beginning of one of his books I discovered these words, which to me in my lowly condition were more than words: 'I am made unlike anyone I have ever met; I will even venture to say that I am like no one in the whole world.'

Here was a sentiment I might have uttered myself. To find such understanding in a book gave me strength. Ever since coming upon Rousseau's writings so long ago, I have tried to live with my dear wife above the glaciers in the condition he would have approved, that of the Noble Savage – in defiance of those citified creatures who multiply in the valleys far below.

The placidity of a late August day lingers over the Swiss Alps. The sound of automobiles wending their way along the road far below does not reach me; I hear only a distant occasional cowbell and the cheerful nearer transactions of insects. I am at peace. The helicopters appeared after noon, when the clouds cleared from the brow of the Jungfrau. They had been active all week, unsettling me with their noise. There were two of them, blue, belonging to the Swiss police. Soon they disappeared behind a nearby slope, and I crawled from under the bush where I had hidden.

Once all was peace here. We did not know of tourists and helicopters.

Now the numbers of the People are increasing. If it isn't helicopters, it's cars on the way to the Silberner Hirsch below, or machines roaring in distant valleys. Elsbeth and I will have to move to a more remote place, if I can find one.

Elsbeth says she does not wish to move again. Our cave on the upper slopes of the Aletschhorn suits her well, but ours is a fugitive life, as I explain to her.

In summer, the People drive off the highway up the track leading to the Silberner Hirsch, with its fine view of the mountains to the north. Occasionally, one or two of them will leave their cars and climb higher, almost as far as the winter shelters. Perhaps they will pick the wild flowers growing in the lush grasses, cornflower, poppy, clover, eglantine and the frail vetch.

They rarely reach the cave on its precipitous slope. I never molest the People. Elsbeth and I stay hidden. I protect her in my arms.

In winter, she and I are completely alone with the elements. My temperament is compatible with the wind and the snow and the storms born from the cold wombs of northern lakes. The People's machines do not threaten us then. We survive somehow. I have learned not to be afraid of fire. I sit over its red eye in the cave and listen to the musics of the atmosphere.

I am kin with the slopes hereabouts. They are steep and treacherous with outcropping rock. No People come to ski on them. In the autumn, before the first snows fall, when fog rolls up from the valley, the hotel closes down, the People all depart. Only a boy lives at the hotel to act as watchman with his goats and chickens. That's far below our eyrie – I go down there to scavenge.

Oh, I have seen that boy's face full of fear as he stares through a window at me passing in a swirl of snow.

Our winter world is without human inhabitants. I can't explain it. I cannot explain to Elsbeth where the People go. Do they sleep all winter, like the waterfall?

This is the trouble: that I understand nothing. Long though I have lived, I never understand better as years pass. I never understand why the teeth of winter bite so cruelly down into the bone, how daylight sickens from the east, why Elsbeth is so chill as I lie with her, why the nights are so long, without word or gleam.

I am troubled by my lack of understanding. Nothing remains, nothing remains.

Best not to think of another winter. It is summer now, time of happiness. But summertime is nearly over.

All this livelong day I lay on my favourite rock in the sun. The flies visited and crawled on me. Also many other small things that may have life and thought – butterflies, snails in curled shell, spiders, maggots. I lay staring at the People below, coming to and going from the Silberner Hirsch. They climb from their machines. They walk about and photograph the valley and the hill peaks. They enter the restaurant. In time, they come from it again. Then they drive away. Their cars are beads on the thread of highway. They have homes, often far distant. Their homes are full of all manner of possessions. They are capable of many kinds of activity. I hear their planes roar overhead, leaving a trail of snow across the sky. People are always busy, like the flies and ants.

This also they can do: procreate. I have mated many times with Elsbeth. She brings forth no child. Here is another thing I cannot understand. Why does Elsbeth not bring forth a child? Is the fault in her or in me, because I am strangely made, because, as Rousseau said, 'I am made unlike anyone I ever met'?

The grass grows high before my sight. I peer through its little ambush at the scene below. Even the grass makes more grass, and all the small things that live in the grass reproduce their kind, until summer is over. Everything conceives more things, except Elsbeth and I.

Elsbeth remained as usual in our cave beside the waterfall. When the good season is spent and cold bites to the bone, the waterfall dies like most other living things. Its music ceases. It becomes rigid and mute. What is this grief that visits the Earth so regularly? How to explain it?

Only in the spring does the waterfall recover, and then it roars with delight at regaining life, just as I did. Then Elsbeth and I are happy again.

My head becomes cloudy as I lie on my rock peering through the grass at the scene down below. After night has fallen, I will climb down the slopes to walk about unseen round the hotel and retrieve what the People have discarded. I find there something to eat, and many other things, discarded papers and books, this and that. The night is my friend. I am darkness itself.

Why it has to be thus I know not. Yet I have taught myself not to feel discontent. Once I was malicious because I was miserable, but no more. Now I have my lovely mate, I have schooled myself to be neither malicious nor miserable, and not to hate People.

In the discarded newspapers I read that there are People far more evil than ever I was. They take pleasure in killing the innocent. This murder they do not only with their bare hands but with extreme weapons, the nature of which I am unable to comprehend. Thousands die in their wars every year.

Sometimes I read the name of my Maker in the newspapers. Even after all this time, they still speak ill of him; why it does not therefore make me, his victim, welcome among People I do not know. This is something else eluding my understanding.

Lying in my cloudy state, I fall asleep without knowing it. The flies buzz and the sun is hot on my spine.

To dream can be very cruel. I try to tear these visions from myself. In my dreams, memories of dead People rise up. One claims that I have his thighs and legs, another that I have his torso. One wretch wishes his head returned, another even claims his internal organs. These desperate People parade in my sleep. I am a living cemetery, a hospital of flesh for those who lack flesh. What can I do? Within me I feel dreadful ghosts and crimes locked within my bones, knotted into my very entrails. I cannot pass water without a forgotten claimant reaching for what is his.

Do People suffer in this way? Being a mere composite from charnel houses, I fear that I alone undergo this sorrow behind the eyebrows. Residual scenes from dreadful other memories play like lice inside veins I hardly dare look on as mine. I feel myself a theatre of other lives and deaths.

Why then do People shun me? Have I not more humanity than they trapped inside me?

While I suffered from these dreams on my slab of rock, something woke me. I heard the sound of voices carried on the thin air. Two People, females, were climbing upwards. They had left behind the Silberner Hirsch and were moving towards the place where I lay.

I observed them with the silent attention a tiger must give its approaching prey. And yet not that exactly, for there was fear in my heart. The People always awaken fear in me. The elder of these two women was gathering wild flowers, exclaiming as she did so. It was innocent enough, yet still I felt the fear.

The elder female sank down on a tree stump to rest, fanning herself with her hand. The other one came on, picking her way cautiously. I saw the brown hair on the crown of her head, gleaming in the sun with a beauty I cannot describe.

She would have passed me by a few feet, perhaps not noticing me. Yet because I could not bear to lie where I was and chance being seen, I jumped up with a great bound and confronted her.

The female gave a gasp of fear, looking up at me with her mouth open, revealing tongue and white teeth.

'Help!'she called once, until I had my hand over the lower part of her face. The look she gave me changed from fear to disgust.

Oh, I've seen that look on the faces of People before. It always awakens my fury. The faces of People are unlike mine, plastic, mobile, given to expressing emotion. With one blow I could wipe that expression and the flesh that paints it right from their skulls.

As I lifted her, her toes dangled in their white trainers. I thrust my face into hers, that female face dewed with the heat of afternoon. As I considered whether to smash her and throw her down on the mountainside, I caught her scent. It hit me as forcibly as a blow to the stomach.

That scent . . . So different from the scent of Elsbeth . . . It caused a kind of confusion in my brain, making me pause. One of those old elusive memories from the back of my brain returned to baffle me – a memory of something that had never happened to me. I have said I understand little; at that moment I understood nothing, and that terrible lack ran through me like an electric shock. I put her down.

'You monster . . . ' the female said, staggering. Beneath us, the descents were toothed with jagged rock. Rather than fall, she clung to my arm – a gesture so trusting in its way as to melt the remains of my anger. I could remember only how vulnerable People were, the females in particular. At that instant, I would have fought a wild beast in order to preserve her unharmed.

As though sensing some abatement of my ferocity, she said in a natural tone, 'I did not mean to startle you.'

When I could not think how to answer this, unaccustomed as I was to conversing with People, she went on, 'Do you speak English? I am just a tourist here on vacation.'

Still I could not answer, my senses reeling from her scent and from the look of her. It was as if a little wild doe had come to me, all quivering with a half-mistrust. She was young. Her face was round and open, without scars from medical science. Her grey eyes were set in a brown skin smooth like the shell of a hen's egg. The hair I had watched from above had become disturbed when I lifted her, so that it shaded the line of her left cheek. She wore a t-shirt with the name of an American university printed on it, and denim shorts cut ragged round her plump thighs. Beneath the shirt I saw the outline of her breasts. That outline held so entrancing a meaning that I was further disarmed.

My difficulty in breathing was such that I clutched my throat.

She looked at me with what I took to be concern.

'Say, you OK? My friend's a doctor. Maybe I'll call her to come on up.'

'Don't call,' I said. I sat down in the long grass, puzzled to understand my weakness. In some elusive way, here before me was the representative of something, some enormous sphere of sensations and transcendent values such as I had only read about, something my Maker had withheld from me which I desperately needed. That I could put no name to it made it all the more tantalizing, like a song when only the tune remains and the words are lost by time.

'My friend can help,' said this astonishing young person. She turned as if to call but I growled at her again, 'Don't call,' in so urgent a voice that she desisted. When she looked up the mountainside, as if searching for help there, I realized that she still had fear of me, little knowing the true state of affairs, and felt herself like an animal in a trap.

'But you're ill,' she said. 'Or else in trouble with the law.'

Her remark released my ability to speak to her. 'My trouble is with the law of humanity, which rules against me. Law is invented to protect the rulers, not the ruled; the strong, not the weak. No court on Earth is concerned with justice, only with law. The weak can anticipate persecution, not justice.'

'But you are not weak,' she said.

Her grey eyes when she looked at me made me tremble. When the moon is high, I roam the mountainsides much of the night. That dear silver dish in the sky is like an eye, guarding me. But in the grey eyes of this female I read only a kind of concealed hostility.

'Justice is only a name. Persecution and weakness are real enough. Those who for whatsoever reason have no roof over their heads are no better than deer to be hunted down.'

My words appeared to make no impression on her. 'In my country, there is Welfare to look after the homeless.'

'You know nothing.'

She did not dispute that, merely standing before me, head bowed, yet sneaking side glances at me and round about.

'Where do you live?' she asked, in a minute.

I jerked my head in the direction of the mountain above us.

'Alone?'

'With my wife. Are you . . . a wife?'

She dismissed the question with a toss of her head.

I listened to the flies buzzing about me and the murmur of the bees in the clover as they tumbled at our feet. These small sounds were the building bricks of the silence that enfolded us.

She stuck out a small brown hand. 'I'm not afraid any more. I'm sorry I startled you. Why don't you take me to visit with your wife? What's her name?'

At that, I was silent with mistrust a long time. Her scent reached me as I took the hand gently into mine and looked down at her.

Finally, I spoke the sacred name. 'Elsbeth.'

She too paused before responding. 'Mine's Vicky.' She did not ask my name, nor did I offer it.

There we stood on the perilous slope. This encounter had used much of my courage. I had caught her, yet still I feared her. While I contemplated her, she continued to look about with uneasy glances like a trapped animal, and I saw her breasts move with her breathing. Now those honest grey eyes, which I associated with the moon, were furtive and unkind.

'Well then,' she said, with an uneasy laugh, 'what's keeping us? Let's go.'

Perhaps my Maker did not intend that my brain should function perfectly. This little thing whose hand I held could easily be crushed. There was no reason for me to fear it. Yet fear it I did, so greatly did the idea come to me that if I took her up to the cave to meet Elsbeth, she would somehow have trapped me instead of I her.

Yet this notion was conquered by a stronger urge I could not deny.

If I led this tender scented female to the cave, she would then be far away from her friend and entirely within my power. We would be private to do that supreme thing, whether she wished for it or not. Elsbeth would understand if I overpowered her and had my way with her. Why should I not? Why else was this morsel, this Vicky, sent to me?

Even at the cost of revealing the whereabouts of the cave to one of the People I must take this specimen there – I must, so great was my urge, thundering in me like the breakers of an ocean. When I was finished with her, I would make sure she did not give our hiding place away. Elsbeth would approve of that. Then our secret life could continue as before, with only the small wild things knowing of our existence.

So thereupon I echoed her words. 'Let's go.'

The way was steep. She was puny. I kept good hold of her, part-dragging her after me. The afternoon sun blazed on us and her scent rose to me, together with her sobs.

The bushes became smaller, more scanty. I had come this way a hundred times, always varying my route so as to avoid making more of a track than a rabbit might do. We came to the Cleft, a shallow indentation, a fold in the flesh of the mountain. Here the infant waterfall played its tune, gushing with pure water which, several hundred feet down the valley, would become a tributary of the Lotschental river. Behind the fall, hidden by a dark-leaved shrub, was the entrance to the cave.

Here we had to pause. She claimed she must get her breath back. She bent double and stayed that way, and her brown hair hung down, and her little fingertips touched the ground.

Great white clouds rolled above us, tumbling over the mountain summit as if eager to find quieter air. Of a sudden, one of the police helicopters shot overhead, startling me with its enormous clatter, as if the thing were a flying tree, streaking out of sight behind the crisp crest of the Jungfrau. I had no time to hide before it was over and gone.

I grabbed the girl and pulled. 'Into the cave with you.'

She struggled. 'What if Elsbeth doesn't want to see me? Shouldn't you warn her first? Why don't you call her out here?'

Not answering, I dragged her towards the cave. She seized at a bush but I beat her hand away.

'I don't want to see Elsbeth,' she screamed. 'Help! Help!'

Silencing her with a hand enveloping her face, I half-lifted her and so we entered the cave, the girl struggling furiously.

Elsbeth lay there in the shade, watching everything, saying nothing. I let the girl loose and pushed her towards my wife.

The girl went motionless, staring forward, one hand to her lips. There was no sound but the high buzz of flies. I waited for her to try to scream again, readying myself to leap upon her and bear her down. But when she spoke, it was softly, with her gaze on Elsbeth, not me.

'She's been dead a very long time, hasn't she?'

Some People can cry. I have no facility for tears. Yet as soon as this activity began in Vicky, a storm of weeping – as I judged the sensation – accumulated in my breast like a storm over the Alps. In Elsbeth's eyes no movement showed. The maggots had done their work in those sockets and moved to other pastures.

As I raised my hands above my head and let out a howl, two male People rushed into the cave. They yelled as they came. The weeping girl, Vicky, threw herself out of danger into the recesses of the cave, where I stored the fruits of the autumn. The men flung a net over me.

Wildly though I struggled, using all my strength, the net was unbreakable. The male People drew it tight, as fishermen must have done when they hauled in a catch in olden times. They shackled my legs so that I could not run. Then they felled me, so that I lay by Elsbeth and was as helpless as she.

Those People treated me as if I were no better than an animal. I was dragged out of the cave, through the waterfall, to lie on my back gazing up at the fast-moving clouds in the blue sky; and I thought to myself, Those clouds are free, just as I was until now.

More male People arrived. I found out how they came there soon enough. One of their helicopters was standing on a level ledge of mountainside above my refuge. The female, Vicky, came to me and bent down so that I could look again into her grey eyes.

'I regret this,' she said. 'I had to act as decoy. We knew you were somewhere upon the Aletschhorn, but not exactly where. We've been combing this mountainside all week.'

My faculty of speech was deserting me along with my other powers. I managed to say, 'So you are just an accomplice of these other cruel beasts.'

'I am working with the local police, yes. Don't blame me . . . '

One of the male police nudged her. 'Out of the way, miss. He's still dangerous. Stand back there.' And she moved away.

I was lifted up and lashed to a stretcher. Her face disappeared from my sight. Still encased in the net, I was dropped on the ground as if I were an old plank. They shouted a great deal, and waved their arms. Only then did I realize they were going to transport me up the mountain. Five male People were there, one of them controlling the other four. They looked down on me. Again those expressions of disgust: I might have been a leopard trapped by big-game hunters, when mercy did not enter into their thoughts.

The male person who ordered the others around had a mouth full of small grey teeth. Staring down, he said, 'We're not letting you escape this time, you freak of nature. We have a list of murders stretching back over the last two centuries for which you are responsible.'

Though I read no sympathy in his face or mouth, I found a few words to offer. 'Sir, I had never an intent to offend. It was my Maker who offended against me, acting so unfatherly against one who never asked to be born in any unnatural way. As for these murders, as you name them, the first one only, that of the child, was done in malice, when I had no knowledge of those states of being which you, not I, can enjoy – to wit, life and death. The rest of my offences were committed in self-defence, when I found the hands of all People were against me. Let me free, I pray. Let me live upon this blessed mountain, in the state of nature and innocence described by Rousseau.'

His mouth thinned and elongated like an earthworm. 'You shit,' he said, turning away.

Another male appeared over the ragged skyline.

'Chopper's ready,' he called.

They swung into action. I was lifted up. It took four of them to carry me. I could not see the female but, as I was raised to their shoulders, I caught a glimpse of my happy home, that cave where Elsbeth and I had been so content. Then it was gone, and they laboured up the slope with me, trussed and helpless.

As we approached the helicopter, a shower burst over us, one of those unheralded showers which sweep the Alps. I tasted the blessed rain on my lips, drinking it even while the People complained. I thought, this is the last time I taste of the benisons of nature. I am being taken to the realms of the People, who hate nature as much as they hate me, who am unnatural.

A chill sharpened the flavour of the water. It carried the taint of autumn, that melancholy transition time before winter. Summertime was nearly over, and my wife would lie alone and lonely in our cave, waiting for my return, looking with her sightless eyes for her lover, uttering never a word of complaint.

BETTER MORPHOSIS

LOOK, I'll put it to you this way, in the hope you'll understand. Literature's OK, but what really grabs me is *scuttling*, right? Like, I mean, scuttling – here and there, anywhere I feel like.

Which is to say that directions are better than sentences. Any direction better than any sentence. Scuttle scuttle bliss. Bliss.

Me and all my friends had been having this really great scuttle. OK? A megascuttle, all round this apartment building in Prague. A moment's inattention and what happens?

– Jesus, I wake up and find myself transformed. Like lying in a BED, transformed into – Look, I have to tell you. Into this huge pale human thing. Well – shit, into Franz Kafka. KAFKA. (That's his name. They have NAMES.)

Where's everyone gone? Nowhere. I don't know. I don't know, I never had a single thought before. Suddenly I'm Franz Kafka, lying there in that bed and thinking fit to bust. THINKING. Yuk . . .

All I'm thinking is just awful. I mean, I'm a fan of oily rags and maybe mildew. A bit of damp in a bad corner and I'm happy. Anything. Grease, know what I mean? But not for fuck's sake *thinking*.

Honest, I didn't even know thinking had been invented.

But there I was, and thinking – I may as well say it, thinking bad thoughts about my father. How he was so oppressive, how he was so strong and hairy and his voice was so loud and when he washed of a morning he made splashes in the wash-basin and blew his nose into the water, both nostrils at once into the soapy water and . . .

Well, look, Christ, never mind thinking, like the whole concept of FATHER was alien. Come on, down there in the basement, we just spawned, remember. We just were. One moment, nothing. Eggs. Next moment, up and running. Dozens of us, *scuttling*. You know?

Scuttling, having real fun, mobile as all get-out. Little legs going like the clappers.

So I felt down the bed. TWO LEGS.

Jesus. What a nightmare!

Just TWO LEGS.

Where had all the others gone? Pity's sake, what the hell was I supposed to do with *two legs*? You think you can get a good scuttle going with two legs? Forget it!

Two legs. I can't get over it. Between the legs some hair of a sort and this stupid flabby thing. I feel it with my mandibles –

Mandibles! – Yow, what have the bastards done to me? I have lost my shagging mandibles. No mandibles. Just these feeble hand things, all pale and pulpy and –

– and I pull at it and it – sort of gets stiff –

– come on, I must be off my tiny thorax –

– it gives out with some mess that I might normally eat but now it sort of blows away and there's a whole muddle of emotion in my . . . MIND I cannot cope with. Look, reproduction should not require such an upheaval.

But almost immediately Kafka – me, dammit – begins *thinking* again, and I get out of bed. No kidding. I. Get. Out. Of. BED.

The horror of it! Those two awful long white legs, not neat at all, covered with a layer of flesh . . . I move them and instead of having a good scuttle across the floor, I stand up on these legs in quite the wrong attitude. And I walk, balancing on these two stilts, high above the floor.

Frightened? Sonny, I was scared out of my wits. Scared shitless, and that's the truth.

There's a chest across the room, of the sort I used to scuttle under. Instead, I pick up the clock on it and I see it is half-past six.

You follow me? I'm reading a clock and I'm thinking it's time to be going to work. Me, who never read a clock or went to work in my life. Look, I've spent days in basements and places like that, but for fun. FUN. Work? I'd never heard of work till that moment, and there I was thinking of myself dressed in trousers and sitting at a desk with a ledger. Sitting. Christ, I ask myself in a panic, how the shagging hell do you SIT? But somehow at the same time I am washing myself – I'm *trying to get filth off myself.*

It's incredible. I thought soap was something you ate, yet here I am, calling myself Franz and rubbing this stuff round my neck. Not at all liking filth. Only yesterday, it used to be a way of life.

And there's Father – OK, don't say it, I'm only telling you – there's FATHER, banging on the door with a fist and calling, 'Franz, Franz, what's the matter with you?'

You think that's odd? Then dig this: I ANSWER.

Yes, I make this noise kind of thing in my throat and I say, 'I'm just ready.' That's what I say. I have never spoken one word before – fine, many a scuttle here and there, but never a WORD. And there I stand, bold as brass, if shaking a bit, saying, 'I'm just ready.' Maybe I'm growing stronger.

And the nightmare goes on. I can't repeat it. You'd think I was round the twist if I told you. I mean, like sitting at a breakfast table with a FAMILY. Not thousands, just four of them, each with two of these legs I've been telling you about. You think I looked funny? Up yours.

I shiver to think of that breakfast. Those people . . . Not a one of them realized I was not human. They looked at me and they pretend I'm someone called Franz Kafka. Maybe they really thought I was Franz Kafka. People who can't scuttle just can't be trusted.

Standing, I sample a bowl of oatmeal.

So after this meal, when I find I'm stuffing foul non-rancid things down my throat – without bad effects – I try a quick scuttle round the room. Can I get up the wall? Can I scuttle across the ceiling?

What, with two legs?

Forget it.

I fall flat on my bonce and break a chair. The other three people all run around screaming – quite fast, admittedly, but you would hardly call it scuttling. Scuttling needs technique. I don't have to tell you.

My idea is to get out of the house. *So I put on a coat.* Don't laugh. I'm telling you, I put on a coat. In this nightmare, everyone puts on coats when they go out. Maybe I'll see the funny side of it one day.

On the way to work, we bump into Milena. That's a female of the species.

'Hello, Franz,' she says. 'Thanks for your letter. How are you?'

This is meant to be the sexy bit, but don't get excited, chums. Franz – me – I – he goes over all shy. Can't even look at her properly. Stutters. In his mind thinks of simply incredible things he would do to her, involving getting her on a couch and going into unrealistic positions without clothes, plus jerky movements.

Of course, EGGS are at the bottom of it all. That at least I can understand. But does he get on with the egg-laying? Do they spawn?

Not a bit of it. They just stand there in the street.

I say, 'I'm not too good this morning. The question of my health is a difficult one, which I shall have to answer at length in a letter, if you can find the patience to read it. I wouldn't hold it against you if you didn't read it. Whatever you think I look like does not necessarily represent the truth.'

This is bizarre. She replies, 'I liked the flowers. They now stand in my room. They bring the daylight into my room. Perhaps you will come to see them, visit my room.'

And I say, 'No, you are not listening.' And he's thinking of her ovipositor. I can hear his stomach rumbling, and long to escape among the cobbles underfoot, where lovely horse droppings lie. I could scuttle scuttle scuttle like fury among them.

'I keep imagining this morning that I have – please believe me, Milena, because when we're married you will have to put up with a lot of this, but I keep imagining that I have lots of little crisp sepia legs.'

'What colour?' she asks, startled.

'Sepia. A sort of light, faded brown, perhaps with a touch of mahogany. Anyhow, I keep thinking I'm a common household pest. Horse shit!'

'What?' Milena backs away in disgust. But this word is mine. I have managed to squeeze out that one phrase, 'horse shit'. Much better than conversation.

Kafka and Milena take fright and run off in different directions. Looks like egg-laying has taken a beating.

Somehow I get to my workplace. All sorts of men there – I'm terrified, of course – in big boots. I keep thinking I'm going to get stamped on, even when the clots are calling me Franz.

I sit down at this desk with a ledger. It isn't as difficult as I'd thought, because I have found how to . . . look, I'm not explaining all this for fun . . . I have found how to *bend in the middle*.

Down I sit, and what do I do?

I shouldn't be doing this. I know I shouldn't be doing this, but still I do it. (Yes, right, figure that one out . . .)

I start writing *The* fucking *Trial*.

In a notebook.

In longhand.

Like there was no tomorrow.

Scared of being caught.

Don't tell me it doesn't make sense. There's that thing, my HAND, utterly repulsive, and it is moving, making tiny scrawls on the paper. Scrawls I might enjoy, on their own, but unfortunately they are not just mere scuttles – oh, no, it seems I'm in some kind of a scuttle-free universe – these scuttles spell something. Spell. SPELL. Don't ask me to explain, just take it that's what they do, see?

'K. was informed by telephone that next Sunday a short inquiry into his case would take place.'

That's what Kafka – that's what *I* wrote. It didn't make sense to me. I'm no fool, but that sentence wouldn't make sense to any insect. Telephone? Sunday? Yet he – I – seemed pleased enough, and kept dribbling these words across the page.

What is all this? I asked him. Who the hell are you?

No answer, naturally.

But he did then stop this scrawling, which was a relief. He rested his head in his hands. He closed his eyes. That is, sorry, I mean I rested my head in my hands. I closed my eyes.

Bad feelings came over me.

An inspector approached, walking heavily between the clerks' desks. When he got to Kafka's desk, he spoke.

'Get on with your work.'

I looked up. At last I found my voice.

'Please help me,' I chirped. 'I'm an innocent cockroach. Sir.'

Kafka – I – was taken before the supervisor. I repeated my sentence. By now, I could say it more loudly. My two pale flabby little paws were waving, as if in protest.

Eventually, a doctor was called. DOCTOR. It seems these humans are often – unwell – a kind of failure even to non-scuttle. He examined me, and was not surprised to find I had only two legs, though of course I squealed about it.

So here I am in this damp cell now. A considerable relief, let me tell you.

There are cockroaches here, thank God. They scuttle over the floor. Scuttle scuttle scuttle. Great. Sense at last.

I lie on the floor so that they can scuttle over me.

'Don't. Please,' says Kafka. Me.

'Sod off,' I say.

Scuttle scuttle scuttle.

Happiness.

THREE DEGREES OVER

ON THE flight back to England, Alice Maynard found herself restless, and in a curious state of mind generally. She avoided conversation with the other passengers, who, she saw immediately, were in commerce and not the sort of people she usually mixed with. She tried to withdraw into herself. Really, she had been *so* outgoing in the States.

So Alice refused all offers of alcohol from the solicitous hostess in First Class, rejected the proffered magazines, donned her eyepads, and lay back as far as possible in what the airline liked to call her armchair.

Gradually, the drone of the Boeing's engines faded into the background of her thought. Yet she remained tense, trying to vanquish that unease which always attended her on transatlantic flights, despite a helpful air-sickness pill.

Perhaps it was not so much the fear of the air – or of the weary hours to be passed before they reached London Heathrow – as the fear of the ocean. On European flights, she felt no such unease; she had made such excursions recently on behalf of her college fund-raising activities. But that great stretch of ocean beneath the plane, directly below her seat, that great stretch of amorphous water, grey, insatiable, impossible to comprehend, represented a threat. Her life, and her husband's, bless him, were so secure, so free of the ghastly crises which afflicted other Oxford people in their mid-forties – so, in a word, if indeed there was such a word, so *un-oceanic.*

Really, the Atlantic was like the subconscious. Drop into it and you were lost. The very notion of falling into that mass of water, as into unforeseen circumstances, and being swallowed – becoming an unconsidered mote and being swallowed – was enough to set the pulses racing.

Of course, one told oneself that that was nonsense – some clever people would call it a manifestation of . . . well, rather personal fears. One thought of other things. A well-disciplined mind could do that with confidence. For instance, one thought of that nearly completed critical edition of Emily Dickinson's poems, to be published by an American university press. It would be a pleasure to return to one's desk in Septuagint College and resume one's ordinary work.

> As freezing persons recollect the snow
> First chill – then stupor – then the letting go

A disconcerting person, Emily Dickinson, but her shrinking from the sexual side of life was something with which one could entirely sympathize.

She roused, removed her eyepads, and looked about the cabin. Everything was as normal. All armchairs were filled, mainly with men, most of them sipping champagne, as if a flight were something to be celebrated, like a wedding.

Alice had thought that a white-haired man was sitting in the chair next to her. She saw she was mistaken. A heavily-built young woman was leaning forward, right elbow on the armrest, writing left-handedly on a notepad balanced on her lap. Her shoulder-length hair obscured her face, though Alice moved position to try and see more than a slab of cheek. The woman wore a dark heavy dress with three-quarter-length sleeves.

This was the source of Alice's unease.

No, what an absurd thought! True, there seemed something vaguely unpleasant about the woman, but that was nobody else's business. Alice did not have to talk to her neighbour.

She lay back, more determined than ever to sleep. It was silly to worry. She was not the worrying kind, any more than Harold was. The fund-raising tour of the States had tired her, which was natural enough. Now she could rest until they reached Heathrow and English soil. Heathrow! Suddenly the word sounded so English.

Alice had enjoyed lecturing about the need of the University, and

Septuagint in particular, for funding. The American audiences had been most receptive, and generous as Americans always were. She had spoken eloquently – and not without quoting American authors – of the opportunities facing Britain in 1988, of Mrs Margaret Thatcher's remarkable drive to revive the economy, and at the same time of the considerable drawing in of horns to which the University had been forced. She spoke of Oxford, that ancient seat of learning, to which universities all over the world still looked for example. And she asked for their support over a difficult period. In fact, she was asking for no more than American colleges everywhere asked of their alumni, and many Americans had benefited from the Oxford system. It had been calculated that there were some six and a half thousand living American Oxonians, many of them leading distinguished careers as a result of their education.

Nor did she refrain from alluding, in the closing passages of her speech, to Mrs Thatcher's wish for a moral revival in England. She approved of that, as evidently did the majority of her audiences, fired by the example of their own President (soon, alas, to step down).

The mere notion had a sense of mission achieved, and Harold would be proud of her. That success would certainly constitute no impediment to his own career in the University. Dear Harold.

She thought of the woman at a mid-Western university she had visited: Frances someone, wife of a lecturer in English Literature. Frances was a New Yorker, totally lost in Nebraska. 'Oh, yes,' she had said, in answer to a remark of Alice's, 'we sure are quiet here.' A quick look round to see if anyone on the faculty might be listening and then, traitorously, raising her glass almost to her lips, 'In fact, I sometimes wonder if we aren't all *dead*.'

Alice smiled at the recollection. How different Oxford was from Nebraska . . . Oxford, the very centre of intellectual life.

Her thoughts drifted, but she was not asleep. Again the drone of the plane seemed to echo a deeper unease, which again came to the surface of her mind. She opened her eyes.

It seemed as if the woman in the adjacent chair had shuffled herself closer. Her dark-clad arm now overlapped the armrest, a loop of sleeve hanging down on Alice's side. An old-fashioned analogue watch and a chunky bracelet on the right wrist might be observed through half-closed lids. The thick dark hair – really, it gave no appearance of having been washed recently – obscured the plane of the cheek. The woman was still writing, writing, with savage intensity.

The nails on the hand clutching the pen were bitten down to the quick – always a sign of savagery. Alice glanced at her own hands, small, neat, the nails immaculately well maintained, and covered with a transparent varnish to protect them from the world.

Drone drone drone went the engine noise, almost as if it were the sound of the pen against the paper.

Somehow, this woman – this *squaw* – seemed immense and, because immense, threatening. Alice herself was of middle height – *petite* was the word her mother had used – with small, delicate, but sharp features. Her body likewise, really. Not really built for child-bearing – and, after all, a modern feminist, a career-woman, had no place in her life for the bother of children. Harold had seemed not to mind. Thank God, they had both made rational choices in marrying each other (she had kept her maiden name because, well, other considerations apart, Maynard was to be preferred to Badcock) . . . Neither of them had ever carried the sensual side to excess. Dear Harold. Somehow, Harold Badcock was Harold Badcock in the way that Oxford was Oxford, an exemplar of rationality and decorum.

Supposing the aircraft went down into that awful grey ocean . . . Then, she was sure, Harold would be the last thing she would think of as she drowned.

Harold, and Emily Dickinson. Certainly not the woman in the next seat . . .

Who was still writing . . .

She knew it, even without removing the eyepads and opening her eyes. Even as she sank, she would know the woman was still leaning forward, great uncouth lump, writing. Writing what? Writing out her soul? Writing out menus, more like? She was a big clumsy woman in middle age, her figure gone, a greedy eater, probably greedy about everything, greedy in the way clouds were greedy when they obscured the sun, just when she was sitting out in their neat little garden in Chadlington Road. That was where she liked to mark papers, under the laburnum tree Harold had planted when they had moved in, many years ago.

Leaning forward to study the papers more clearly, she realized that she could get a better view of the pad on which the squaw was composing. The woman, writing in that cramped way, left hand curled about the pen, used a bold sloping script. It unravelled itself across the page. Now it was forming a name.

Alice read the name. Harold Badcock.

She uttered a grunt of dismay and surprise.

The squaw turned head and shoulder and looked at her. Great dark eyes stared up from under broad brow and untidy hairline. Generous lips drew back in a smile to reveal small, pearl-like teeth. Little beads of moisture dotted the upper lip.

'Did you say something?' The enquiry was couched in a low voice, almost a murmur, although it contained a hint of a rasp on the 's' sounds.

'My husband . . . ' Alice said. She did not know how to complete the sentence, an unusual slip for a lady with an Oxford degree in English. She gestured towards the squaw's pad.

'Is your husband a writer, too?' asked the squaw. 'I am a writer of sex novels.' She gave her name. Alice missed it, as she groped to orient herself. Those large eyes were disconcerting and somehow overheated.

A dangerous woman, no doubt of it.

'How do you do. My name's Alice Maynard. I'm from Oxford.' There were always polite formulae to which one could adhere. But the mention of Oxford in no way deterred the squaw, as intended. She leaned closer to Alice, so that Alice could smell a warm perfume, reminiscent of a flower, the name of which could not be called to mind.

'Oh, you're from Oxford. Then you can help me. I'm heading for Oxford, and this is my first time away from the States. I'm real excited, as you can imagine, and greatly looking forward to the adventure.'

This was said with a direct simplicity which normally would have had its appeal for Alice. The woman was younger than she had supposed, although it was difficult to judge her age at all precisely.

'And whereabouts are you from?' Alice asked, rather sharply.

'Oh, you won't have heard of it. A place in Nebraska. Just a hick town, I guess. Right off the map.'

There were formalities in these exchanges.

'I was in Nebraska recently. Lecturing.'

The squaw extended her hand.

'I'm sure we are going to be friends, Alice.'

Reluctantly, Alice accepted the hand.

It was noticeably warm, as if it had been hiding somewhere snug.

'You can show me all the delights of Oxford,' said the squaw.

And so Felicity Paiva arrived in Oxford, England. Alice was not entirely sure how.

The Victorian house in Chadlington Road seemed curiously dim – dim and cold behind its formal stone exterior, although the month was June. In this context, Felicity (Alice was still trying to banish the word 'squaw' from her mind) Felicity gave off an impression of light and warmth, as if she had never presented herself as dark. She strode with a determined step into the hall, and in no time was going from room to room, throwing open doors, exclaiming with interest and delight.

'Such a heavenly home! So British! And you've kept it in period, which is such a smart move!'

Alice was vexed by this remark, since she and Harold had updated the house in many ways, only five years earlier. While tearing out the old central heating and installing new, they had daringly put in new patio windows looking on to the rear garden (where they had done away with mouldy flowerbeds full of Michaelmas daisies and had built a tiled area complete with ornamental pool and a lion's head which dripped water into the pool), as well as redecorating most of the house in a lighter, more 'eighties', way. They had also knocked down the wall of the old breakfast room to extend the kitchen, and put in a super scarlet Aga such as the Vice-Chancellor's wife possessed. This was not what Alice called 'keeping it in period'.

Besides, they had David Gentleman prints on the hall walls, framed in aluminium frames.

Felicity cooed over her bedroom, though in a rather disappointed way, and inspected the bathroom without comment. It was true that the shower curtain should have been renewed. She strode over to her single window and looked towards the Cherwell, over the garden.

'Nice yard you have. Well, well, I wonder what's going to happen to me in a place like this . . . '

'I expect you'll do much as our other American tourists do,' said Alice. 'I anticipate that my husband will be home in about an hour.'

Her intention was to speak to Harold and prepare him before he got sight of the girl. She was sure he would be serious, although, Harold-like, he would attempt not to show it. Harold was as well-mannered, she considered, as anyone in the University, including the stiff old Prebendary Porkadder, who lived in the next-door house with his housekeeper. And Harold could not abide young women – though of course he was too polite to manifest dislike, even of *trendy* young women.

She sat down at her dressing table, feeling a curious lethargy overcome her. Her shoulders sank, her head sank. Perhaps she even went into a doze, which was very unlike her usual alert self.

When Alice roused herself, it was with the realization that her husband was already in the house. She heard his voice downstairs, talking in the rather affected boom he put on for strangers. Drone drone drone.

It seemed a longer walk than usual from the bedroom, along the passage, down the stairs and into the living room. The house really was surprisingly dark. And chilly. And quite unfriendly.

Harold Badcock, Tyndale Lecturer in Medieval European History, shot his wife a look of hate as she entered the living room. He stood by the empty grate, resting an elbow on the mantelpiece, so as almost to prod the Meissen shepherds and shepherdesses. Upon his wife's entry, he drew back slightly from Felicity Paiva and straightened. She had changed into a golden dress of a loose-flowing kind, and had brushed her hair back to reveal a high, broad brow. She was smiling at Harold. One hand, with its bitten nails, rested on the mantelpiece, also close to the innocent shepherdesses.

Harold Badcock conquered his glance of hatred immediately, and came forward with his arms out to greet his wife. She went to him. He clutched her elbows.

Harold was slightly fleshy at this time of his life, in his mid-forties. They lived well in Magdalen, no doubt of it. He was balding fast, with a monk's tonsure. That, and his pointed nose and small moustache, gave him a rather naughty, pixie-like look, quite at variance with what Alice considered his real character. Harold was a tie-wearer, against the fashion, but he had already removed it, and his grey jacket, which surprised her. The room was full of a tension Alice had not known before, not even during their sometimes rather stiff North Oxford dinner parties.

'So, we've got a visitor, Alice. How jolly!'

This remark was so out of keeping that Alice became alarmed.

'I hope you don't mind, Harold dear.'

'Mind? Of course I don't mind. Felicity may find us a bit stuffy in our ways.' This was surely one in the eye for Alice, but Harold, without pause, turned to address the golden visitor. 'But are you all right, my dear, after your long journey? Not running a temperature, are you? I thought your hand felt rather hot.'

'Three degrees over,' she said, as if quoting, languid of voice as she stared across the hearthrug at him, one hand up to her bosom, as if protectively.

Or as if saying, the hussy, Look at my ample – too ample – bosom, Alice thought. Really, she could not think what had come over Harold. He was eyeing the young woman as if she were a – well, a confectionery shop.

'What's that?' she asked in best classroom style. 'What does "Three degrees over" mean?'

'"Three degrees over." That's my permanent body temperature. There's a medical term for it. I'm always three degrees above normal blood temperature. Have been ever since puberty.'

It was amazing, thought Alice. Almost as if key words had been uttered – body, blood, puberty – Harold was drawn across the hearthrug to Felicity's side. He put a hand on her forehead, an unusual and disturbing expression on his face.

'By George,' he said. 'You're not ill? Don't want to go to bed?'

'I'm not sick, no. Just kind of feverish compared to other folks. One of my boyfriends said that it's as if I was from another planet. Venus, most like.' She was grinning at Harold in what could only be construed as a saucy way.

He kept his hand on her brow, smiling in a little-boy manner.

'I expect you have a lot of boyfriends.'

'You don't get the effect in full force on my forehead, Harry. Try a hand a little lower – in my armpit, for instance.'

'Really! Why should Harold want to place a hand in your armpit?'

There was no response to Alice's question. Harold was more preoccupied with medical matters. The girl lifted her arm, he slid his hand in. Immediately his face lit up, as if he had found a treasure.

'Mm. Quite a fever . . . Amazing. And of course it's like that all over, one gathers?'

Felicity laughed. 'What do you reckon? Want to check it out?'

Although not loud, her laugh seemed to reverberate in the room, destroying its solemnity. For a moment its two square bay windows, which stared across the road to the rear of the Dragon School, seemed to lighten as if with sunlight, and the carriage clock on the mantelpiece chimed five as if in sympathy.

'I expect you have a lot of papers to mark, Harold,' Alice said.

'Could we have some tea, do you think, Alice?' he asked her, in a remote tone. He looked at her impersonally, solemn-faced, as if they had never met before.

Fifteen years of determined feminism dropped away. She turned to do as she was told. As she did so, she saw her husband remove his hand from Felicity's armpit and place his fingers daintily to his nose.

She slammed the door behind her, then instantly regretted that she had left them shut in alone together.

She had no memory of making the tea. All she knew was that she was back at the closed door with a tray, wondering what Harold and

Felicity might be doing on the other side. The cups rattled in response to her uncontrollable trembling. She knocked.

Harold and Felicity were sitting together on the sofa, heads close. They straightened as Alice entered, laughing in a conspiratorial manner.

'We're out of ginger-nut biscuits,' she said severely.

Barely looking at his wife, Harold said, 'I thought I'd drive Felicity down to see the College after we've had a cup of tea.'

'Harold, Felicity may not want to see Magdalen, she's probably tired after her journey. I expect you're tired – you generally have a sherry and a nap when you come home at this time, and, besides, there are those papers to correct and I hoped you'd help me unpack. I want to have you about the house because I brought you a little souvenir from New York, only it may take a while to get it out of my suitcase. Don't you think it looks like rain? I should save the trip until the weekend, when we can all go, besides, she'll be bored with all your old historical studies, she'll want to be with other people of her own age, other Americans, perhaps – I mean, there are plenty of them about the place, goodness knows, and that shirt should really go in the wash straight away.'

'Let's have our tea, dear,' he said, with a show of patience. 'Why is there no chocolate cake? Felicity writes sex novels, you know? *Skirts* was her last title – just that, *Skirts*, one word, very cute. Arouses the interest at once. Not published over here yet.'

'I should imagine not,' said Alice. 'And the traffic will be so congested at this time of afternoon, you'll hardly get down the High at all, and it's clouding over, and Felicity should acclimatize herself before she goes out, particularly since Magdalen is so cold at this time of – '

'I'll be just fine, Ally,' and

'My study's always warm,' they said simultaneously.

When they had left the house, Alice went back upstairs to her bedroom. She undressed. Naked, she walked into the bathroom and there surveyed herself in a way she had not done for some years. She put her hands under her breasts and lifted them slightly. True, they were not particularly large, but they were keeping their shape well. She had not ruined them by child-bearing.

She ran the bath, loading it with bubble-bath, and sank down into the water. Again she felt overwhelmed with fatigue, but sly, lecherous images slunk into her mind, like a guilty dog sneaking in after a roll in something bad. She was simultaneously pleased, revolted and delighted. The thought of Harold's penis, erect and engorged, slipping between the hairy lips of Felicity's vagina was something that no counter-thoughts of the corridors of Septuagint could dispel. She moaned and clutched her sudsy breasts.

Perhaps she drifted off in the bath. In a vivid dream, someone offered her a plate of peacock breast. She refused, as she usually did. She woke and dressed, spraying on perfume in a manner quite unlike her usual self. A good burst between the thighs.

It was after ten o'clock, and almost completely dark, when Harold and Felicity returned to the house. He was holding her arm, looking peculiarly young and unprofessorial.

Alice had the impression, as she rose from her chair, that again Felicity was dark and hag-like, her eyes glittering from a wigwam of jet-black hair. It was difficult to make out the essential nature of the girl: it seemed to change with the time of day, the season.

'Did you care for the look of Oxford?' she asked, striving for a conversational tone.

Felicity merely shrugged and looked up at Harold, as if expecting him to answer for her. Then she gazed at Alice through languorous and drooping eyelids. It was dim in the living room, and Alice could find nothing else to say. She seemed to stand staring at the two of them, and they at her, for a long time, while outside, where night was making of the road a strange country, the vegetation grew black and monstrous.

'I think we'd better go to bed,' Harold said, shuffling impatiently.

Alice's heart stopped.

He clarified his statement by adding, 'Felicity's tired and wants to unpack.'

Watching the girl slink from the room without so much as a goodnight, Alice took hold of her husband's hand. She could almost hear him sub-vocalizing the dreadful phrase – how vulgar it was – 'three degrees over'. As soon as Felicity had left, she let go of him and they stood side by side, as if waiting for someone to photograph and frame them, listening to the slow ascent of Felicity up the stairs. She was heard to pause before going into the bathroom, the latch of which gave its distinctive click.

Harold raised a finger, to indicate that they should listen. They heard nothing until the sound of the toilet flushing. He smiled and licked his lips.

'Let's go to bed, my dear,' Alice said. 'I want you to make love to me tonight.'

'It's been a long time . . . ' he said, letting his voice die away.

'I expect we shall remember how to do it. Come on.'

'You look very tired, Alice.'

'Come along, Harold.'

'Haven't you got a headache?'

Up in the bedroom, she switched on her bedside light, leaving off the other lights. Rapidly, she undressed, to prance before him, coquettishly covering and uncovering breasts and quim with outspread hands.

'Disgusting,' he said. 'A Septuagint fellow . . . '

But when he also stepped out of his clothes, she saw he had an erection. She flung herself upon him, going down on her knees to kiss the ramrod. A long time since she had done that. It felt marvellous, both hard and upholstered. Perhaps it had grown fatter since she had last stroked it. She wondered about the other men who had been on the plane, and what theirs felt like. What fun to have them all lined up for inspection . . .

Once in the bed, they fell on each other, doing it sideways, Harold bending over to get her nipples teased between his teeth, while he placed a middle finger over her anus in the way he knew she enjoyed. She groaned and cried, feeling, oh, so much readier than usual. That it was all undignified, that it was really rather unpleasant, that it was somehow dehumanizing for Harold – these considerations went by the board as he finally rolled on top of her, grunting fiercely in a tone no one at Magdalen would have recognized. She called her affirmatives and gasped, clutching him tight as she had not done in years.

'Oh, that was so lovely,' she whispered, gazing into his eyes.

He was smiling too. 'OK, dear, fine, *great*, now, if you don't mind, I want to pop into Felicity's room and just say goodnight to her. Won't be long. You get some sleep. You must be exhausted.'

Alice sat upright, heedless of her swinging breasts, still wet with his saliva.

'Harold, how dare you? I forbid you to go.'

'No, dear, it's OK,' he said, reassuringly, although he never used the word 'OK'. 'I promise I won't be more than an hour. Only she is feeling desperately homesick. She misses Nebraska. I'm sure you understand. Poor girl, so far from home, and, you realize, her sexual quarters are also three degrees over, and what man could resist the thought of that? Can you imagine how deliciously hot they'll be? It would be preposterous – and cruel besides – not to go in and comfort her a little. She is our guest, after all.'

'Harold, please, what are you saying? After all these years – that's adultery . . . What would Prebendary Porkadder think?'

'Now, Alice, dear, don't get worked up, it's just a little hospitality. We don't want Americans to think we aren't hospitable, and besides, she's bound to be lying there thinking of sex, poor little thing, and it'll be all wet and hairy, and so deliciously – '

As he was talking, he was sliding out of bed, still trying to face his wife, but finally leaping up with a glad cry and rushing for the door, clad only in his pyjama top, his penis smacking against his thighs as he ran, as she noted.

'Bugger,' she said. Seven years ago, she had allowed a man from Christ Church to do it to her on a sofa during a Commem ball, and really she had not liked it. His breath had smelt of beer and his shirt of mothballs. And he had asked her afterwards if Oxford had moved.

Since then, nothing but virtue. Now this. Bloody Felicity. What was the creature? A harpy? One of the harpies . . . Harpies with herpes.

'I hope you get bloody herpes,' she shouted – rather an old-fashioned shout in Oxford in 1988, when the younger dons were talking about nothing but the case of AIDS in Merton. Of course, it was hushed up, like everything else in the University.

'Did I really say "bugger"?' she asked herself, in an awed whisper.

Slipping into her silk bathrobe, she crept to the door and listened. She could hear nothing. Not a sound. Perhaps that foul seductress had developed a way of doing it absolutely noiselessly, and without movement. She had once been told by a graduate in oriental studies – Studmeyer? Studebaker? Shuckskin? – some foreign name – rather handsome, actually – that such things were possible as far as Japanese women were concerned. Apparently it involved developing the muscles of the pelvic floor. Foreigners were really very odd . . .

'I'll damned well buy a book and learn the art. It's not too late . . . ' She sighed. 'And practise on someone other than Harold,' she added.

Of course, Felicity was not oriental. Not even a squaw with Indian blood. She had announced that her father was Albanian. Who knew what strange rites went on in the savage mountains beyond Tirana, what musical instruments they played, where mad King Zog had ruled.

Noises. Definitely. Felicity's door opening.

Oh, God, her heart failed her. They were going to rush into her bedroom, to annex the double bed, in order to thrash about. What was she supposed to do? Bring them tea while they copulated? No doubt they would find new and disgusting ways in which to do it.

Rushing over to the open suitcase standing on a side table, she snatched from it the long paper-cutter she had brought back for Harold from New York. She would stab him to death if he dared bring that hideous hag in here, even if it involved blood spurting over the recently redecorated ceiling.

. . . But the footsteps went past her door. They were neither hurried nor stealthy – the sort of footsteps old acquaintances might leave behind.

With great caution, she opened the door and moved breathlessly into the corridor. It was dark and airless. She put out her hands so that her fingertips brushed the wall on either side, almost as if she were floating. The water was thick and murky, full of currents that ran rudely against her face.

Alarmed, she thought she saw a black man lurking just behind her. Not that she had the slightest prejudice against blacks. In fact, one of her students who was black showed a remarkable sympathy with Emily Dickinson, and had written a good essay on the short poem beginning, 'Drowning is not so pitiful/As the attempt to rise'. It was not a black man, just a dolphin.

Floating down into the depths, she heard the kitchen door into the back garden close the very moment she switched on the hall light.

At that, the door opened, and her husband looked back at her, his moustache bristling. 'Don't come out, dear, you'll catch your death of cold. Go back to bed. We're just going to have a fuck in the flowerbed.'

'Mind the bloody peonies,' she shouted, but too late. The water went sluicing out of the house into the garden. She heard the prebendary's cat from next door weeping in feline fright.

Trembling with rage, Alice rushed to the refrigerator and flung open its blind white door. As she might have expected, it was almost empty, except for an air hostess sitting on the toilet, smoking. There was not even any ice in the ice compartment – the ideal antidote to this whole obnoxious 'three degrees over' pretence of Felicity's.

Felicity! What an absurd name for that primitive slut! There were decent Felicitys at the University, along with the Penelopes and Rosalinds – all acceptable high-protein English names. Why there was even a Felicity at the other end of Chadlington: Felicity Chugg, who lived with her widowed sister, Deborah Hensprawn, and her two cocker spaniels. Felicitys were not supposed to be irresistible to men. That was left to the Valeries, Tinas and Marilyns of this world.

Either she could hear jungle drums or the beating of her own heart. Drone drone drone. Why, there was a positive orgy going on out there, in her respectable garden! The Medes from over the way were joining in, perhaps, or the dreadful Throckmorton brothers from Number Thirteen. Surely not . . .

She ran upstairs again, heedless of the dolphin thrashing wetly on the upper landing. Damned creatures – Harold had been leaving the landing window open again. Climbing over Felicity's tousled bed, she shone a torch out and down on the garden.

The sight was confusing. Evidently the garden had been badly neglected during her ten days' absence. It looked as if Old Hubbard had been drinking again and had not shown up on Tuesday. The laburnum had gone. Where the lawn had been grew a large clump – you could hardly call it a copse – of coconut palms. She could scarcely believe her eyes. But she could believe her ears. Sexually coarse – no other term for it – sexually coarse laughter sounded from the region of the raspberry canes, on the other side of the goldfish pool. The balmy Oxford night air was alive with lechery.

She ran downstairs again, clutching her wicked New York paper-cutter. My God, she would have vengeance for this! She had never killed before: in her heart, she foresaw what she had missed. Intense though Emily Dickinson was, Emily had never experienced the spume and spray of arterial blood. Many though the pleasures of Septuagint were, they did not include *crime passionel*. Or only very rarely, and then Alice Maynard had not been remotely involved.

On her feet were no shoes. On her slender body was only the bathrobe, which fluttered out behind her as she ran into the steaming night. She could smell the lust, tainting the air like distant barns burning. Night birds screamed, rejoicing.

Pushing her way through the hordes of little black boys with bones through their noses, she looked up at the sky. A full moon hung above the distant mountains. Over New Marston way, the volcano flared briefly, its great tit black against the last bars of sunset. Something roared down in the swamp. Prickles formed over her flesh at the sound. Well, we know where we are, don't we, Alice? This is Papua New Guinea, and the remote end of it at that. A tell-tale phrase came back to her as she ran over the dew-wet marsh grass: The White Girl's Grave.

My God, but there would be blood-letting this night.

It hardly surprised her that the goldfish pool had spread so much. She had been away too long. The natives had run amok without her firm guiding hand. Something lumbered and crashed out on the sandbank. The hippos, she thought, with a sure hunter's instinct, the hippos always mate at the full moon, to whelp during the monsoon, as they had since Tertiary times.

Harold and the girl were dancing ahead or, rather, pursuing each other at a ritual pace round and round a flat white sacrificial stone. They paused when Alice came up to them, their bodies painted with symbolic whirls and animals.

'What do you do here, white woman?' Harold asked, raising his great fists threateningly. 'Dis de sacred mating place of de tribe. Meat dagger belong me he quench flaming tip along passage she belong she-minx. You go vamoose from here plenty chop-chop, tuck up in him blanket, take sleeping pill.'

But the girl cried in a clear voice, 'No, Mighty One, let de old lady stay. She come to do worship, ain't it, She-Who-Carries-Torch?' She had a bougainvillaea blossom in her tousled mane.

Alice set the torch down on the sacrificial slab. She was not going to be fooled by their silly voices and accents. As she began to tick them off, a manservant rushed up with a magnum of champagne. When she waved him away, he poured the foaming liquid reverently over the stone.

'You two don't deceive me,' she said. 'Harold, come inside at once before you disturb the Prebendary. You're simply making a spectacle of yourself. This is not a College Gaudy.'

The hell-cat rushed up to her, pointing to Harold. 'He sing. He dance. He know secret how place de stick in de hole of flesh. He Mighty One.'

'Nonsense, he's my husband Harold, and don't you forget it.'

Felicity was wearing nothing but the great swirl of hair and the flower in it. Her breasts wobbled as if with a slow rhythm of their own. Her hips vibrated with energy. Down in the forest of her sex hair, something glinted in the moonlight like a jewel. She came closer.

Harold pointed to her and chanted, 'She sing. She dance. She shake it like you don't know how. She screw like rattlesnake all the same one-piece.'

They chanted together, leaping up and down, 'We sing. We dance. We shake it.'

An infant's skull tied by a thong rattled round his loins. It did not conceal his monstrous organ, the end of which had temporarily found lodgement in the eye socket of the defunct toddler. He and Felicity moved nearer. He snatched the knife from Alice's hand.

'He armed. He know no fear,' Felicity chanted. 'He sweat like pig.'

Alice was powerless. Yet she had lost her terror. Tearing off her single garment, she stood naked before them, proud little breasts pointing upwards as if to offer the cherries of her nipples to the Papua moon.

'Take me, take me,' she said, her voice low and thrilling, 'penetrate me – only, for God's sake, don't wake the neighbours.'

Felicity flung herself down on the sacrificial stone, opening wide her legs, arching her back, so that her pudendum rose in the air like some nocturnal flower. Her labia opened in a welcoming smile. Her orifice steamed. Moet & Chandon was poured over it.

'Worship, Alice, do de female stuff, dear! You come makeum pact along us,' she called.

Impelled by an instinct greater than herself, Alice slunk forward, walking between the bent legs, looking that magical organ in the eye, caught by its immodest yet complex configurations. She could hear her own animal noises. A scent came to her nostrils, like the mingled smell of laburnum honey and lobster thermidor. Her tongue came out, waving with a life of its own. She bent forward to the glistening flower, amid the cries of the others. The jungle drums were beating again. Her lips met those luxurious other lips.

Orgasmic shudders seized her body.

'Three degrees over!' she cried.

Now she knew what the heat meant. The heat birth of the universe. The terrible tandoori oven of the womb, the essential kindling of sex, the force that woke the dormant dog of philoprogenitive penis.

'Three degrees over!'

Now the lust was in her head, burning in her body. Everyone was shouting and singing and chanting.

'He sing. He dance. He take us both.'

And he did. The infant skull went flying. They writhed upon him, writhed under him. The great lip-smacking moon flailed their flanks with silver as they tumbled in ecstasy. For a while they were more than human. Inexhaustible, like creatures of legend, Indian sculpture, pornography. Once more, Zog gloried and drank deep in his distant palace, while the head-hunters ran on the fevered margins of the lagoon, a frieze from prehistory.

'He come. He go. He come again.'

She knew she was more than human – a goddess, born for the eternal burn of love. There had been many nights like this, and she had been furiously ridden before, as now, by this tireless Mighty One, face fixed in the inhuman lineaments of lust. Something in her drank in his savage juices, as the mango trees suck up rain, and, in her turn, she spurted liquid from every pore and orifice. Even from her ears, golden treacle flowed, which the others lapped like nectar.

'He suck. He blow. He know. He got de rhythm.'

And indeed he had. Now they were all three degrees over. There seemed to be many of them. No longer was it necessary or possible to tell which limb was which, which body. Oh, oh, that there should be nights like this – and her mother need never know.

'He shout. He shag. He got de rhythm.'

They all had the rhythm. She heard her mouth calling strings of obscenities, sweet to be heard, lullabies, jocularly jurassic love songs, meaningless aphrodisiacal noises. And there was another voice, a new voice.

And the new voice was saying, 'Mrs Badcock, what do you think you are doing?'

Only one person was brave enough, fool enough, to address her as 'Mrs Badcock', a name she hated; that was their obstreperous old neighbour, Prebendary Denzil Porkadder. He had climbed on a garden seat to peer over the wall at their activities. Although she could see he wore pyjamas, he had on his head as usual his old straw hat with its black band.

'Are you fornicating with those persons, Mrs Badcock? They're not Oxford people, are they?'

Alice was immediately embarrassed, and shrank back into her

usual self. It felt extraordinarily like the process of detumescence she had witnessed in her husband on many an occasion.

'They are members of the University, Prebendary,' she muttered, covering her nudity.

Although not exactly a religious person, she was pained to think that a senior member of the Church of England should get (albeit by moonlight) a good glimpse of her sexual organs in their present somewhat engorged state. Abashed, she tried to shrink behind the sacrificial stone, and hid her eyes.

'Get inside, the lot of you, or I'll call the police,' shouted the prebendary, foaming at the mouth. 'The gardens of North Oxford are designed for peaceful horticulture, not these heathen goings-on. Besides, it's gone midnight.'

But Harold and Felicity were less easily cowed than Alice. Harold gave a murderous cry of rage and jumped up on the stone, aiming the knife straight at the holy old blatherer. It flashed in the moonlight.

Alice saw that murder was going to be done, and shrieked uselessly. To kill off the prebendary, a reverend old man whose one hundredth birthday was going to be celebrated on the next Sunday, the second Sunday after Trinity, at St Andrew's Church and just about everywhere else in Oxford . . . Well, it would be the end of her career and of Harold's. They would be imprisoned, and, when released, would probably have to live out their stained lives in Cowley, or Kidlington. Old acquaintances would cut them dead when they chanced to meet in the Covered Market.

She lifted a hand to stop her husband, to grasp the knife. But she fell back, reading in both Harold's eyes and Felicity's an unstoppable blood lust. It was a life they needed now, a life they were going to have.

'He hate. He conquer. He know.'

The prebendary was still ranting on, unconscious of danger, as he quoted scripture and mentioned the Prime Minister, whose determination to get rid of sex and violence, and anything else amusing on TV, he commended.

Harold was flexing his muscles for the perfect balance, teeth bared, knife poised over his head.

And the savage woman shouting, chanting, naked and outrageous, goading him on.

'He throw. He kill. He throw.'

Alice covered her eyes and groaned. All round was a hubbub. People were pressing against her.

And still the squaw was shaking her and repeating the chant.

'He throw. He throw.'

A LIFE OF MATTER AND DEATH

A Novel in One Chapter

I

VERY WELL. Here I sit looking out over the sea, on this little rag of an island, Uskair. I may as well tell the story, though a new generation, growing up since the Odonata arrived on Earth, will find it incredible.

Do you wonder why I have hesitated until now? Because it isn't really my story. It's my brother's.

Yes, my brother Alec. The Man Who Changed the World, damn him.

Last year, before I decided to settle here for keeps, my business took me to one of the great northern cities, chief among those of the prosperous world. From the air, it seemed a place of beauty, from ground level often horrifying. From the city's government and economic centre, the destinies of billions of people round the globe were decided, yet the population was still not under control. The problem of the living remained, though the problem of the dead had been solved.

To the man who had solved that problem, a statue stood in one of the main squares. On the plinth were the simple words:

ALEC GREYLORN

1975–2026

He Brought a Cleansing Force

To Human Affairs

My brother's figure stood in bronze, and on his shoulder was an Odonata.

Many cities have erected similar memorials. All his fortune went to institutions; only the island came to me, the younger brother he spurned as a liar.

All cities have changed their appearance in the last decade. Even villages and hamlets have changed. Odonatist towers stand everywhere, glass towers resembling translucent vases. They say that such towers stand in Alice Springs, in Cove, Oregon, in Timbuktu and Petra and downtown Samarkand. The vase towers bring beauty to the ugliest place, and have altered human perceptions of what is sublime. Sometimes as the light of the sun catches them, you see the Odonata fluttering down into them to receive the gifts that mourners leave there.

It is not only the landscape that has changed. So have religions. It is laughable now to imagine a single one of the world's multitudinous dead being burnt by fire or buried in earth.

Much has changed for the better, thanks to Alec's discovery. All the same, there's no glass tower on Uskair.

The Odonata themselves are pretty splendid, I admit. Another generation will grow accustomed to their beauty, and no longer marvel at them. I take a shot at the odd one that flies over Uskair – strictly illegal, I know. In general, their iridescence, their startling speed, remain a joy. It is easy to see why a new religion has grown about them. Besides, people will worship anything.

But the Odonata are not spirits. They scarcely resemble the order of dragonflies after which they were named. Some have been sighted more than thirty feet in length, cruising almost a kilometre above sea level. Wing-spans are recorded of up to forty feet.

They are intelligent, although it is an intelligence unlike humanity's. There's no aggression. Odonata have never attacked a living human being. They avoid planes and helicopters. What they do is basic: they fly, feed, breed sparingly and look beautiful. They do good. They inspire musicians. They make me sick.

And it was Alec who let them loose.

*

Alec took after my father. He was a man of action. And a boy of action.

He was two years older than I, taller, more handsome, better at sport. On his fifth birthday, he climbed a tall tree until he reached twig level, where he sat contentedly as the wind rocked him to and fro. On the ground far below, Father applauded while Mother cried for him to come down. I stood and licked my ice-cream.

Later, I asked Alec if he liked being perched so high.

'Oh, no,' he said.

It was an irritating answer. I believed him to mean that he climbed trees not for enjoyment but because he felt danger was his natural environment. Perhaps he did it to hear Mother scream.

While I was always told I talked too much, Alec was quiet. That was because he was athletic.

We used to go sailing on the estuary when we were boys. Father taught us everything. He taught us how to ride out a storm. That was when my sister drowned. Father wanted her to be buried at sea; Mother did not. They quarrelled terribly over that. I'll never forget how they quarrelled.

Alec liked sailing more than I. I got seasick. Fortunately, we spent more time mountaineering than sailing. Father was a mountaineer; he made his fortune from the ski resorts on a mountain Grandfather had bought cheaply in Colorado. So we were forever heading for the rocky interior of continents, to regions of crags and barrenness. Father was at his most hearty in places where there was an echo. Alec liked solitudes too.

Father was a big square man, very freckled and covered with sparse sandy hair. He perspired a lot, he enthused a lot. He liked to sing hymns as he worked his way up cliff faces. He was a schoolboy at heart – as I realized later in life.

He used to tell us that on our expeditions we were 'confronting the Unknown'. The phrase gave him satisfaction; he used it a lot. Mother – another sandy person, with pretty green eyes – would nod to herself when she heard the phrase, as if in recognition, and smile a little secret smile.

Personally, there were things other than the Unknown I would have preferred to confront. But there's no doubt this activity stood Alec in good stead when he finally came across the truly Unknown.

When we were not at school, we were under canvas, often as not, and far from the crack-crazed cities of Europe. In the 1980s and 1990s, there were still remote places, and if there were remote places we found them. Although I was no linguist at school, I could still say a few useful words in Spanish, Nepali, Urdu, Carib, Slovak and Bahasa Malay. We often slept under the stars. I knew the word for star in about twenty languages.

So it was that, just before my fourteenth birthday, I found myself with my parents and brother at the foot of an unprepossessing mountain called locally El Jocoso, the Jocund. I had tried many lies and devices to avoid this mountain, including a realistic limp and stories of leg cancer. To no avail. Even my bloodcurdling tale of the Curse of El Jocoso had not prevailed. There I was, there the mountain was.

We were camped amid the little-visited Calaste chain in southern Bolivia. The mountains are no great height, but the ascents are steep, the country wild, and the snakes prolific – all plus factors as far as my father was concerned. Another irritating item was that the place was swarming with tortoises, clashing against each other in their anxiety to mate. One can only question the wisdom of a god who gave shelled creatures a sex life.

We had experienced great difficulty in procuring bearers and mules, since a small war was raging in valleys and hills. Several rival revolutionary armies were challenging the central government and each other. Father dismissed all this as typical South American ferment, and believed that all would be well as long as we sang a hymn before breakfast.

The fact that we had ventured into disputed territory meant nothing to my father. Guerrillas warned us that the CIA were about to spray the area with a new defoliant and anthrax contaminants. How often have I heard Father, after listening impatiently to similar warnings, exclaim, 'Oh, don't be an idiot – let's get on with it, man!' and stride ahead, swinging a machete.

Men thus instructed often found it easier to get on with it than to try and explain the danger all over again.

So it was that – ill-equipped, ignoring all warnings, and unable to pick up the BBC World Service on our radio – we confronted El Jocoso without guides and in a thunderstorm. Even my mother, normally so placid with her three great boys, was in a bad mood. There had been shelling in Casa Tampica and she had left her hair dye in the Holton Hotel.

'Onward, Christian soldiers!' boomed my father, as he hammered in his first piton.

It was on 8 August that Father suffered his fall. The three of us were scaling an almost vertical face. I was bored. I had just discovered boredom, and it was magic to me. To my left hand was a small ledge and on it, rather surprisingly, a tortoise appeared.

Pitching my voice to a tone of mild puzzlement, I called, 'What's a rattlesnake doing up here?'

My father looked round, startled. He slipped on the naked rock. The fifi hook attached to his étrier slipped. He reached too violently to grasp it, a tape snapped on the étrier, and he was gone. He slid fifty feet down a chimney, and became wedged there. When we called, he replied, although he soon must have lost consciousness.

Alec and I had been climbing on his right-hand side. We had to pick our way down and scale a different shoulder of cliff before we were able to lower ourselves to where Father lay. By then it was late afternoon.

Shadows began to fill the valleys below us. The sun swung round towards the west and the Pacific Ocean. Once we heard the sound of firing, but the crackle of guns came up to us tinny and diminished. In the mountains, humanity becomes an abstraction. Night approaches fast in those altitudes. Alec and I realized that we would only endanger our lives by trying to extract Father from where he lay and make a night climb with him. We slept on a narrow ledge, clinging to each other. Once in the uneasy hours of dark, I heard my father singing to himself. 'From Greenland's icy mountains . . . ' He sounded drunk.

It was after noon on the following day before we got a rope round Father and managed to haul him slowly out of the chimney.

He was badly injured.

'Just a scratch,' he said, before passing out again.

His left leg was broken, together with several bones in both feet. The flesh had been scraped from his stomach, chest and face. His right hand was smashed and that shoulder dislocated. There was massive bruising, and he had lost a lot of blood in the night.

'That was all rather spectacular,' he said, as we sat him up and got him to sip some rum.

We had a six-mile descent, down El Jocoso to the little camp by a stream where Mother waited with the mules. Alec and I lowered and carried Father by turns. We were well aware of him stifling cries of pain, but there was nothing for it but to proceed. Darkness overtook us again. We camped uncomfortably, one on either side of Father, to keep him warm. Although we had little to eat, the water held out, and we bathed Father's wounds, which were beginning to look nasty. The flies were a problem.

The three of us reached the camp by the stream on the following afternoon. Mother wept to see Father's state, and proposed that we set out for Chiguana, the nearest town where we might expect to find a hospital, immediately. Unfortunately, as chance would have it, a few villagers had passed the camp on the previous day; finding they were friendly, my mother traded one of our two mules for a gallon of hair dye. We had only one mule left, an unfriendly beast called Estrelita.

On to the back of Estrelita Father was loaded, and we started off, leaving much of our kit behind. Alec and I were exhausted. Happily, the way was mainly downhill to Chiguana, not far from the frontier with Argentina.

The night was filled with my father's delirium. He called persistently for his old schoolmaster to beat him. We decided in the morning that Alec should press on ahead and try to find a doctor in town, while I came on with Mother and the recalcitrant mule.

What a journey that was! Father appeared to be sinking, day by day. In order to avoid a stretch of forest, in which Mother thought she had heard firing, we crossed an expanse of igneous rock, red, potholed and uneven. The potholes, rarely bigger than Estrelita's hoof, were filled with little brackish puddles in which minute things swam – mosquito larvae.

In one of these potholes, Estrelita's front right hoof became trapped. She bucked and reared in fury in her efforts to get free. We had to calm her and untie my father, laying him down tenderly while we tried to extricate the mule.

'I'll light a fire under her,' I suggested.

But we were afraid she might then escape. Mother poured hair dye round the hoof; even that did not act sufficiently as a lubricant to set the poor beast free. Eventually, after dosing Father with more rum, Mother and I sank down exhausted to sleep, leaving the animal to kick and struggle throughout the night.

When I woke, the mule was still stuck. My first thought was for Father. I went to him. In his delirium, he had drunk several potholes dry, and was dead.

The heat on the rock flow became intense only an hour or two after sunrise. Mother and I decided that in the interests of hygiene we could not take Father's body into Chiguana, but must bury him where he lay.

I set to work with the pick. The rock splintered and flew, alarming the wretched mule, whose leg was now badly inflamed. After two hours' work, I had managed only to hack out a shallow hole hardly large enough to bury a tortoise. Father had been burden enough when alive; dead, he was nothing but a nuisance.

While I was still labouring away, my mother screamed in a rich contralto. I looked up. She was staring at a party of five men, heavily armed, who had appeared from behind a rock pile and now stood, several metres away, pointing machine guns at us.

'Are you any good with a pick?' I called.

Evidently they had no English. They wore camouflage uniform and, from the looks of them, had been living long in the jungle. Perhaps that accounted for their nervousness. They would not venture into the open where we stood, but shouted their demands at us.

'What can they want?' Mother asked me. When I had no answer, she addressed them directly, stressing each word for their convenience.

'Who are you? Can't you go away? We have a dead person here. He died of the plague.'

Gun barrels waved at us, but the men stood their ground. One of them, a handsome man scarcely more than an adolescent, shouted something in a high voice. It sounded vaguely political, chiefly because it went on for some while.

'I think he said they are the Chiguana Revolutionary Liberation Army,' I told Mother. 'We'd better be civil. Offer them your hair dye.'

The man was shouting and gesticulating. Now his meaning was clear. They wanted Estrelita. I understood something of his heavily accented Spanish. He said, 'Bring the moke over here and we will not shoot you.'

Picking up a stick, I whacked Estrelita on her rump. She kicked out but still could not move. The more I whacked, the more she kicked, the more the members of the Revolutionary Liberation Army shouted and raged. They clearly believed I was trying to trick them.

The leader let off a few rounds which went bellowing over our heads.

My mother lost patience. 'Come and get the bloody animal yourself, if you want it,' she yelled.

The revolutionaries charged. Possibly they were accepting my mother's offer; more likely they, like her, lost patience.

Mother turned and ran. I threw myself flat beside the corpse. The mule uttered its insane bray and broke free of its prison at last. Forgetting us, the revolutionaries ran in pursuit, firing sporadic shots as they went. They disappeared over the rocks, often falling.

'We'd better get on to Chiguana,' Mother said, coming up to me, panting.

'What do we do with Dad? We can't leave him here.'

She looked up at the sky, where vultures were gathering.

'Can't we?' she said.

Alec met us in the cobbled streets of Chiguana with an English-speaking doctor. I practically collapsed in his arms.

The doctor was efficient and kind. His surgery was well equipped. In his care I remained, delirious. I had contracted dysentery, of a type known locally as 'cordillera killer'.

The doctor's house was on the main square of Chiguana, with three steps up to his door: 'to deter the crippled and the halt', he told me, genially.

I lay for several days in a small wooden room, convinced for some reason that I was on an ocean-going ship. My father made irregular appearances, singing hymns lustily as he climbed a mizzen-mast like a mountain.

Filth and ugly matter poured from my body. A little square woman – to be identified when sanity returned as the doctor's wife – came to change my bedding and cleanse me regularly.

I sat up weakly one morning, and the ship's cabin had transmuted itself into a little square room in an isolated town in South America. Where had the illusion of the ship come from? Where had it gone?

The doctor's name was Santos. He was of medium height and middle age, rather a square man, to match his wife, with square capable fingers at the end of square brown hands. His face was open and honest and smiled readily, the generous mouth turning upwards into a handlebar moustache.

'You're back on land again, my lad. You've been raving about galleons and sea creatures.'

'I did believe I was at sea, sir.'

'You gave me orders from the poop deck. The only poop was in your bed.'

'I'm sorry for that.'

He smiled. 'I'm used to humanity's mess. It's my stock-in-trade.'

Dr Santos told me that my mother would pay his bill. She and Alec were staying with a 'grand friend' of the doctor's, a Senor Porua, who lived nearby.

I was strong enough next morning to go and look out of the front window. A market was in progress. A stall selling apricots, peaches and melons stood outside the doctor's house. There were earthenware pots for sale, and men rode through the crowd on horseback. The scene was more reminiscent of the nineteenth century than the twenty-first.

When I remarked on this to the doctor's wife, she explained that the town was under virtual siege, cut off from the central government. The airport had been seized by one revolutionary force and the communication centre by an opposing one. Both forces shelled the town periodically. Chiguana had virtually no contact with the outside world.

My small room adjoined the doctor's surgery. I could hear him bullying his patients in a good-natured way.

'Of course you're ill. Look at the way you live. Your house is a pigsty. Cease to neglect your wife and she may not neglect your home. You eat too much. You smoke too much. You drink too much. You go to the whores of the Calle Minotauro. You have guinea pigs in your bed.'

That night I dreamed I was on a ship again, and Alec was captain. But when I awoke I was sane.

I washed myself and walked out the back of the house. The ground was steep, and soon gave way to the cemetery. Among the graves were small tombs like English beach-huts which, in the Catholic way, sheltered the remains of whole families, their likenesses memorialized in framed photos on the carved stones.

Remember my age and make allowance for it. I was just an English schoolboy. I remarked on what to me was exotic to the doctor over a hasty breakfast of coffee, bread and cheese.

'What's odd?' he asked, smoothing his moustache with a linen napkin. 'A surgery, like a chapel, should be near the cemetery. I cure no one. For all my medicaments, the peasants all wind up there, under slabs, sooner or later.'

'Does not that make you melancholy, sir?'

'For all these people's piety and prayers, they finish up out there, in decay. Worms get them all in the end. Do you think that makes the priests a wit less jolly?'

I saw he liked simply to converse. I was astonished. I had never met such a characteristic before. That was part of my inexperience.

After the surgery closed, he loved to drink wine and talk. To my ears, much of the talk was about death, a subject which made me nervous. I said something to that effect, in a churlish tone – manners are something else we have not learnt at that age.

'I've nothing against death,' said the doctor, ignoring my tone and answering in good humour. 'If we didn't all turn into disgusting lumps of decaying meat, men would be even more arrogant than they are. Civilization is the art of concealing the corpse in us. The Church conspires towards the same end. There's too much pomp in funerals. We need a better way of disposing of bodies – something less ostentatious.'

This remark, which struck me as silly and offensive at the time, was to be recalled later. Reminded of my defunct parent, I said, 'Father believed in the Resurrection.'

The doctor laughed. 'My grand friend Porua has visited Italy more than once. He enjoys all this renaissance art, full of noble statesmen, florid gestures and people being resurrected. Yet what are people under their fine robes? Just matter – matter in decay.'

I noticed he himself dressed well.

'Sir, my position in the world is precarious enough. I don't wish to know what it is to be mortal, thanks. I intend to live for ever.' Despite the boast, I spoke rather miserably.

'What you want is a woman, young feller-me-lad. I'll get you one when you're fully recovered. You have a sound prick on you, as I've observed. I'll find it a billet in a few days.'

At the mention of its name, the member referred to leaped up in hope. I was recovering.

Next evening, I was drinking his wine. Perhaps it made me too outspoken. Night had fallen over Chiguana and, as the doctor's wife had predicted, the Lower Bolivian Liberation Force had driven through the town, firing randomly and inspiring fear in all.

'Well, it's not so bad,' said Santos. 'Only one old woman killed, and she with a frightful goitre and her husband long ago disappeared in the hills. We've known worse. There's a treat on Saturday. I'm going to take you to the Bioskop to see a great old film from ancient days. Charlie Chaplin, in *Modern Times*.'

'That's ages old,' I said, contemptuously. 'Sentimental rubbish.'

He jumped up, spilling his wine. 'What, you dare say that, you impudent young frog? You dare call *Modern Times* rubbish?'

I was alarmed, but stood my ground. 'I just don't like Chaplin.'

'Then what an unfeeling little brute you are to be sure. The comedy, the poverty, the pathos, the loneliness, the hope – all beautifully in balance . . . If you don't enjoy that then you have no feeling for your fellow men.'

'He's not half as funny as Buster Keaton.'

'You dare say that in my house! Chaplin grasped the whole complexity of the human heart, its goodness, its beastliness – and you dare call that rubbish! Jesus!'

He grasped my collar. I struck out feebly in self-defence and hit him across the chest, which increased his rage. Next moment, I found myself frog-marched out to his front door. He kicked it open and flung me down the three steps into the street.

It was my fourteenth birthday.

Alec and my mother had taken shelter under the wing of Santos's 'grand friend', Porua de Madariaga.

Porua's house was large, rambling and decaying. At the time, I took this decay merely as a sign of the times; I was comfortable with decay. I liked my room, reached by an open staircase, at one end of the mansion. It looked out over a garden so long overgrown it was returning to jungle. Porua's vineyards, long the source of the fortune of the de Madariaga family, were in the hands of one or other of the revolutionary parties.

While my mother attempted to sort out our family finances – no easy matter with the capital, La Paz, virtually divorced from all communication – I took on a job of work for Porua.

In his great house, almost bereft of servants and filled with damps, glooms and moulds, Porua lived like a soldier under siege. He was a tall man, heavy in build, his hollow voice making him sound empty, like an old wooden drum. Yet his great blue jowls appeared sufficient fortification against the world; while so immense was his dignity that it was some while before I realized he spent his nights in the arms of my recently widowed mother.

She, poor woman, had at last found a grown-up man, and showed her pleasure by fawning on Porua. Callowly, I was disgusted by all this; I avoided my mother and threw myself into the job of telling lies for *La Clava*.

Porua had three cars. They mouldered outside the *casa*, a-thirst for the gasoline which no longer arrived in Chiguana. He rode to work every morning on a fine stallion. I followed on foot to the offices of his newspaper.

With most other lines of communication knocked out by the civil war, Porua's *La Clava* played an important role in informing that isolated community. Not only had the various guerrilla movements cut all land means of communication; the staff of the paper, including the reporters, had left to join one side or another in the hills. Some would say this made him the ideal publisher of a newspaper.

So I respected him, and was glad to work long hours in his stuffy little offices, learning better Spanish and the workings of a paper; learning also something about Porua, whom I studied with almost servile interest. This was my first real relationship with a grown man beyond the charmed circle of father, uncles, cousins, in which Alec and I had previously moved.

The coldness of his character shocked me. While Porua would spare a fly buzzing against his window pane, he was never better than harshly civil to anyone he considered his inferior. He was unsparing of anybody who worked for him. Only to his great black horse, which he rode about the town, did he show affection. I failed to see how tolerant he was of me, with my callow questioning of everything: I flinched under the coldness of his eye, yet did not perceive his isolation.

We sometimes worked almost till midnight, with a sub-editor, to get out the next edition of the paper. I could hear gunfire in the hills on occasions when I walked home. In response to some implied criticism I made of his treatment of the sub-editor, Porua regarded me in a sneering silence and then said, 'Why should I have regard for my fellows? Consider the stories we print in our columns. Are they not bulletins on the nastiness of mankind? Murders, theft, rape, calumnies, graft – our daily bread. Not one grown man, aristocrat or peasant, is worthy of respect when you really know him. Women are little better, only weaker in carrying out their ill intentions. Dogs shit in the street, children in their trousers. Only the horse has nobility.'

I was secretly thrilled by such misanthropy, arguing that such views were in conflict with his profession of Christianity, for Porua was a regular churchgoer.

He gave a short laugh, as hollow as his voice.

'You've much to learn. Christ was a fool to die for men. That's my opinion. What improvement did he make in the world? The sight of him hanging on the Cross – are we really supposed to worship that, defeat and death? Christ's preachings have merely made us more aware of the darkness surrounding us. I have a scorn of him.'

He made a curt gesture.

'My visits to the church are to set an example to the brute population of Chiguana. They need a fear of heavenly retribution to keep them in order. Sometimes I also enjoy the music and the wailing. I am not entirely averse to the compositions of Monteverdi.'

He left the room abruptly, with the air of a man who has revealed too much of himself. I returned to the clutch of reports on my desk.

My father's nature had been sunny. To Father, every man had been 'a good chap'. The darkest villain was 'a rather jolly fellow' in Father's book. I remembered a banker friend of my parents who was on trial for having raped his twelve-year-old niece; Father had tut-tutted and said, 'I suppose he could not help himself.' This lack of judgement, of the judgemental impulse, was revealed in Chiguana as weakness.

It was a part of becoming adult that I grew aware of the great invisible universe of personality which controls us as surely as do physical laws. This dawning knowledge made me aware of my isolation. I needed the woman Santos had promised me to share experience with. My state was an unhappy one compared with the other members of my family: my mother had become attached to the grim Porua, and Alec had formed a liaison with Nuria.

Nuria was the daughter of the de Madariaga family. She had an older brother, but he was studying architecture in Italy. Their mother had died when they were little more than infants and, I gathered, it was from that moment that Porua's misanthropy had set in.

Nuria's was a solemn beauty. She was not lively as are many girls of eighteen. She was studious, read much, and liked to talk about the cosmos. Her face was pale, her eyes grey, and therefore quite startling, her mouth prettily shaped, indenting at the corners in a permanent half-smile. Oh, I often studied that face covertly! She wore her dark hair in plaits about her head. She had a penchant for long grey velvet dresses which marked her, in my youthful estimation, as foreign and sophisticated.

'I mean to go to Italy one day, as my brother has done,' she told me, when I discovered her on a stone bench in the garden, reading a book. 'That is why I read Dante now. Do you read Dante?'

'No. Never. At least, I don't think so.'

'I am teaching your brother.'

Alec had never before shown any interest in Dante – or in women. He and I, together with that great boy, my father, had spent our lives in a world of eternal boyhood, being good chaps and climbing or sailing. Now Father had gone, and here was Nuria, with a strong physical presence, as challenging in her way as her father.

The poisonous philosophies of both Santos and Porua were banished by the sight of the latter's daughter in her grey dress, red book in hand.

My relations with my mother were also marked by coolness. She resented my dislike of her relationship with Porua. Once, when I told her a lie about what I was doing, in order to evade hostile questioning, she said, severely, 'You're growing too like your father.' I thought about that for an hour before deciding to ignore her, as Father always did.

As I rarely watched TV or read newspapers, my knowledge was scanty. There had been a story about secret arms deals with a Middle Eastern country involving the suicide of a French diplomat, but I recalled no names or figures.

'Make them up,' Porua said. 'We have to enlighten our readers. They are so insensitive to matters of veracity that accuracy is no virtue.'

So I made up my stories. There was the fictitious crisis involving tourists dying of food poisoning in Portugal, and another concerning a foreign minister who vanished without trace in Budapest, and there was the Chilean dope smuggler arrested in Miami who was found to have sixteen wives.

These reports had at least a grounding in real events, or my memory of them. But I soon had to rely more and more on my imagination. So the news became more and more sensational. Porua made no complaint. Nor did our readers.

One day we carried a headline SECRET OF IMMORTALITY DISCOVERED. It was the story of a German scientist working on seaweed in South Korea who had found how to elude death. A small queue formed in the dusty street outside our office doors to ask for the scientist's address. Then Porua gave his short laugh and said, 'Why should those pigs wish to live a day longer?'

One evening after night had fallen, I returned alone to the Porua mansion. Lightning flickered noiselessly in the western sky. I had been drinking in a bar with the sub-editor, who had become a friend. The town lay dead, exhausted after the day's heat. Some eternal quality in the atmosphere seized me and I stood silent, listening to dogs barking distantly in the hills.

A figure moved on a balcony above my head. It emerged from Nuria's room. The man came down the steps and began to cross the courtyard. I saw it was Alec, walking slowly as if in a daze, his right hand held up to his nose and mouth, his eyes downcast.

He saw me, apparently without surprise, and spoke tonelessly. 'This night I am in heaven.'

There was no pause in his stride. He did not look directly at me. He simply walked on towards his own quarters.

How my heart sank at his words. I understood their meaning and was full of jealousy. Next day, *La Clava* carried the bloodthirsty story of how the king of one of the United Arab Emirates had murdered his brother for love of a gorgeous American woman named Maria Nuria Nussberg.

As far as I can tell, Alec never went with a woman again, or had dealings with women. It was as if that one experience had been so charged with meaning it had forever changed something in his being.

It was a blow to Alec – I too had my regrets – when Mother got papers and money through from La Paz. Suddenly we were preparing to return to the real world; Mother, advised by Porua, was bargaining for mules in the market. I was reluctant to leave, being in the midst of fabricating a sensational case in which a Soviet spy ring had been discovered in Israel and an old ex-Nazi had admitted that he had helped liaise in secret South African military strikes against the colony on Mars. A pretty grey-eyed woman was being held, pending enquiries.

When bidding farewell to Porua, I tried to extract from him some word of praise for my activities on behalf of his paper.

'You are no better than our readers,' he said, fixing me with a look it took me years to forget. 'You found an opportunity to lie and seized on it avidly. You took pride in your lies. Do you consider that warrants praise?'

We made our way past the strongholds of the revolutionary armies to Antofagasta on the coast. At the sight of the Pacific Ocean, Alec was overwhelmed. Tears burst from his eyes when we were leaving South American soil and stepping aboard the cargo ship that would deliver us in Panama. The tears fell like raindrops on the deck, and he would not speak.

Within a year, Alec, with his share of Father's money, had bought himself this small island of Uskair, off Barra in the Outer Hebrides. Perhaps he had already formed a notion of sailing alone round the world.

I lost touch with him. When I had finished with university, I qualified as an ecologist. In no time, I was established in the small world of the university as lecturer.

Someone once said to me, 'Nature creates women, but society has to make its own men.' I still think of Porua de Madariaga as a real man.

Alec became a real man. Somehow my father and I remained in

boyhood, not developing, turning into big hairy ageing boys. So we were popular, and courted popularity, because we happened to be the sort of person society preferred, neotenic, forever in the larval stage.

I married a big hairy freckled jolly girl called Ruth. We have three children, all girls. Ruth is Chairperson of the local Consumers' Association.

Just the other month, I met my mother in Kensington High Street. I was going to walk by, but she grasped my sleeve.

'Why do you hate me?' she asked. 'You and Alec?' She does not get on well with Ruth. She was looking much older.

Alec never married. Instead, he sailed alone round the world.

He was twenty-five when he began the voyage. In his thirty-two-foot ketch, *Nuria*, he set out from the small harbour under the shoulder of his Hebridean island. He was gone from sight of man for eight months. He slipped away one dawn. Five islanders, the total population of Uskair, not counting his dogs, waved him on his way. It was Father's 'confronting the Unknown' again.

Although we took little heed of his departure, Ruth and I watched Alec being interviewed on TV when he returned.

'I was fortunate in my choice of boat, and my equipment gave me little trouble. All the electronic tackle performed without hitch. You just need to want to sail on for ever . . . No, not for the notoriety, for the experience, for one's own sake. I reckoned that I needed to chance everything on a – well, it's a bit like roulette, when you feel an inexplicable urge to stake everything on one number . . . Yes, of course I was scared occasionally. It doesn't matter. Some of those waves at the bottom of the world – I mean you can tell by the look of them they have come from the beginnings of time and will roll right over you and go on rolling for ever. Afterwards . . . I suppose I have told myself I must be a lunatic. But after all, other men have done it. Captain Slocum did it at the end of the nineteenth century.'

He looked modest when he said all this. It was the irritating Alec I remembered as a boy, perched twig-high in a tree.

'The best thing about it? You escape the twenty-first century. The Southern Ocean is absolutely apart from man – I mean in time as well as space. The seas are high and grand and you're in the rushing air all day, surrounded by stars at night, and the whole universe might be yours. You share it with dolphins and whales and albatrosses and the lonely satellite orbiting overhead. Oh, when you're down there, everything is worth it, everything . . .

'Sure, yes, it's good to come home. One of the most moving things of the whole voyage was when I saw Uskair loom out of the mist. In all the previous months, I had rarely seen land, never wanted to. But there was my island, Uskair. And as I changed tack, the harbour came into view round the headland, with the hill rising behind it, where pines grow in a sheltered spot, and then I could make out the white walls of my house through the binoculars. I was sure my dogs would be waiting for me. That was a great moment.

'No, I shall never do it again. Not twice. That would be tempting providence . . . '

With his manly modesty, my brother became something of a hero. He came to my university, lectured, and met Ruth and the girls. He seemed uncomfortable with us. Later, after Mother died, we heard he was looking for a sponsor and planning another solitary voyage.

It was on that second voyage he encountered the Odonata.

Alec's autobiographical book, *Far from Land*, was published before he sailed. In view of what was to come, one passage is particularly striking:

> In the Southern Ocean, in that great reverberating blue-green world I shared with nature, I became intensely aware of the way in which men and women have trapped themselves within cities. Cities re-create in concrete the restrictions humanity has imposed on its spirit. The land had been left behind. The world chokes with people, living and dead. On Mars, the colonists are repeating the errors of Earth. We pollute our globe on an increasingly massive scale because something has died in us.
>
> Our civilization has become a cage in which we choose to imprison ourselves. In that great clean ceaseless world towards the Antarctic, all this became clear to me. I saw then that we shall

die, wish ourselves into extinction, unless we find a new course. I would have been content then to die myself, rather than take my body back eventually to encumber the continents with yet another corpse.

In *Nuria II*, Alec sailed back to that distinct world of high oceans. He was again his own master. I suppose few of us have imagination enough to project ourselves into his place. I am convinced that a special kind of solitary mind is required to endure such a voyage.

He was on latitude fifty-six, somewhere to the south of Heard Island, when he sighted wreckage on the water ahead. Something like a fin protruded from the water. Alec took it at first for a whale. Nearer, he thought it might be the tailplane of an aircraft, possibly Australian. A figure clung to it.

The wreckage was sinking gradually. The *Nuria II* made slow headway. The figure waved. Alec waved back.

Evidently the wreckage was becoming unstable. The figure suddenly jumped into the water. As it did so, Alec saw that it appeared deformed. He said later that the body was curiously broad, rather like a turtle's. There the resemblance to a turtle ended, for, after one or two splashes, the figure disappeared below the waves.

When Alec reached the spot, the wreckage lay waterlogged below the surface, sinking slowly deeper. He saw lettering on it he could not make out, although he had the presence of mind to record the scene on a video. Of the figure there was no sign. Drifting nearby, however, was a sort of transparent inflatable dinghy, low in the water, resembling a cocoon. Alec pulled it in with a boathook, and got it on deck with some difficulty.

Peering through the transparent cover, he saw what appeared to be bundles of bandages. He believed it was a kind of first-aid package from a life-raft which had failed to inflate. After tying it to the mizzen-mast, he did not investigate further.

This indifference on Alec's part has been the subject of comment. My belief is that my brother wanted no intrusion from the outer world. It disturbed his peace of mind. His wish was to be alone in the deserts of ocean, as others crave the solitude of deserts of sand.

He had taught himself to sleep in brief snatches. He thought he heard noises in the night but did not bother to look. At dawn, he found that the transparent covering had split and thirty white insects had emerged on deck, each the size of a rabbit.

His impulse was to kick the creatures into the sea. Their very oddity deterred him from doing so. To discover a new species would be a wonderful thing. He continued with his tour of inspection, in which every knot, cleat and screw came in for daily scrutiny.

With the sun shining on them, the insects became more active, and climbed the mainmast. My brother observed them, and captured them on video. Their bodies are carried on ten multi-segmented legs. Their heads have a horizontal split which gives the appearance of a visor. Within the split, vari-coloured eyes can be seen. The creatures might pass for terrestrial were it not for the thick twisted cable-like sensors which connect head and tail and run on either side of the body, lending a machine-like appearance.

Clustered at the top of the mast, the insects became immobile. Alec lost interest. The wind was freshening and he took in the mizzen-sail. When he next looked, great winged things were circling his boat. The backs of the insects were splitting, and new forms emerging from the husks – the adult forms we know as Odonata. The larval stages remained clinging to the mast, to blow away in the next gale.

The adults are beautiful and metallic. Shimmering moire tints in fugitive pink, blue and green suffuse their wings, while their bodies appear clad in abalone and mother of pearl. Their wingspan exceeds that of an albatross. Although they metamorphose like terrestrial insects, they have a lung-bladder which sucks in air or extracts oxygen from liquid. Along their flanks are arrays of proprioceptors which in part act like external arteries. These Odonata may never have been on Earth before, but they circled the *Nuria II* in an assured way and then set off northwards towards Australia with leisurely beats of their wings.

Glistening wing colours could still be seen after the insects themselves had faded into the blue.

Alec monitored a variety of radio signals, but rarely responded himself. However, he did consider this event important enough to send a report to an Australian station on Lord Howe Island.

Nothing more was seen of the Odonata for a couple of years. In that time, they adapted to the new environment, established themselves, and bred. In saying this, I subscribe to the generally held view that the creatures are of extra-terrestrial origin. The notion that they were mutated terrestrial insects does not bear inspection. We may never be certain, but it seems most likely that the Odonata were part of a cargo in a trans-stellar vessel which crashed on Earth by accident. If it had not been for my brother, the Odonata would have drowned, just as the turtle-shaped biped drowned.

After two years, Odonata sightings in Australia began to mount, to be met by incredulity from the rest of the world. Next, sightings were reported in the Philippines and Singapore and Malaysia. The first living specimen was caught in a suburb of Sydney, where it was perched under a hedge, devouring the carcass of a dead dog.

At this early stage in the Odonata's existence on Earth, such incidents led people to believe that Odonata killed dogs, other animals, and even humans. Scare stories abounded. In consequence, the creatures were exterminated whenever possible.

Still they spread. In the following year, they were sighted in India, spreading rapidly north. They were sighted in China, where those who attempted to eat them reported them to be tasteless or unpleasant. Within eighteen months, the Odonata appeared in Africa, southern Europe and in South America. At this time, serious attempts were made to eradicate 'the new plague', as a phrase of the period went. The attempts failed, and soon the whole world was confronting the unknown.

Photographs of Odonata were to be seen everywhere. They were regarded as both beautiful and terrifying. Already, their arrival stirred fresh religious beliefs. In some quarters, they were regarded as being sent by God to destroy man.

A more scientific approach to the problem was forthcoming. As clouds of the invaders reached Texas, a UN fact-finding commission reported that the Odonata (it now became their official name) lived for only seven months in their adult winged phase. In that time, they fed exclusively on carrion; specimens kept in captivity refused to sample any living thing.

Almost concurrently, a report came from Bombay that the Odonata had been observed all over India, feeding on the corpses of Parsis. The burial customs of the Parsi sect involve dead bodies being exposed on a grating at the top of a Tower of Silence. All that is mortal of the body, except the skeleton, is devoured by vultures and the ubiquitous kitehawks of India, after which the bones of the departed fall through the grating into the tower below. Word even came out of Tibet that the Odonata had been assisting at sky-burials, where corpses are left in sacred mountainous places for the attention of scavenger birds.

Before the Odonata invasion, the morbidly repressed cultures of Europe and the United States were unable to face death, or to discuss the subject with the same openness of the inhabitants of India and the East. But the ever-mounting numbers of their dead were, in fact, a subject for concern. Millions of people had a horror both of burial and of cremation. Europe, in particular, was filling with old graveyards. The immense graveyard in Queens, New York, was famed as a particularly depressing city of the dead.

Almost spontaneously, people began to dispose of corpses via the Odonata. Some say the idea originated in Greece or Turkey as a tourist stunt. Others speak of a Spanish grandee who offered up the corpse of his lovely young wife in this way, hoping in his grief that her elements might be dispersed about the air. Yet others say that the poor countries of Africa put out their corpses to be devoured – by creatures regarded with superstitious awe – as the least burdensome method of disposal. Yet others accused bankrupt nations of Eastern Europe of adopting 'Odonata funerals' as a way in which the state could economize on electricity and wood.

All these developments certainly happened within a few months of each other. Once fear of the glittering new flying things was lost, they became worshipped. They were clean creatures which did not excrete during their lifetime. They did not ruin crops or attack living things. They would not enter buildings. When they died, their carcasses were not corrupt, and contained useful minerals in small but quantifiable amounts. In the air, they introduced an element of beauty and grace.

It was inevitable that new religions should develop round them. As the Odonata became generally revered, so the tall towers grew up round the world's cities. Cities vied with each other to build more beautiful towers. None was built higher than six hundred metres, for the Odonata were low fliers. To the top of Odonatist towers the dead of all nations were taken, to be exposed to the four winds – and to the Odonata. As the habits of death changed, so did the habits of life.

Since then, a curious peace has descended on the world. No major wars have been waged, and few minor ones. Just as the dead might be said to take readily to flight, so the living found their spirits lifted. An unsuspected shadow had faded and gone.

Alec died suddenly in his sleep one night. His hair was white, as my daughters reported when they went to view the body before it was given to the Odonata.

Now he is known as The Man Who Changed the World, and there are statues to him everywhere. No one remembers he had a younger brother. But Ruth and I have inherited Uskair, and that's worth something.

A DAY IN THE LIFE OF A GALACTIC EMPIRE

IBROX Villiers Cley remained entirely within his chambers while the Second Galactic War was waged. He saw few people.

His leisure time, which was ample, was spent mainly in aesthetic contemplation of the moral and social degeneration of which he considered himself a part, if apart.

Cley was ill, subtle, devious, sardonic, and a servant.

His manner was cheerful, even metallic, to cover his deep-rooted depression.

Cley served the Emperor of the Eternal Galaxy under the Banner of a Thousand Stars. He served him well by telling him the truth and by refusing to scheme against him. His distaste for other people kept him aloof from plots and treacheries.

The Emperor ruled over a million suns and three and a half million planets. Most of the planets were inhabited, by robot task forces if not by human beings.

The Emperor was himself a prisoner. The Emperor had been born and would die in what was called the Galactic Paradise. Guards never left his presence.

Every man and woman was his slave. And he was theirs. The Conventional Rules of Duty bound him as they bound his subjects.

The Conventional Rules of Duty constituted, or rather replaced, all metaphysical systems within the Eternal Galaxy.

Ibrox Villiers Cley was almost as respected as the Emperor. His chambers were in the Galactic Paradise on the planet Voltai. His official title was Adviser of the Computers. He saw the Emperor in person every third day.

Those meetings were enclosed within a Fifth Force Field, so that no one ever knew what passed between the Emperor and his

Adviser of the Computers. No note was taken, no record was made.

The edicts continued from the Throne Computer. The Galactic War continued, as it had for many generations.

The war was going well for the galactic empire. Twenty-four solar systems held by the enemy had recently been destroyed. Countless populations were starving.

Whole armies fought and died under the Conventional Rules of Duty. They died without questioning the cause. The number of their deaths was reported to Ibrox Villiers Cley.

Cley's chambers were built of one of the new metals created through the exigencies of war. Cley himself had a sheen as of metal about him. His temples were pallisades against the world of outside iniquity.

The perpetual light of Voltai came in through his long windows. Cley's chambers had no internal lighting. It was the fashion. He preferred to live in chiaroscuro.

His rooms differed little, one from another. In the sombre main chamber where most of his days were spent, there was no decoration, no contrasting texture. In a case along one wall were stored the six hundred and seventy-seven volumes of the *Eternal Galactic Encyclopaedia*, each cube awaiting activation.

Cley rarely referred to the encyclopaedia.

His modest needs were served by an android called Marnya. Marnya had beauty of a severe kind. Her smiles were few and wintry. She had been designed by Cley's father, long ago.

Marnya was always about in Cley's chambers as a silent presence. She was like a shadow within shadows. She was like an embodiment of the Conventional Rules of Duty. She provided most of the company that Cley needed. She was calm, loyal, without deceit and self-lubricating.

Reports came to Cley on his desk screen of the numbers of men, women and children who died every day for the sake of Empire. Sometimes he read these casualties aloud to Marnya.

'There are always more people,' she said.

He tapped the screen. 'These people are lost for ever.'

'But were they precious?'

'Not to me or you, Marnya, but to someone. And to themselves.'

'They became most precious when they fulfilled the Conventional Rules.'

'Certainly that is conventional wisdom.'

She sat down beside him and laid a velvety hand over his. 'They had no existence until the report showed on your screen, as far as you and I are concerned. Their existence was as brief as a phosphor dot.'

'They lived and died. No doubt in a brutish way.'

'It happened far away.'

'Yes, it was far away.'

Sometimes, Ibrox Villiers Cley had Marnya play him a piece of music composed long ago on a planet now forgotten in a remote galaxy. The music was written before the Conventional Rules were imposed on musicians. It was good, sensible, male music, without display, yet with a poignance of which Cley did not tire.

In a case beside the encyclopaedia stood a solitary cube. Marnya occasionally activated it for Cley. The cube contained the works of a poet who had died in the distant town where Cley was born. On the last pages of the cube, the infant Cley had inscribed a map.

The map showed the kind of town which did not exist anywhere in the empire. It had not been formalized. The street system did not accord to a grid pattern. Roads ran here and there, houses were of various sizes. The house where the old poet died was marked.

The whole map spoke of a rampant but vanished individualism.

The cube was Cley's only personal possession.

Cley did not pretend to or aspire to be a friend of the Emperor's. There was too much power, there were too many regulations, in the air for emotions to flourish. The Emperor merely consulted him. He was merely one of the Emperor's tools. This function he understood. It was reliable, as things go. Friendship he found more difficult to comprehend.

Nor did he cultivate relations with those on Voltai who admired him. They thought of Cley as a guru.

He mistrusted ravishment by charm, spiritual appeal, force, wit or other blandishments.

Power favoured coldness, just as the empire favoured ruthlessness.

All empires are unscrupulous.

If Ibrox Villiers Cley was one thing, he was scrupulous.

Cley's closest acquaintance was Councillor Deems. Councillor Ardor Deems was Galactic Minister of the Arts.

Deems was a soft and highly coloured man who spoke always in a low voice. So low was Deems's voice that his auditors had to give it close attention. This habitual quietness had earned Deems the reputation for subtlety in his dealings. As he adapted himself to this reputation, Deems indeed grew subtle in his affairs, until man and reputation became one.

His gowns were always of softer material than the gowns of other ministers. His cheeks remained stubbornly rosy, even as his thought grew more pallid.

He came one day softly to see Cley, to discuss with him whether to ban, as it was in his power to do, a new play entitled *Forgotten Robe, Abyss, Glitter.*

'Certainly the play advocates a continuation of the war, as plays nowadays are required to do,' said Deems, folding his hands and placing them gently on the table before him, as if to show that he concealed nothing. 'But it also advocates extreme cruelty against animals as a matter of imperial policy, in order to dismay the enemy. Is that not obscenity?'

'The cruelty to which animals do you consider most obscene?'

'The play specifies long-drawn-out public torture for many animals, especially those the playwright deems most to offend against the Conventional Rules of Duty. To wit, cats, monkeys, meekrahs, jewkes and miniature elephants.'

The fine lines of Cley's face could be studied as he gazed towards the ceiling before speaking again.

'You ask if this cruelty is obscene. The play's not a covert satire against the state, is it? It seems to me no more – and no less – obscene than the new Ministry of War headquarters just built on our satellite. We ban plays. No one bans architecture.'

'The rules for censorship of architecture might be difficult to draw up.'

'The Computers could do it without trouble. But humanity has a basic need for ugliness and brutality in its public buildings.'

'But not in its plays?'

'The majority of people do not care to hear of the torture of elephants. Except, of course, in our Eastern Region.'

Deems's eyes were soft, and did not rest long in one place, as if they sought something they feared to find. 'And the torture of children?'

'The majority do not mind that as much. We are accustomed, almost from birth, to hear of children being maltreated. Accounts of child abuse sell newsfaxes.'

'If there is some hint of sexual abuse, certainly . . . Ibrox, I am a liberal man. I have wept to hear of children ill-treated. Even children on quite distant planets.'

'Congratulations. Your grief did you honour, as you know. You could relish both the pain of the children and your grief at the same time.'

'Oh, I am sincere.' He spoke without emphasis, and removed a white cloth from his collar with which to wipe his lips. 'Such crimes are common on Voltai. Other worlds, other mores . . . '

Although Deems spoke of other planets, Cley's chamber was perfectly prosaic, apart from its melancholy air. There was no sign that decisions were taken here which would affect populations on distantly scattered worlds. Cley's chambers suited the mentality of the entombed rather than the star-conscious.

After a pause, Deems said, 'I take it that you would not ban performances of *Forgotten Robe, Abyss, Glitter*?'

'Last galactic day, seven billion people were destroyed by a panthrax bomb on the planet Jubilloo. Do we ban panthrax bombs? Until we do, why bother about banning plays? They kill no one.'

Councillor Ardor Deems took a turn about the long room. His slender figure was plunged first into light then into shadow as he passed before the slitted windows.

Ibrox Villiers Cley did not stir in his seat. His gaze remained fixed on the polished surface of the table, which dimly reflected the glooms and gleams of the room.

The councillor approached nearer to Cley than custom demanded.

'I hate this war. I hate it as much as you do, Ibrox. It has become a part of life.'

'War has always been a part of man's life. Ever since the days when we were creatures of one world.'

Deems nodded. 'I heard just recently that a first cousin of mine was destroyed in the Battle of the Lesser Sack.'

'Did you love him?'

'I hated him. I hate his destruction more. There's the family to consider . . . '

Cley smiled and nodded. 'The Lesser Sack was a great victory for the empire.'

Deems's manner altered. He pulled his chair nearer to Cley's and spoke in his softest voice.

'You will be seeing the Emperor again tomorrow?' He then repeated the question with variations, as his custom was, as if unable to rely on the understanding of even his most intelligent listener. 'You have an audience with him at nine hours?'

When he received a glance of affirmation, he leaned forward, to speak even more quietly.

'The war must end, Ibrox. It must be terminated. We are destroying worlds we should be using. The Emperor will not consider proposals for peace. His will is set on continuous war.'

When Cley made no comment, Deems continued. 'As long as we are winning the war, and there are victory parades and banners and speeches, the vast majority of the population is also for the war. Their personal miseries become insignificant when compared with bloodthirsty accounts from our various war sectors. They can feel their petty lives caught up in great events. They forget they are mere statistics. Their psychic health – '

'I am Adviser of the Computers, Deems, not a rabble to be addressed.'

'Pardon me. I will approach the central question. Let us get to the point. Factions of the enemy hierarchy have made contact with me. They are prepared to sue for peace. Before peace can come about, something must be done about the Emperor.'

The steely profile of Ibrox Villiers Cley appeared not to be listening.

Deems's voice sank further.

'Something must be done about the Emperor. His mind must be changed. He must prefer peace. I have in my possession a new drug which will have the required effect upon him.'

He paused and then said, in a whisper, 'My party wishes that you will administer the drug to the Emperor during your audience tomorrow at nine.'

From his pocket Deems produced an object which resembled a short pencil. He laid it on the table halfway between him and Cley, his head on one side as he appeared to measure the distance precisely.

Cley did not touch the weapon.

'There are, I take it, inducements to – encourage me to use this drug against the Emperor?'

'Not "against", Ibrox, "on".'

'The inducements?'

'We do not put pressure on you. We believe that your own high intelligence will suffice to induce you to use such a weapon which will stop the war at last.'

'You think well of my intelligence.'

'Come, Ibrox, you are considered one of the most intelligent men who ever lived.' He allowed a whisper of reproach into his tone. 'Hence your position. You will do this thing, won't you? It is a noble undertaking, no less.'

The long room contained a long silence.

'How does the drug work?'

'Its name is mascinploxyrhanophyhaninide, or MPRP for short. It is delivered by aerosol. You have but to press a button. It sedates areas in the limbic brain from which the instincts of aggression rise. Permanently sedates them . . . You have but to press the button at nine, Ibrox, and at nine-five our beloved empire will be moving towards peace. Otherwise the drug is harmless, apart from some side effects.'

'What side effects?'

Deems eyed Cley narrowly, watching for his response. 'Blindness.'

Cley made no response. After a moment, he said, 'An aggressive weapon is not the most promising way through which to try to achieve peace.'

'We all depend on you, Ibrox. Not to be melodramatic, but the empire awaits your decision. Your name will be imperishable if you do this thing in the name of peace. You must do it for humanity's sake.'

He put a finger delicately on the MPRP weapon.

Cley rose to his feet and stood gazing down at the councillor.

'I want you to examine this act in which you propose we should conspire with the enemy against our emperor. Whatever its motives, it represents a physical attack. It is by physical attacks that battles and wars begin rather than end. Yet, as a preliminary to peace, you wish to make an attack.

'Do you not see that over a million wearying years of galactic history, so-called peace has invariably had its prelude in attack, so that the seeds of further conflict were sown? You merely perpetuate a status quo of constant warfare.

'How can war be eradicated? It is a permanent human condition. The baby emerges from the womb crying anger. Even the excision of the entire limbic brain would not suffice to remove aggression. This aggression of yours, represented by this MPRP weapon, springs not from the limbic brain but from the neocortex. It is an intellectual form of aggression, born of ambition, self-seeking.'

'I seek only peace.'

'Humanity is an aggressive species and no drug will alter those inherent characteristics.'

'You are being cynical and evasive.' As he spoke, Deems rose, clutching the MPRP weapon.

'I prefer my cynicism to your self-deceiving optimism.'

'Ibrox, my party wishes merely to see an end to conflict. We desire to finish with galactic war for ever. Is that self-deceiving?'

'It is nothing if not self-deceiving. Your party wishes to elevate itself. It would conduct conflict by means of backdoor dealing.'

'Backdoor! Our aspirations are of the loftiest.'

'That is what plotters always say. Deems, it happens that I have read this play which so disturbs you. It is written by a self-seeker. You should conscript him to your party. We do not have great writers any more, men to whom we can turn for enlightenment and discussion of the most engaging problems. The Conventional Rules of Duty have swept such men away. They languish in our reformatories. Those remaining seek fame or money, preferring those trumpery things above an immovable integrity. Your play is written for a materialist and spiritually bankrupt society – the people of Voltai. It is designed to shock and titillate them. It can do no harm since its audience is already corrupt. Any public which did not rise up in protest at the expense and ugliness of the Ministry of War edifice is corrupt.'

'But that magnificent building on which you pour such – '

Cley held up a commanding hand. 'Humankind condemned itself a long while ago to a perpetual diet of catastrophe. It burdens itself with the consequences of its own indifference to what is best. Go into a tavern tonight and listen to the music played there. What is of merit, what is not ephemeral, is shunned. The good in man is out of fashion. Mankind has chosen – or perhaps it was never a choice – a perpetual diet of catastrophe. Since it cannot and will not save itself, it cannot be saved by anything you or I might do. Not to mention your party. No, not even by killing the Emperor.'

Deems's voice barely reached Cley's ears. 'We have evidence that the Emperor is mad.'

'Then he represents the people well. People like mad rulers. They relish the rhetoric. Words like blood and loyalty and revenge and endurance awaken something primitive in their auditors, who enjoy the sensation of adrenalin coursing in their veins. They enjoy enmities.'

'They enjoy defending themselves against enemies. They are not cattle. The Emperor has become the enemy and must be destroyed.'

'For the sake of our enemies?' Cley folded his arms and stared at

Deems. 'The Emperor is not your enemy, Deems, except in so far as he stands in the way of your advancement. He aids and abets you in the task of self-destruction. We have no real enemies. You realize that? We have no real enemies throughout the whole galaxy. Our battlefields were once a cathedral, silent until the congregation of mankind entered. Enemies are as much an ancient invention as God.'

Deems made to speak but thought better of it.

'Mankind has always been alone, ever since it left Earth, millennia ago. Mankind had been unable to endure the – the purity of that situation. And the responsibility that situation brings. It has thought only about building "empires", absurd, repressive and unstable power-structures. Empires failed on our mother planet – how much more philosophically untenable are they across a dozen, a hundred, a thousand, a thousand thousand planets? Yet, rather than think out new and just ways of distributing the riches to which we have all fallen heir, it uses those riches as the basis for deadly quarrels.

'Mankind's real love is not of life, but of self-destruction.'

Deems raised the MPRP weapon and pointed it at Cley's face.

'We have to get you out of the way before we deal with the Emperor.'

Cley said, 'If that weapon kills aggression, as you claim, then it will have no effect on me. My cynicism, to which you have drawn my attention, prevents my aggression. I have never wished for power. I have no ambition. I am used. You have used me in the past. In order to enjoy solitude, I am prepared to be used. But I fancy MPRP is unlikely to change my character.'

He spoke easily, spinning out his words, until Marnya had come softly up behind Deems and taken the councillor in her grasp. The arms that held Cley tenderly were strong.

As Deems struggled fruitlessly, the MPRP weapon fell from his grasp and rolled under the table.

'You could have fired your drug at Marnya, Deems, and it would not have harmed her. Androids have no limbic brain, and no desires.'

Deems was pale. His voice was husky. 'I'm sorry to have

threatened you, Ibrox. My desires ran away with me. I cannot bear your diseased view of mankind.'

'How is that, when you are diseased yourself?'

'Is to desire change a disease in your eyes?'

'You don't desire change. You desire power. That's the disease.'

Deems was silent, hanging his head and then asking in a subdued voice, 'What will you do with me? Remember I am an old man.'

'You are free to leave. Everything that has transpired in this room has been recorded. Take your drug with you. It does not work.'

As Marnya released the councillor, the latter said, 'The drug does work.'

'You lie. I also know who sent you to me. You were ordered by the Emperor to test me. There is no wish for peace, on our side, even on the enemy's. Only I wish for peace.'

'It's useless talking to you.' As he made to leave the chamber, Deems said, 'If you perceive that the Emperor does not trust you, why continue faithful?'

Cley gestured with his left hand. 'Through cynicism. I like being tested. It interests me. One day in the future, the treacherous Deems-figure who arrives to make the test will employ an argument so sophisticated that I shall be convinced by it, and enter the Emperor's Council Room and kill him.'

'I will report on what you say. So you do still have hope, of a sort?'

'So does the Emperor, of a sort. He prays for the Deems-figure to win.' Ibrox Villiers Cley permitted himself a smile. 'I have no hope for humanity, if that's what you mean. Only for myself. Hope that the day may come when I am surprised by goodness.'

He crossed over to Marnya and took her patient arm.

'Goodbye, Deems,' he said.

Deems wiped his lips on his cloth. He left the chamber without answer, knowing the fate of those who failed on an imperial mission.

Cley was left once more in his chambers, in the shadowy silence which was now his greatest pleasure.

CONFLUENCE

THE INHABITANTS of the planet Myrin have much to endure from Earthmen, inevitably, perhaps, since they represent the only intelligent life we have so far found in the galaxy. The Tenth Research Fleet has already left for Myrin. Meanwhile, some of the fruits of earlier expeditions are ripening.

As has already been established, the superior Myrinian culture, the so-called Confluence of Headwaters, is somewhere in the region of eleven million (Earth) years old, and its language, Confluence, has been established even longer. The etymological team of the Seventh Research Fleet was privileged to sit at the feet of two gentlemen of the Oeldrid Stance Academy. They found that Confluence is a language-cum-posture, and that meanings of words can be radically modified or altered entirely by the stance assumed by the speaker. There is, therefore, no possibility of ever compiling a one-to-one dictionary of English–Confluence, Confluence–English words.

Nevertheless, the list of Confluent words which follows disregards the stances involved, which number almost nine thousand and are all named, and merely offers a few definitions, some of which must be regarded as tentative. The definitions are, at this early stage of our knowledge of Myrinian culture, valuable in themselves, not only because they reveal something of the inadequacy of our own language, but because they throw some light on to the mysteries of an alien culture. The romanized phonetic system employed is that suggested by Dr Rohan Harbottle, one of the members of the etymological team of the Seventh Research Fleet, without whose generous assistance this short list could never have been compiled.

AB WE TEL MIN The sensation that one neither agrees nor disagrees with what is being said to one, but that one simply wishes to depart from the presence of the speaker

ARN TUTKHAN Having to rise early before anyone else is about; addressing a machine

BAGI RACK Apologizing as a form of attack; a stick resembling a gun

BAG RACK Needless and offensive apologies

BAMAN The span of a man's consciousness

BI The name of the mythical northern cockerel; a reverie that lasts for more than twenty (Earth) years

BI SAN A reverie lasting more than twenty years and of a religious nature

BIT SAN A reverie lasting more than twenty years and of a blasphemous nature

BI TOSI A reverie lasting more than twenty years on cosmological themes

BI TVAS A reverie lasting more than twenty years on geological themes

BIUI TOSI A reverie lasting more than a hundred and forty-two years on cosmological themes; the sound of air in a cavern; long dark hair

BIUT TASH A reverie lasting more than twenty years on Har Dar Da themes (cf)

CANO LEE MIN Things sensed out of sight that will return

CA PATA VATUZ The taste of a maternal grandfather

CHAM ON TH ZAM Being witty when nobody else appreciates it

DAR AYRHOH The garments of an ancient crone; the age-old supposition that Myrin is a hypothetical place

EN IO PLAY The deliberate dissolving of the senses into sleep

GEE KUTCH Solar empathy

GE NU The sorrow that overtakes a mother knowing her child will be born dead

GE NUP DIMU The sorrow that overtakes the child in the womb when it knows it will be born dead

GOR A Ability to live for eight hundred years

HA ATUZ SHAK EAN Disgrace attending natural death of maternal grandfather

HAR DAR DA The complete understanding that all the soil of Myrin passes through the bodies of its earthworms every ten years

HAR DAR DI KAL A small worm; the hypothetical creator of a hypothetical sister planet of Myrin

HE YUP The first words the computers spoke, meaning, 'The light will not be necessary'

HOLT CHA The feeling of delight that precedes and precipitates wakening

HOLT CHE The autonomous marshalling of the senses which produces the feeling of delight that precedes and precipitates wakening

HOZ STAP GURT A writer's attitude to fellow writers

INK TH O Morality used as an offensive weapon

JILY JIP TUP A thinking machine that develops a stammer; the action of pulling up the trousers while running uphill

JIL JIPY TUP Any machine with something incurable about it; pleasant laughter that is nevertheless unwelcome; the action of pulling up the trousers while running downhill

KARNAD EES The enjoyment of a day or a year by doing nothing; fasting

KARNDAL CHESS The waste of a day or a year by doing nothing; fasting

KARNDOLI YON TOR Mystical state attained through inaction; feasting; a learned paper on the poetry of metal

KARNDOL KI REE The waste of a life by doing nothing; a type of fasting

KUNDULUM To be well and in bed with two pretty sisters

LAHAH SIP Tasting fresh air after one has worked several hours at one's desk

LA YUN UN A struggle in which not a word is spoken; the underside of an inaccessible boulder; the part of one's life unavailable to other people

LEE KE MIN Anything or anyone out of sight that one senses will never return; an apology offered for illness

LIKI INK TH KUTI The small engine that attends to one after the act of excretion

MAL A feeling of being watched from within

MAN NAIZ TH Being aware of electricity in wires concealed in the walls

MUR ON TIG WON The disagreeable experience of listening to oneself in the middle of a long speech and neither understanding what one is saying nor enjoying the manner in which it is being said; a foreign accent; a lion breaking wind after the evening repast

NAM ON A The remembrance, in bed, of camp fires

NO LEE LE MUN The love of a wife that becomes especially vivid when she is almost out of sight

NU CROW Dying before strangers

NU DI DIMU Dying in a low place, often of a low fever

NU HIN DER VLAK The invisible stars; forms of death

NUN MUM Dying before either of one's parents; ceasing to fight just because one's enemy is winning

NUT LAP ME Dying of laughing

NUT LA POM Dying laughing

NUT VATO Managing to die standing up

NUTVU BAG RACK To be born dead

NU VALK Dying deliberately in a lonely (high) place

OBI DAKT An obstruction; three or more machines talking together

ORAN MUDA A change of government; an old peasant saying meaning, 'The dirt in the river is different every day'

PAN WOL LE MUDA A certainty that tomorrow will much resemble today; a line of manufacturing machines

PAT O BANE BAN The ten heartbeats preceding the first heartbeat of orgasm

PI KI SKAB WE The parasite that afflicts man and Tig Gag in its various larval stages and, while burrowing in the brain of the Tig Gag, causes it to speak like a man

PI SHAK RACK CHANO The retrogressive dreams of autumn attributed to the presence in the bloodstream of Pi Ki Skab We

PIT HOR Pig's cheeks, or the droppings of pigs; the act of name-dropping

PLAY The heightening of consciousness that arises when one awakens in a strange room that one cannot momentarily identify

SHAK ALE MAN The struggle that takes place in the night between the urge to urinate and the urge to continuing sleeping

SHAK LA MAN GRA When the urge to urinate takes precedence over the urge to continue sleeping

SHAK LO MUN GRAM When the urge to continue sleeping takes precedence over all things

SHEAN DORL Gazing at one's reflection for reasons other than vanity

SHE EAN MIK Performing prohibited postures before a mirror

SHEM A slight cold afflicting only one nostril; the thoughts that pass when one shakes hands with a politician

SHUK TACK The shortening in life-stature a man incurs from a seemingly benevolent machine

SOBI A reverie lasting less than twenty years on cosmological themes; a nickel

SODI DORL One machine making way for another; decadence, particularly in the Cold Continents

SODI IN PIT Any epithet which does not accurately convey what it intends, such as 'Sober as a judge', 'Silly nit', 'He swims like a fish', 'He's only half-alive', and so on

STAINI RACK NUSVIODON Experiencing Staini Rack Nuul and then realizing that one must continue in the same outworn fashion because the alternatives are too frightening, or because one is too weak to change; wearing a suit of clothes at which one sees strangers looking askance

STAINI RACK NUUL Introspection (sometimes prompted by birthdays) that one is not living as one determined to live when one was very young; or, on the other hand, realizing that one is living in a mode decided upon when one was very young and which is now no longer applicable or appropriate

STAIN TOK I The awareness that one is helplessly living a role

STA SODON The worst feelings which do not even lead to suicide

SU SODA VALKUS A sudden realization that one's spirit is not pure, overcoming one on Mount Rinvlak (in the Southern Continent)

TI Civilized aggression

TIG GAG The creature most like man in the Southern Continent which smiles as it sleeps

TIPY LAP KIN Laughter that one recognizes though the laugher is unseen; one's own laughter in a crisis

TOK AN Suddenly divining the nature and imminence of old age in one's thirty-first year

TUAN BOLO A class of people one meets only at weddings; the pleasure of feeling rather pale

TU KI TOK Moments of genuine joy captured in a play or charade about joy; the experience of youthful delight in old age

TUZ PAT MAIN (Obs.) The determination to eat one's maternal grandfather

U (Obs.) The amount of time it takes for a lizard to turn into a bird; love

UBI A girl who lifts her skirts at the very moment you wish she would

UDI KAL The clothes of the woman one loves

UDI UKAL The body of the woman one loves

UES WE TEL DA Love between a male and female politician

UGI SLO GU The love that needs a little coaxing

UMI RIN TOSIT The sensations a woman experiences when she does not know how she feels about a man

UMY RIN RU The new dimensions that take on illusory existence when the body of the loved woman is first revealed

UNIMGAG BU Love of oneself that passes understanding; a machine's dream

UNK TAK An out-of-date guidebook; the skin shed by the snake that predicts rain

UPANG PLA Consciousness that one's agonized actions undertaken for love would look rather funny to one's friends

UPANG PLAT Consciousness that while one's agonized actions undertaken for love are on the whole rather funny to oneself, they might even look heroic to one's friends; a play with a cast of three or less

U RI RHI Two lovers drunk together

USANA NUTO A novel all about love, written by a computer

USAN I NUT Dying for love

USAN I ZUN BI Living for love; a tropical hurricane arriving from over the sea, generally at dawn

UZ Two very large people marrying after the prime of life

UZ TO KARDIN The realization in childhood that one is the issue of two very large people who married after the prime of life

WE FAAK A park or a college closed for seemingly good reasons; a city where one wishes one could live

YA GAG Too much education; a digestive upset during travel

YA GAG LEE Apologies offered by a hostess for a bad meal

YA GA TUZ Bad meat; (Obs.) dirty fingernails

YAG ORN A president

YATUZ PATI (Obs.) The ceremony of eating one's maternal grandfather

YATUZ SHAK SHAK NAPANG HOLI NUN Lying with one's maternal grandmother; when hens devour their young

YE FLIG TOT A group of men smiling and congratulating each other

YE FLU GAN Philosophical thoughts that don't amount to much; graffiti in a place of worship

YON TORN A paper tiger; two children with one toy

YON U SAN The hesitation a boy experiences before first kissing his first girl

YOR KIN BE A house; a circumlocution; a waterproof hat; the smile of a slightly imperfect wife

YUP PA A book in which everything is understandable except the author's purpose in writing it

YUPPA GA Stomach ache masquerading as eyestrain; a book in which nothing is understandable except the author's purpose in writing it

YUTH MOD The assumed bonhomie of visitors and strangers

ZO ZO CON A woman in another field

CONFLUENCE REVISITED

WHEN AN Earth ship discovered the Myrinian system, the planet Myrin's civilization was already eleven million years old. The Myrinians traced their history back that far; they had erected a memorial of vertiginous beauty to the passing of the ages every million years, either in reverence or fun.

Most of that lengthy period was passed in what one Earth philosopher has termed 'fruitful stagnation'. Stagnant or not, the Myrinian cultural complex is to be envied for the general level of contentment in which its peoples live, referred to as *Bi Jo*, (approximately, Stylized Submerged Individualism). The people eat moderately and sleep well at night.

Bringing back with it many records of the venerable Myrinian culture, the Tenth Research Fleet has just returned to Earth, android-manned, since the human crew in the main elected to remain on Myrin in the state referred to as First Lobby. Unfortunately it has not yet proved possible to receive a visitation here from representatives of the Myrinian system, despite many pressing invitations. Doubtless we may expect acceptances when levels of radiation decrease. Meanwhile, terrestrials must be grateful that Myrin does not ban all human visits. Even the unfortunate incident involving the Earth ship *Bombast* has been clemently overlooked.

The complexity of the chief Myrinian language, Confluence, has already been noted. That it is a language-cum-posture, or lingopost, was established by the Seventh Research Fleet, members of which were privileged to attend special lectures at the Oeldrid Stance Academy on Myrin Centre, in Sector Ten. Meanings in lingopost can be radically altered by the stance assumed by the speaker (or *S'Ih Hin*, the Intoner, also a rather transparent curtain), or even by that of the listener. The positioning of a single finger can negate or reverse the meaning of several classes of lingopost words. It is clear that there is no possibility of compiling a dictionary within the ordinary meaning of the term.

The Tenth Research Fleet was confined to Sector Nine on the chief Myrinian planet. As is well known, the Myrinians have for convenience (or some say for amusement) divided their territories into squares, so that they resemble a gigantic checker-board. There the researchers spent considerable time investigating Confluence. Their special report on terms for wine will be published separately. They also compiled a holographic record of various stances assumed in lingopost. Findings will be available shortly.

Meanwhile, the brief listing that follows displays something of the interest of a lingopost which far excels Solar English in its nuances. Definitions must be regarded as tentative.

The romanized phonetic system employed here is that suggested by the leader of the Etymological Division of the Seventh Research Fleet, Dr Rohan Harbottle.

AH BLAK HOO Oblong eyes; the inhabitants of Sector Nine say that persons with oblong eyes live longest

AH SHEN SHI Having learnt any classical book by heart

AK IH WAN Courtesy to an old lady in cognizance of her previous beauty; an overcooked egg or fish

ANEY A place much used by great-grandfathers

ARP RUH HIG LO TON Being busy in an office after lunch; a dotard studying history; sounds of leaves falling in early autumn

ARTH Conversation; a cave with echoes

AS DIN A family holiday less than a complete success; a fever

BACH HOANG A machine factory; a long worm in a tiger's intestine

BA YEF NA One's recognizably second-rate thoughts

BAZ YEF HO Striving to better one's thoughts; restocking a lake with fish of improved quality

BI A reverie sustained for twenty years; crowing like a cockerel without making a sound

BI JOWA Ninety per cent contentment; half of a chocolate egg

BOL I PEIU Those who worship tigers; perhaps a ceiling with blood on it

CH'N DOGBA HAN The kind of conversation one expects between two robots; singing for the sake of it

CHUK CHEE Answering back to owls; laughing at one's own jokes; a concoction of raw egg and alcohol

CHU PAT A learned person in a low tavern

CUR Persistent attempts at flight; any hilarious suicide

DA EST KO A hypothetical form of reason which will reach to the roots of unreason, at present being developed by sages in Sector Nine

DI CHI'FAN I The laughter of women in the next room; restaurants with doubtful reputations

DOBGAT An irresistible tendency to laugh at what is not funny

FAN Beloved female

FANG TO A rarity; cream on mare's milk

FAN N'M A slightly less beloved female

FANOW A surprisingly pleasant female cousin; a miniature painting

FAN SEE KIT MEE An undiscovered continent; a well-cultivated female mind; cream

FEE MAABA An obsolete weapon once used for beheading robots; the shinbone

FEET A kind of hedgehog skilled at climbing trees; old hair brushes

FOH TAT A dog singing; laughter towards nightfall

HA LIT A special dish of jelly fish; jokes told to the wrong people

HANG TAK A robot which thinks it thinks

HE'CHI YAY Borrowing and not returning books; a certain smile

HE HANG TUK TI A robot which thinks it can walk straight but deviates to the left consistently

HI HANG TUK TIN A robot which thinks it can walk straight but deviates to the right consistently; a devious politician

HI IH HI Listening to choirs and similar activities

HI IH HU YA Making a habit of listening to choirs; conversation with a green bear

H'KAI TURK The malfunction of a semi-computer; a small child farting

HO HOO'FAN Dining on Farinese oysters and wine; having eyes only for the beloved

H'YA TO An unintended gesture; a posture; a furry type of fish from the Clement Sea

ICT P'EEM SHA To be pulled apart by four carthorses; any similar punishment

I JOW N'A Poor forms of contentment; on the Southern Continent, a game with fingers as counters, some say, cat's cradles

IMOO A kind of pudding; a planet

IMSK IMOOT Thinking of worse people

INA O YEF Achieving perfection of thought

JA A type of depraved underground mammal; mathematics; one's appearance on certain mornings

JA LULI Any depravity, especially if practised in brothels

JAL UM Standing in such a way as to annoy a mother-in-law; a pimple not concealed by garments; the young pig or eagle

JALUM PI A preoccupation with money; an elusive ache; diseases of middle age

JIN PAH T'HA A waterwheel beginning to work again; kissing a lady on her private parts

JOW TSEE The division where soft ends and hard begins; a tiger's tale

KA'RENI Visiting a distant country; an assignation with a sister-in-law

KEY HANG Annoying thoughts: robot with a conical head

KO HO LAM Two people looking sideways at each other

KOISAL T'PEEM The Four Realizations:

EEM AD AH The realization that one is eighteen and already a failure

EEM HA WAK The realization one is eighty and has achieved nothing

EEM YA AK The realization one is popular only in vulgar company

EE 'OH MOI The realization one is shunned by one's own family

LEONG M'BEE Congested bowels; an overpopulated city

LIEM TU'H Highest form of art; in Sector Nine, also the stories one tells children in order to prepare them to conduct themselves wisely in adulthood

LI LIH JUH Superconductivity; an orgy; illicit communication with a female prisoner

LUH PU SMAK TI Constant dripping of water; conversation in which one cannot join; listening unwisely

MAK TI IH Talking only slightly to impress

M'BEE GOH General discourtesy to old ladies as a principle

M'BEE WA An old city; ancient thing; article; or a certain desolation which descends when one sees a beloved house demolished

MEE KIT A well-cultivated mind; fatness; like a little continent

MEN TATI YI Discerning the differing qualities of each hour of darkness; 'parting the night breeze'

M'FEE BAH An obsolete instrument used for giving exact measurements of genitalia; any kind of one-armed lobster

MIN RETSO Thinking of someone dear but distant; a row of little houses, perhaps a village

M'KO HA BLIT Avoiding a friend who has written a book one has not read; bad sunrises

NAH Purity; blue sky before the eleventh hour

NA TAT MA DATO Divorce while one's partner is not looking; having a chimney relined

NIK TRIT A state between something and nothing; scarcity; abundance

NIN TU WOL Any form of behaviour lacking inward control; a child's toy

N'JAH TUR Mild depravity; a spring fair for children only

NUT IMGI Managing to die without causing inconvenience to others; cooling egg custard

NUTRED JOW Achieving death in an amused daydream

OI PAH SMA GEE A young lady seen through a looking glass; a little cress growing between storms

OPI NIN Any form of behaviour which improves on what has been before; a drink that wards off intoxication

ORAN BAL The uneasy feeling that change is on its way; death of the Ruler

OTA TI HA Gesturing circumspectly to the left; the picturesque

OTA TIN HI Gesturing circumspectly to the right; a mystery

OUTA Several feet washed under the same tap; a haul of squid; a parliament

PEET Four people sitting companionably round a table

PUH TIH Oh, hell!; also used for urine

QUAM Delicate feelings towards older persons; poetry of an especially obscure kind

REEN Getting in touch with a distant country

SHEN Any fruitless task undertaken through embarrassment

SHIN HOI BAA The toes; playing a musical instrument with strings, some say by blind musicians

SIN LIN H'KAY A robot pretending to belch; anything above its station; also, some say, low comedy, such as a custard pie about to be delivered

SMAK T'HAH A one-eyed fish; so that two have to swim close to see the way forward; the place; any silly behaviour by twins

SNI TO'SI Compulsory counting; 'he is adding up the stars'; any venerable astronomer

SZE PU LO LO An icicle of urine; cryonic superconductivity

TEI FEET PU Excessive hairiness; a great victory

THEE DO Examining three or more graduate-level students; an owl's nest

TH'HOW Boundless lapses of time since the universe began; what astronomers say

TIG TRAG Creature most resembling mankind, said to smile in its sleep; a rival imitating one's best garment

TRIH H'YA A gesture with the fingers where one wishes to speak but cannot

TRIH YA An imaginary world where it is worse

T'SMAK TH'HOW CHE Rattling of reeds by a flooded lake; any northern breeze; useless thinking about boundless lapses of time

TU LA LAT Holding a high note in opera; letting sunshine into the back of the mouth; speaking purely to please; a lizard

TURK TOH A little child laughing; gutters; like firecrackers thrown into water

UK'WAN AS To hasten towards one's death; in general, to enjoy oneself

UK'WAN TA To hasten towards marriage

UK'WAN TAMA To hasten towards an unwelcome marriage

ULI WAS Fasting; going a year without food

UNIMGAG BA A machine dream which takes some time to recall; a lethargic flea

URK AY A custard pie after delivery; a deficiency of wit

USANO NUTO A novel about love written by a computer; a vain thing

WAN A type of tortoise used in races

WOON HA Parking a chariot; the smell of over-heated horses

YAG ORN Passing on knowledge; the honourableness of passing on knowledge; a president (archaic)

YEP YAY Disillusion

YEEF Any place more than a thousand miles from the ocean

YEEF N'YI One day in adolescence; a pale lemon

YUK NA Predicting the future; looking through a bamboo blind into the night; certain low autumn fogs

YU UZ'NIT A very large person who fails to realize he resembles his father

ZEI TAI' A short-haired dog with dignity

NORTH OF THE ABYSS

> I am not yet born; provide me
> with water to dandle me, grass to grow for me, trees
> to talk to me, sky to sing to me, birds and a
> white light in the back of my mind to guide me.
>
> Louis MacNeice: 'Prayer Before Birth'

THE WEST bank of the river, so the old legends had it, was the bank of death. There the dead went to their tombs, among the sands and the sunsets.

However that might have been, a barque emerged from the mists veiling the west bank and moved towards mid-channel with steady purpose. It was high in prow and stern. In the stern, a dark figure guided the boat by means of a large steering oar.

The figure was alone in the boat. At its feet stood pottery coffers of curious design, their lids taking the form of heads of owl, wolf and cat. More curious was the figure of the ferryman himself. He wore a short tunic with stiff pleated kilt, from the belt of which hung a sword. His brown arms were bare, adorned with ornamental metal bands at wrists and biceps. Round his neck was a wide bead collar, and he wore a thick blue wig to show that this was an official occasion.

The wig enfolded a narrow bony head. The ferryman's sharp nose and shallow jaw, the black fur covering his face, the two sharp erect ears – pointing alertly forward at the *felucca* he was approaching – were those of a jackal. He was not of the world of men and women, although his traffic was with them.

No less disturbing was the unnatural fact that his barque, in its stealthy approach to the *felucca* over the sunset waters, cast no reflection on the darkening flood and no shadow into the depths below its keel.

*

The *felucca* had departed from the Aswan Sheraton hotel on the east bank of the Nile, and was making its way upstream, its sail taut in the light wind blowing from the north. Not one of the fourteen passengers on the boat had anything to say, as if the gravity of the sunset bore upon their spirits. All fixed their gaze on the distant west bank which, while the sun sank lower, turned apricot against the cloudless sky, as if composed of material more precious than sand.

Oscar North sat in a cramped position in the stern of the *felucca*. He was pervaded by feelings of isolation. There was no one in the boat he recognized, although he believed that they, like him, had embarked on this trip from the immense concrete honeycomb of luxury now falling behind them in ashen distance. No one he recognized, that is, except for a small thin man with sparse hair and hooded eyes into whom North had bumped in the foyer of the hotel on the previous day; this man now turned and regarded North as if he would speak. North evaded his gaze.

North was nearing forty. He had been making every effort to retain a youthful figure, entering into all the sports organized by the department which employed him, while at the same time spending evenings drinking with friends from the office. The features on his wide bony face, in particular his narrow colourless eyes, appeared rather insignificant.

In the files of the multi-national company for which Oscar North worked was a note against his character which said, 'Unpromising background'. Another note consisted of one word: 'Conformist.'

Evading the glances of the thin man, North stared about him. To be on water generally excited him, yet this evening he felt only unease, as if this were a journey into the unknown instead of nothing more than a tourist outing. The great river seemed to gather lightness to itself as the sky overhead darkened. Already stars glittered and a horn of moon shone superb and metallic overhead. The faces of the other people in the boat dimmed, becoming anonymous.

The thin man leaned forward and tapped North's arm.

'There's Philae,' he said.

He pointed in the direction the *felucca* was heading. His voice was confidential, as if he imagined himself to be sharing a secret with North.

All North could see ahead was a confusion of land and rock, black against the cloudless evening sky. The odd palm tree showed like an angry top-knot. The sound of their progress over the waves could almost be the noise of night coming on, closing over Upper Egypt.

The thin man rose from his place and inserted himself on the stern bench next to North.

'I visited Philae with my father, fifteen years back. I've never forgot it. It's magic, pure magic – out of this world, to coin a phrase.'

He shook his head dismissively, as if in contradiction of his own words.

North found himself unable to make any response. He recognized an obligation to be pleasant to a fellow American, yet he had come on vacation to Egypt largely to escape his compatriots – in search of what exactly he had yet to discover.

Worse, he felt that somehow this guy understood him, understood his weaknesses. Accordingly, he was defensive and reluctant to talk.

The thin man hardly paused for response, going on to say, 'We had an encounter in the lobby of the hotel, if you recall – you and your wife. Pleasant-looking lady, I'd say. She's not accompanying you on this little trip?'

'She didn't feel like it,' North said.

'Why's that, may I enquire? They say the new *son et lumière* on Philae is just great.'

Again, North found himself unable to reply. Anger and resentment welled up in him as he thought of the violent row with his wife in the hotel room before he left.

'My name's Jackson, Joe Jackson, and I'm from Jacksonville, Jax, Florida, mortician by trade, married, divorced, three kids, two grandchildren,' said the thin man, offering his hand and shaking his head.

'Oscar North,' said North, taking the proffered hand.

It was as if the name released a flood of information from Joe Jackson.

'Night's coming on. The ancient Egyptians would claim that Ra, the Sun God, was sailing under the world with the sun safe in his boat . . . They had many odd beliefs like that. Still, people believe pretty strange things even today, in this age of progress, even in the United States. When the *Jacksonville Bugle* ran a poll on education recently, they found that sixty-two per cent of the people questioned believe that the sun goes round the Earth, instead of vice versa . . . '

'Well, I guess people in cities . . . '

'That don't make no difference.' He shook his head. 'They got an alternative frame of beliefs here – different mind-set, as they say. It's a Muslim country. You and your fair lady ever visited Egypt before?'

'This is the first time I've been outside the United States and Europe. Europe's pretty Americanized – we own a good piece of it, as you know.' He laughed uncertainly.

'Belief – that's the important thing in life,' Jackson said. 'Me, I'm a religious man. It alters how you look at facts.'

Afraid the man was about to become philosophical, North said curtly, 'Well, I believe in the Protestant work ethic.' He turned a shoulder to the man from Florida and stared across the bows of the boat.

It had seemed that the *felucca* was scarcely making progress, but suddenly dark shapes of land were swinging about them as the steersman changed course. Rocks moved in close by the side of the boat, intent on invasion, smoothed into elephantine shapes by the countless past inundations of the waterway. The effect was as if they entered among a concourse of great beasts at a waterhole.

Flat-topped stone temples loomed above the mast of the *felucca*, only to disappear behind a shoulder of land. Ahead, as the vessel swung about, they sighted a line of torches illuminating a landing stage and a flight of steps beyond.

Almost as one, the passengers in the boat rose and stood silent, aware they had made a transition from one world to another. Darkness now wrapped them about. Nobody spoke. Couples held on to each other.

The crew jumped ashore and moored the boat at the bottom of the steps. The passengers climbed on to the island and began the ascent. The steps they trod were broad and shallow. Turbaned Egyptians stood by, motioning them on. Other vessels were arriving out of the dark like moths at a flame, other people setting foot on Philae, looking tense and serious.

While climbing ashore, North tried to evade Joe Jackson, but the thin man appeared at his side. North made no sign. He wanted to give himself over entirely to Philae, without distraction. This was his last evening in Egypt.

'My profession being mortician, I've made a kind of hobby of studying the ancient Egyptians,' Jackson said. 'They were wonderful folk. In the arts of embalming they were second to none. Second to none.'

Again he shook his head, as if denying what he was saying.

'They had secrets and techniques unknown to us today despite all our modern advances. Some experts think they used magic. Maybe they did use magic.' He chuckled. 'Of course, they had gods and goddesses for everything. I know quite a bit about them. Like this island of Philae is dedicated to the goddess Isis, who was worshipped hereabouts for over a thousand years . . . She was a tricky little bit of goods and no mistake.'

Climbing the stairs, North made no response.

'Philae's dedicated to Isis,' Jackson repeated. 'I guess you knew that from the guidebooks. How long you and that wife of yours been in Aswan?'

'Two days.'

'Two days. That all? What have you seen so far?'

'Shit, we've been resting, Mr Jackson, taking it easy by the pool. What's it to you?'

'You and your lady are on the fringe of a wonderful world. Vanished but mysteriously still here.' His tone suggested he took no offence at North's tone; bores could not afford to take offence. 'By day, Egypt's blanked out under a blaze of light. Quite different from Florida's light. Then you go down underground into the dark of the tombs and – wham! – a wonderful coloured picture-book of the past opens up. Gods, goddesses, the lot. They sure aren't Christian but they're a lot of fun. Don't miss it.'

'Back to Geneva in the morning,' North said.

Flambeaux burning in the low wall on their left made stygian the waters beyond. The visitors were cut off from the rest of the world. As they mounted the steps, various imposing stone buildings rose into view. Even Jackson fell silent. A general solemnity gripped everyone, as if they were not merely tourists, in search of little beside sunshine and some distraction, but pilgrims to a sacred shrine.

When they gained level ground, before them stretched several temples, picked out of the dark by hidden spotlights, their walls embellished by some of the best-loved gods, Horus the falcon-headed, Hathor, Nephthys, sister of Isis, and Isis herself, alert, slender, her breasts bare. These giant figures stood as they had stood for three thousand years, incised in the stone with a conviction which seemed to grant them immortality.

Above the temples, night had closed in with its glittering horn. Only in the cloudless west a line of ancient rose light remained, fading, fading fast, the colour of regret.

The beauty and tranquillity of the scene before him – a tragic quality in it – made North pause. He wished he had it all to himself, without the intrusive Jackson, without the other tourists. Tomorrow it was back to the pressures of commodity-broking in the Geneva office.

The posting to the Swiss office had represented promotion for the aspiring Oscar North. Winifred had hated leaving the Washington area where her family lived. Their marriage had been in decline ever since. Perhaps he should pray to Isis for better things, the thought occurred to him.

He evaded Jackson in the crowd of anonymous people. Attendants were urging everyone across a paved area. More *feluccas* were arriving at the landing stage, materializing out of the dark, more people pouring in for the show. North moved forward with them, determined to get a good position.

He found a place by the rope which held spectators back. The Temple of Isis presented itself ahead, before it a great stone pylon, dating from the period of the Ptolomaic pharaohs. Its two towers were illuminated so that their tops faded away as if aspiring to the stars themselves. A measure of calm entered North as he took in the spectacle; it was a sensation he hardly recognized. He reflected on the venerable age of the structures, their solidity and grace, and the way in which so many generations had found peace on this small island in the Nile, worshipping the goddess. A feeling of sanctity still prevailed. The little island had been preserved: no one lived here. There were no houses or shops, only the majestic ruins.

Jackson was at his elbow again.

'Lost you for a minute, Oscar. You don't object if I stand with you? I just don't care too much for all these strangers. Guess I'm more accustomed to folk who've passed on, being a mortician.' He chuckled, shaking his head at the same time.

'It's a wonderful place,' North said.

'Too bad your wife isn't with you.'

He was not going to be led into a discussion of what had happened to Winifred.

Winny and Oscar North came in from the hotel's pool area and showered in their room. The heat outside had been almost too intense to bear.

'Let's go and sit in the bar and sink a few,' he said, drying his hair.

'You were drinking all the time we were out by the pool. Haven't you had enough?'

'You would keep talking to that woman, whoever she was.'

'She's nice. She's from Arizona. She's staying a whole two weeks in the hotel. She was telling me – '

'She's a pain in the neck.'

'Osk, you never even spoke to her. How do you know what she's like? She's very well-heeled, I tell you that.'

The phone rang. He moved quickly to answer it.

Covering the receiver, he made a face and said to her, 'It's a call from Geneva. Larry wants to speak to me. Can't be good.'

Winny was sitting on a chair arm, putting on a shoe. She flung it to the floor in anger. 'No, not Larry. Tell him you're not home. Don't speak to him. Tell him to get lost.'

But Larry, North's immediate boss, was on the line, and Oscar was listening and smiling and saying, 'No, glad to hear from you, Larry, great, just great. How's tricks in Geneva?'

When his face grew serious as he listened, Winny went over and listened too.

'But the Armour account is fine, Larry. Can't you possibly handle it till I'm back Monday? We're only away a week.'

'You know I have to be in Paris, Oscar.' Larry, unremitting. 'If the wrong people get a hold of this story . . . '

'Tell him to get lost,' Winny said. 'We've only just arrived.'

'We've only just arrived here, Larry.'

'Well, if you are prepared to let it slide . . . That's your decision, Oscar. You know the stuff Armour handle.'

'I really don't think it's that urgent, Larry. Look, I mean – '

'If that's your decision, Oscar, old pal. Of course I'm going to have difficulty explaining it to the meeting tomorrow . . . '

'Can't you just tell them – tell them I'll be back Friday? . . . Look, suppose I came back Thursday? . . . Wednesday, then?'

'Tell him to stuff his fucking job, Osk!'

'That's entirely up to you, Oscar. Entirely up to you. I don't want to pressure you, but you know how these things go. And there's your future in the company to think about.'

'How about if I come back Tuesday, Larry?'

'Do you think Armour would understand? I have to ring them back pronto. You know how it will look if I say you are on vacation and are unavailable. But that's entirely your decision if you want to play it that way.' Larry's voice was flat, cold.

'Oh, Jesus, look, Larry – OK, look, I'll get a flight back tomorrow morning, OK?' Forcing sarcasm into his voice he asked, 'Will that be soon enough to please you?'

'I leave it entirely up to you, Oscar.' The line went dead.

North set the receiver back in its cradle without looking at his wife.

'Oh, you asshole!' she shrieked. 'You spoil everything.'

A slender moon shone down on the isle of Philae with sceptred gaze. No wind stirred. The great dark flow of the Nile opened its lips to breathe the island as it ran its course from south to north of the ancient land.

Still the tourists were emerging from the river into the light. They felt the dryness of the air. Rain never fell here; life depended on the artery of the river. Vegetation stayed close to its banks, a thin embroidered strip woven into boundless desert sands. And Joe Jackson pointed to one of the giant figures sinuously carved on the temple wall and said, 'See that one? The god with the jackal's head? That's Anubis.'

'I think I've heard of him,' North said. 'What's he do?'

'Anubis mediates between the living and the dead. He connects the visible and the invisible worlds. Quite a boy. He conducts the Act of Judgement which decides whether you spend eternity in the summer stars or the Abyss.'

'He's frightening.'

'I've got a special interest in Anubis.' The hasty shake of the head, the nervous mannerism denying what the mouth had spoken. 'See, he's the god of medicine and embalming. That's why I've got a special interest. He removes the intestines from corpses and embalms them in pots – pots often shaped like animals – so's they are ready for you when you arrive in the Underworld. And what is the special – hold it!'

He interrupted himself, for music suddenly welled out of the dry earth, the shrill music of an earlier day, music of heat and wine and nudity and the Bronze Age.

Illumination faded from the temple walls. They were washed pale and then sank away into dark like ghosts. For an instant, only the night reigned over Philae.

And the moon shone down, transfixing the island with its purity.

Then coloured spots awoke, green, bronze, orange, and the *son et lumière* was under way.

Measured voices, male and female, hired from London, told ancient tales of the gods and goddesses who had once ruled the two kingdoms of Upper and Lower Egypt. Of Ra, the god of the sun, of his grandchildren, Geb and Nut, god of earth and goddess of sky, and of their children, who included Osiris, the god of the dead, and his sister, Isis, later his wife.

As the preposterous story unfolded, new areas of the temples opened, and turbaned attendants ushered the spectators on to hear the next chapter of the tale in a further chamber of the holy ruin.

The visitors filed solemnly past a long colonnade of which no two capitals were alike. Its ceiling was decorated with stars and flying vultures. Two granite lions guarded the way to the inner temple complex. In the Great Court stood the Birth House. Here was represented Isis giving birth to Horus, Horus as a hawk crowned with the Double Crown, Horus being suckled at the breast of Isis. All the weird progeny, alive on the walls, smouldering in ambers and sullen mauve, appearing or disappearing at the will of the narrative.

And the story went on. Incest, murder, mutilation, brother fighting brother, a great conflagration of mortal sins and aspirations, all played out in an earlier world where the reed beds were full of wild fowl and the woods of deer and leopard and the skies of geese and doves and the minds of human beings with the lees of previous existences before intellect was born.

In all this walking between hypostyle hall, sanctuaries, ritual scenes of offerings to the dusky gods, and tales of flood and fury, Oscar North proceeded in a daze, half attending to the task of avoiding Joe Jackson. As the coloured lights led the crowds on, shepherding them like dogs controlling a flock of sheep, he was aware of the moon, raining down its light on him between the ornamented columns. It seemed to offer refuge from tormented emotions.

As he moved between light and dark, following narrative and physical path, the story conveyed by remote modern lips got to him. It overtook him like an old belief. He was filled with desire for the vivid world that had vanished thousands of years ago, for the hot sunlight that had once contained its people, animals and birds within the narrow ribbon of Egyptian dynastic life. As in his own day of the twentieth century, people had conflicting ideas of the afterlife: some holding that death released one to dwell for ever among the summer stars, others that death led to a tomb where Anubis would come, dog-faced and dark, to pickle one in preparation for judgement – a judgement that would lead either to the Abyss or to another life, where there were still slaves and dancing girls and wine and perfumes and strips of land to plough.

With all this he compared his own existence, his years in offices and bars and high-rise apartments, his imprisonment by desk and VDU, his anxieties over work and marriage and income. There had never been an Isis in his life, dainty and bloodthirsty. He had submitted to circumstance. There had never been belief. Only fear and a wish to conform.

'I believe we're coming to Trajan's Kiosk,' said Jackson's voice at his shoulder. 'That's if I remember after all this time. You going to have a bite of supper when you get back to the hotel, Oscar?'

'I don't feel like food,' he said.

His mind was in a torment. He had to escape this little man. Then he could think. Perhaps it would even be possible to set his life back on course.

As the crowd filed into the mighty rectangle of Trajan's Kiosk, North obeyed an impulse – he ducked away and hid behind a massive block of granite. Shadow enfolded him. The attendants had not seen him go.

From where he crouched, the narrative could still be heard. Disembodied voices acted out the ancient drama of Osiris and Isis, and the death of the god at the hands of his brother.

He paced about the hotel room, wearing only a towel round his midriff. Winifred had turned her back on him and stood looking out of the window at the Nile and the desolate expanses of west bank beyond.

'What else could I do? I had to give in to Larry. You know how these guys ride me. The Geneva office is worse than Washington in that respect. You know that. Besides, the Armour business – '

'Don't tell me about the Armour business,' she said, in a low controlled voice. 'This isn't the first time you've done this to me.'

'What do you mean, to you? I haven't done anything to you. It's what's been done to me. Do you think I can help it?'

He never told her what his work involved. Either Winny did not want to know or could not grasp the details. He felt compelled to explain to her that Armour was one of his most tendentious clients. Through sub-agents, Armour exported thousands of tonnes of nuclear waste from industrial countries to Third World countries. Now a crisis threatened operations. A customer in an African country had used radioactive waste bought from an Armour sub-contractor as hardcore for a new road through the capital city. People were getting sick. The facts, long suppressed, had been leaked to a German news agency.

'You think I care?' Winny said, interrupting. 'All of Africa can drop dead as far as I'm concerned. What gets me is how you in your stupid dumb way have just loused up my vacation. You wimp, why don't you tell Larry and these Armour people to get lost? How long do you think I'm going to put up with this crap?'

He clutched the nape of his neck, feeling one of his migraines coming on. 'Get off my back, will you? You think it's my fault? You think I'm responsible for this almighty cock-up?'

She had finally turned round to face him, looking white-faced and mean. She folded her arms protectively over her breasts.

If North tried – as he sometimes did at night before sleep enfolded him – he could remember a time back in Washington when Winny did not bitch at him. She had changed only when he had been posted to the Geneva office, when promotion became slow.

He had done his best. Taken her on trips with his office buddies at weekends into the Alps or the Haute Savoie. Humoured her wish to have her stupid sister to visit.

The magic between them had long departed. He suppressed the knowledge that what he had done for her – the favour – had been done grudgingly. Her responses now were conditioned by his own lack of grace. But he could not be to blame. Could he?

Once Winny's face had looked so cute and placid in repose. Now it was flabby and had a dull, cold expression which her grey eyes reinforced. Winny turned that cold expression on her husband now, continuing her diatribe.

'I heard what Larry said. He said it was your decision. You could have told him to get lost. You made the wrong decision one more time.'

'What Larry said was a threat. Can't you understand that, you bitch? Larry's a mean careerist bastard.'

'Oh, and what are you? You always put the company first. You're a lackey, Osk, that's what you are, a – a minion! I hate you, you're a creep, an asshole.'

'Don't call me an asshole. I'm Assistant Regional Director and you know how hard I've worked for the post. The Armour account is volatile. If there's a blip, I have to be there. It's as simple as that. What Larry's saying is that they can't do without me. Can't you respect that?'

She crossed the room in fury and confronted him. 'Can't you see what a miserable life we lead? Can't you really? Ever since before we married you've put everything into that company. You've slaved and toadied and kowtowed. I've seen it. I've watched every inch of the way. I've seen the people you brought home. Friends, you call them. Enemies, I call them. People you had to be nice to, drunks, bullies, sadists, hardly able to hide their contempt for you while you proceeded to get smashed before I served dinner. Oh, yes, don't deny it. And all their fancy compliments. Freesias for me – God, how I hate freesias. All the time you've put in – '

'Oh, for Christ's sake, can it, will you?' He turned his back on her and struggled into a clean shirt. 'I have to earn a living. If I was pissed that was your fault. If only you could have been friendly to all – '

'Friendly! Friendly! Listen, you are about as friendly as that wall.' Winifred paused unexpectedly, as if past resentments choked her. She clutched her throat. 'You weren't friendly with these people. We got no friends. Larry you call your friend. He just rides you. As you ride me. You get what you can out of me, he gets what he can out of you. It's the filthy system. What about our one and only beloved son? Why do you think he ran off from home at the age of fourteen? Just because you – '

'Leave Alex out of this. It's a sore point.'

'Of course it's a sore point. Everything's a sore point with you because you've never lived. You've spent your whole life being an asshole. Now you're doing it again, lousing up our one chintzy week off in the sun. Asshole.'

He hit her hard with an upward blow of his right hand, feeling his knuckles strike the right side of her jaw. He was amazed how flimsy she was. She seemed to blow away. She tumbled across her bed, knocked over the lamp on the locker, fell against her open suitcase, tumbled to the floor in a shower of articles, and lay hidden by the swell of the duvet.

There was silence. North heard a radio playing in the next room.

'Winny?' he said.

Voice of Osiris: 'Our treacherous brother, Seth, held a lavish feast for me when you were away, O divine Isis. With him were seventy-two conspirators and a conniving queen of Ethiopia. We drank and sang while the dancing girls danced in their diaphanous robes and slaves scattered flowers about the room.'

Voice of Narrator: 'Osiris was then King of Egypt. At the moment of his birth, a heavenly voice announced, "The lord of all the world is born." Osiris was the first man ever to drink wine. Thus he brought a new thing into the world, and showed his peoples how to plant vines for grapes and cultivate them for the new beverage. He refined the rough customs of his peoples and taught them to honour the gods, and gave them laws. By the same token, he persuaded the ibis-headed god Thoth to invent all the arts, music, sculpture, astronomy and its attendant arithmetic, and, above all, the letters of the alphabet, in order that wisdom might be recorded to pass from one generation to another, in the way that the waters of the Nile were canalized to irrigate distant fields.'

Voice of Osiris: 'But my brother Seth was jealous of me, and coveted our sister, Isis, for his wife.'

Voice of Isis: 'While you were away in distant lands, O my Osiris, Seth caused to be made a chest of great value, richly decorated, its metals and jewels worked by the finest artisans. The interior of the chest fitted your measurements exactly.'

Voice of Osiris: 'At the feast, Seth announced, "He who can lie down in this chest and fit into it exactly, to him shall I give the chest as prize." No one could win the chest. Then my brother challenged me to try. I did so. The conspirators slammed down the lid upon me.'

Voice of Isis: 'O my king, how you were trapped! Hot lead was poured about the joins of the chest, so that you suffered and died. I knew you had gone from this world without the need of telling. Seth threw your coffin into the Nile, where it drifted to the sea and was lost. My sister, Nephthys, the wife of Seth, gave birth to a baby boy whom she deserted. The dogs saved him. Because he had the head of a jackal, I called him Anubis and looked after him. He grew fierce and loyal and joined me in the search for Osiris's body.'

Voice of Narrator: 'The faithful Isis's search was at last rewarded, and she found the chest, some say in the Nile Delta, some off the coast of Syria. Placing the body of her dead husband on the deck of a boat, she sailed home in triumph.'

Voice of Osiris: 'Such was her warmth and her love that she roused me back to life for a brief while. I returned to this world of circumstance, and was so stirred by the beauty of Isis when she revealed herself to me naked that I was able to take her unto me and impregnate her before again returning to the Underworld, there to reign as Lord of the Dead.'

Voice of Isis: 'So I could continue the line of the gods. With the aid of Anubis, I gave birth in the spring to Horus, who flew from my womb fully fledged as a bird. Later, Horus would avenge his father.'

Voice of Narrator: 'This early resurrection myth comes to us from an epoch before the birth of formal religions, from the long golden days of the Bronze Age, when humankind remained still on a par with nature and did not tyrannize it. For her powers as wife and mother, Isis was worshipped here on Philae, her island, sacred to her name, and here, on a night such as this, we may imagine that she still has power over living men and over their hearts.'

Oscar North peered above the slab of masonry which hid him. The crowds of spectators at the light show were now far away. He saw them merely as a black mass, insignificant below the ancient capitals and architraves, a herd who would be leaving shortly and dispersing to their Western-style hotels.

He would be staying.

Tomorrow, he must fly back to work, to the offices in Geneva. Tonight, he would stay here and exorcize – whatever had happened in the hotel room. When he tried to turn his thoughts in that direction, he met with a frightening blank. But the island of Philae would be a sanctuary in which he might be able to repossess himself before confronting the world of Mammon again. The moonlight might remake him. Or the solitude. Or Isis. Or whatever it was lingering out of reach which he had never tasted. It was OK for Osiris, but he, Oscar North, had been imprisoned in a chest all his damned life.

Trust her to complain. Winifred came from a reasonably stable background. Tyrone North, Oscar's father, had always drifted in and out of jobs. There had been no security for the family, little education for the boys, as they moved from one big city to another. When adolescent, Oscar had run away from home, to seize on what opportunities he could. Sure, he had stayed with the company – and had educated himself at night school. Had made something of his life. Of course there had to be sacrifices.

Too bad about Alex, their kid. Alex had taken after his old grandpa, he was a bad coin, and no use thinking about it. Why didn't Winny shut up about Alex? Well, fact was, he'd never hear from her on that subject again.

The *son et lumière* was over. Music came up, and white lights. From his hiding place, North could see the turbaned attendants directing the crowds away, tramping towards the point where the *feluccas* were moored against the harbour wall. That fool Jackson would be among them.

Mortician! What a profession!

The tramp of feet died. The electric lights were switched off.

Moonlight shone down on North. He looked up at the silver horn, thanking it for its light, sub-vocalizing the words. As a small boy, he had been afraid of the moon, afraid that monsters would jump out at him from the shadows it cast.

He rose slowly, and went to stand in the shelter of Trajan's Kiosk. It was probable that the island remained unoccupied during the night; there was no habitation as such; but he could not be sure. What he greatly wished was to be alone here, communing with Isis.

The sound of footsteps came to him, of sandals slapping against stone. North stood rigid. He watched as a shadowy figure approached, carrying a dim torch. It processed through the ancient ruins, passing on the other side of the wall by which North waited.

Slipping off his shoes, North followed the man at a distance. It was a robed Egyptian who smoked a cigarette as he walked along, no doubt checking to see that all was well after the day's intake of visitors.

The man came at last to the water's edge. A little way out on the flood, lights with trembling reflections marked where the *feluccas* had begun to carry their freight of passengers back to their hotels.

As North's gaze searched the boats, he saw a passenger stand up and wave. It was Jackson. North believed he had been sighted. A moment later he realized that the man from Jacksonville was merely making a dramatic gesture in the direction of the island. It was good to know he was out of the way.

Mindlessly, a woman passenger caught Jackson's gesture and stood up to imitate him. The idea caught on. In no time, everyone stood up sheeplike and was waving to Philae as it faded from their view into the stillness of the night.

Uninterested in the tourist antics, the Egyptian had walked down to the bottom of the shallow steps, where a second man waited. As they talked, the first man threw his cigarette into the Nile. Its spark was instantly quenched. After some while, as North watched and waited, the men climbed into a small boat, hoisted sail, and set their backs resolutely on Philae.

North was left in sole possession.

He stood erect. He raised his arms and stretched.

'Isis!' he called.

The word echoed over the stones, fading towards the ancient buildings, clear and ghostly under the moon. A sense of sanctity came to him like a piped melody.

Cautiously at first, he began to walk about.

The moonlight, raining down, embalmed him in light. It caught under his eyelids. The silence, the mildness of the night, the sense of ancient stones underfoot, the almost unheard meditative utterance of the river – these had the effect of altering his consciousness. He was no longer himself. Rather, he was sensitized to a number of impressions which moved through his mind like a breeze through a copse. All the gods and goddesses of ancient Egypt became possible, in their variety, their human failings, their mischief, their grace. He found himself in tune with their music.

There they were, elusive as a breeze, beauty, night, sunlight – life. Fresh areas of his brain opened to him, like the unsealing of a long-closed tomb. The conventional Western idea of the old Egyptians as being obsessed with death was wrong; they had been possessed by life, their lives lived under an eternal clear sky, and so in love with that existence they had invented an afterlife which echoed as nearly as possible the delights and freedoms of this, their ribbon of Nile-bound existence which flowed all too swiftly from birth in the far mountains to death in the low delta.

The West had imposed a negative image. It was a transference wish. It was in the West that life had perished, not here. Life in the West had turned itself into a series of non-biodegradable boxes. The hours in the office, the hours spent commuting, the hours spent in negative ways, gossiping in the golf-club bar, watching television. Departmentalized life, shut away in cities, in small apartments.

These notions arose wordlessly in his thoughts, amazing him.

Winny was right. He had never loved her. He had found no way to express his love.

Yet always on the fringes of his mind – somewhere – had been an awareness of the desert and the river of life flowing through it, of wild life rattling in the marshes and flocks of birds winging overhead. Almost within reach. Just not for him.

And that absurd plurality of gods – perhaps these vanished peoples did not believe in Life with a capital L. They merely had lives, not the abstraction of Life, and the multiplicity of gods reflected that human immediacy. A fecundity of beings! – How much more to be desired than a joyless monotheism!

All this poured into North's awareness.

Instead of bringing despair, it brought him joy. Joy that at last – even if late – even if too late – he had touched a secret reality and found it something to be embraced.

'Isis!' he called. 'Where are you? Come forth.'

He was on her island. This moment in moonlight contained the whole of his imaginative life. It expanded to embrace the world.

He was overwhelmed – or not overwhelmed because not himself.

The night was absolutely still except for a distant bark of a dog, the fluid note of the river accentuating a waiting quality.

Walking in a trance, North patrolled his new-found territory, treading from shade to brightness, brightness to shade. His island was a mere stepping stone between the two banks of the Nile, one hundred and fifty metres long by four hundred and fifty metres wide. He made a circuit through the echoing temples and arrived back at the landing stage.

As he stood looking down the flight of steps at the water, dark in the moonlight, a barque moved noiselessly to the mooring. It carried a black sail, which the sole occupant of the boat expertly hauled down. He stepped ashore almost immediately, ascending the steps without pause, towards North.

North shrank back, but was unable to avoid detection. The figure was beckoning him.

He took in the newcomer's oddity with an ill tremor which ran through his body. His eyes were small and black as black coral. He wore a white tunic, with bracelets at biceps and wrists. And he had the head of a jackal. His ears pointed alertly at North.

'I want you, Oscar,' said Anubis.

There was no sound in the bedroom after the last article had fallen out of Winifred's suitcase to the floor. From where Oscar North stood, his wife's body was out of sight behind the bed.

He remained where he was, dressed only in shirt and towel. After a moment, she began to make faint scrabbling noises.

His mouth had gone dry. Padding into the bathroom, he poured himself a glass of mineral water from their bottle and drank it. Then he put on a pair of slacks.

Winifred was sitting up groggily, patting her mouth, which was bleeding.

'Maybe that'll teach you not to call me names,' he said. 'Just keep your trap shut in future.'

She said nothing.

He felt an urge to continue the quarrel. 'I don't want to go back to Geneva any more than you. It's just something I have to do, and you know it.'

She said indistinctly, 'I'm not coming back with you, you bastard.'

He went over to her and looked threatening. 'Oh yes, you are. Let's not get into that hassle again. Remember we had that one when we left Washington. You didn't want to go to Europe.' He put on a silly voice. 'You didn't want to go to Geneva. You were afraid the terrorists might get us. You were afraid the Commies might get us. You were afraid – Christ knows what you weren't afraid of. Fact is, our standard of living has been enhanced since we left the States – not to mention my pay scale. There's a price to be paid for that, and we have to be realists and pay it. That's why we're grabbing a flight back tomorrow, and that's all about it. Now get up and get dressed. Move it.'

She did not reply. She drew up her bare knees and rested her head on them, so that her streak-dyed blonde hair fell forward.

'Come on, Winny,' he said, more gently. 'I didn't hurt you.'

'You did hurt me,' she said, without looking up. 'You're always hurting me. You don't care one bit about me, any more than you cared for Alex. You've even ceased to fake caring about me, and that hurts, too.'

She began to weep.

'Oh, for Jesus's sake,' he said.

He began to pace about the room, threatening her with all kinds of things if she did not pull herself together, threatening her with leaving her on her own – 'alone in Egypt', as he put it.

'You didn't want to go to Switzerland because it wasn't America. When I grabbed this chance of a winter holiday you didn't want to come to Egypt because it wasn't Switzerland. What the hell do you want?'

'I want to be consulted, damn you, I want to be a part of your life.'

'Oh, you're part of my life all right,' he said, sarcastically. 'You're my anchor – the part that drags me down.'

Winny looked up then, ghastly, muzzle blood-red, face pallid, like a tormented animal.

'Will you show pity for me, Osk? You think I like to be so miserable? I don't drag you down. You were down. You've never grown out of that slum boyhood of yours, that slum father. Try to see beyond your own eyes.'

'That comes well from you! Spoilt brat, Daddy's little girl! You're always phoning him, the old bastard. He poisons you against me, he tells you not to trust any of my buddies, he – '

'Oh yes, and when did you ever like any of my friends?'

It was true. He disliked her friends, she disliked his. He tucked his shirt into the top of his slacks and turned away.

'Get up and start packing, and just don't cross my tracks.'

Quietly, she said, 'I told you, I'm not coming back with you. I'm through.'

'You'll come if I have to drag you on that plane by your hair.' He swung back towards her, face ugly. She knelt up behind the bed, elbows on it to steady her aim, and pointed a gun at him, clutching it with both hands to control her trembling.

'You're not going to touch me again, you bastard. Stay away from me.'

He recognized the weapon at once. It was a small pearl-handled revolver her father had given her some years ago – father, big in electronics, fancying himself as having links with the Old West, buyer up of dude ranches and Remington paintings. Winny had insisted on taking the weapon to Europe, 'to protect herself', she had said when they first argued about it. He had no idea she had brought it with her to Egypt.

'Don't you dare point that thing at me, you little bitch!'

'I'll fire!' she yelled as he rushed at her. The revolver went off almost simultaneously.

He stopped dead, raising both hands to his chest.

'Oh, Jesus, Win,' he said. 'I loved you . . . '
It was amazing how people didn't understand.

When the flagstone was lifted, a black rectangle appeared in the expanse of moonlight. Steps led down into the stony night. The sound of rushing water came up from below, and a smell of mould.

Anubis had mysteriously acquired followers, human in shape, blank of face, white of eye. One of the followers came forward, carrying a large concave shield of polished bronze. He positioned the shield at such an angle that moonlight was reflected into the opening, to light a way down the steps.

The jackal-headed god motioned North to proceed. Reluctantly, North moved to the first step; his legs carried him almost automatically down into the depths. He heard Anubis stepping behind him, saw his shadow with its pointed ears extended on the steps in front of him.

The obscurity was lit by the ghostly reflected light. They came to a landing and a bend in the stone staircase. Another of Anubis's slaves was positioned there, with another shield. He reflected the moonlight round the corner, so that they could see to descend still further into the earth.

They reached a quayside where a wooden boat, moored by ropes secured to iron rings set in the stones, awaited them, rocking to and fro under the force of a strong current. Half-naked oarsmen saluted the dark god as he strode up the narrow gangplank. Following, North saw for the first time the tail of Anubis, curling from under his skirt. Sight of it scared him terribly.

Although another slave was positioned with a burnished shield at the quayside, there was little light to see by as they cast off – a mere nimbus of a suspicion of moonlight. North supposed that the blind black beads of Anubis's eyes saw everything.

They swung out into the stream. The oarsmen rowed furiously, the helmsman shouted the time, and they headed for the west bank.

Water rushed by. The ceiling above the river was painted with golden stars and lines of baboons.

After a long battle against the current, they arrived at a mooring and went ashore. North's eyes were now better accustomed to the gloom. He saw immense colonnades with imposing buildings behind them, incised with columns of hieroglyphic inscription. People moved here like shadows, silent on bare feet. No music sounded, no sun or moon shone; only a ghost of light reflected from shields manoeuvred by slaves paraded along the quayside, each man appearing much like his neighbour and chained to him by a bronze chain, like some grotesquely enlarged Christmas decoration.

Anubis padded forward without looking back. North was torn between fear of following and fear of losing his only guide in this forlorn necropolis. He had little choice but to follow the sturdy figure with its long brush-like tail.

Beyond the imposing façade of the colonnade were buildings of lesser majesty. These inferior buildings soon deteriorated into hovels of mud, their windowless eyes gaping into the street, squares of greater darkness within the darkness. They were thatched casually with branches of palm. North was reminded of the villages he had passed outside Aswan. They came to fields where bare-chested brown workers laboured in the corn. He could see that the corn was poor and thin, the heads withered. A chariot rumbled by, but the horse pulling it was a skeletal beast without eyes. Overhead were doves; their wings were paper-thin; he saw that they were in fact mere papyrus birds suspended from a painted ceiling and designed to simulate reality. When they reached a crossing of the ways, a farmer stood over a fire, but the flames were mere spirit flames, like St Elmo's fire. The farmer himself looked mummified, his features withered and afflicted.

The dirt under foot was dry and rose in clouds as they walked. Dust sprinkled down from nearby palm trees.

'Where are we?' he called in his apprehension.

Anubis made no response, plodding on with dull footfalls.

But an answer to his own question occurred to North. Gods were sustained by religious belief. Belief was their lifeblood. Without belief they withered like vampires without blood. He came from an America where the official god, the Christian god, was withering under many forms of disbelief, science and capitalism among them.

Even omnipotence had its day. The great thriving world of belief in ancient Egypt had drawn on centuries of worship from priests and congregations. But that belief – like all beliefs – had gone out like a slow withdrawing tide, defeated by Christianity among other things.

Only on the isle of Philae – perhaps only then by the light of the moon or the artificial lighting of *son et lumière* – could the old gods still find nourishment. Gradually, the great department store run by Ra, the sun god, and Osiris and Isis, was having to close. It was reduced to showing only second-rate goods in its window. Its lease had expired.

He regretted it.

He knew what had brought this situation about. History. Technological development. The swing of so-called 'progress', the most deceitful word in the dictionary. Change. Simple change. The old order changed, giving place to the neo. He was a neo in this old place.

They had arrived at a building like a barn, with an inelegant square door.

'Hall of Judgement,' announced Anubis.

The jackal-headed god looked back, reached out, and grasped Oscar North's hand. He felt the clasp of that dry feral hand as a psychic shock. Anubis dragged him forward into the building.

Isis was there.

He did not need telling who she was.

She was dainty, young, eternal, supreme. She at least – at her Philaean shrine – still had psychic energy and could generate light. The interior of the building glowed with her vitality.

She was dusky, slender, sleek, tall, imposing yet infinitely available. Her great eyes were rimmed with kohl. Hers was the Eye, the great eye of life. She wore on her head as if it were part of her skull a crown of the horns of Hathor, with a solar disc between the horns. From the disc, from her whole body, light flowed, and evil was trodden under her sandal. A golden cobra coiled from her forehead, denoting power.

A plain white sheath dress covered her body. A diadem of green malachite adorned her hair and wig, which were coated with beeswax and resin. Bracelets and anklets of similar stone decorated her limbs. She carried an *ankh*, symbol of life, in one hand.

Anubis raised his hands in the symbol of greeting. North sank to his knees. The goddess radiated powerful perfumes, *balanos*, hibiscus, and other flowers. And a goddess scent . . . at once rousing and quelling.

She did not even glance at North, instead exchanging a few words with Anubis, who then dragged at North, pulling him powerfully to his feet again.

The manner in which her glance slid so humiliatingly away from him brought Winny to North's mind. Towards the end, she too had not wished to look at him – until she had to take aim with the revolver.

And she could have been his personal Isis, his woman of radiance and power. Instead, he had slighted her by seeking for power elsewhere, in the air-conditioned offices of the multi-nationals. She had caught a chill from him. He had ruined Winny more thoroughly than he had dehumanized himself . . .

These belated insights vanished as soon as they dawned, washed out by the luminance pouring from Isis.

Having had eyes only for the gleaming figure of the goddess, North realized belatedly that the chamber they were in was crowded with figures coming and going on mysterious business. Many had human bodies with animal heads. Those with most authority – often directing slaves – were most animal. They wore striking tunics with the Egyptian kilt, and were bewigged, like Anubis, with blue matted hair which hung heavy on their shoulders.

Some of these formidable beings crowded about a gigantic table, one end of which was scrolled. A horrifying surgical operation was taking place on the table, supervised by a stunted being with the head of a crocodile and eyes of a goat. To see this creature engaged in some kind of co-ordinated activity – wielding a large scalpel, indeed – brought home to North how deeply he was caught up in myth. Here in this dungeon of life were the hieroglyphics of human concern: he was witnessing one corner of what had once been a self-sufficient world-view, embracing the desires and torments of a species emerging from the animal to seek explanations for the wonderful natural world in which it found itself, with its waters, vegetation, wild life, storms, and succession of days and nights ruled over by sun, moon and stars.

As Anubis dragged him nearer the operating table, he saw that a man in the garb of a warrior lay on the table. The warrior still wore a helmet of ferocious aspect, with basketwork armour on chest, abdomen and legs. In attendance on him was a formidable woman dressed in red, very broad, with powerful arms. She had the head of a lioness, which she turned languidly in North's direction; taking him in at a glance, she then swung her head away again. North recognized her from a guidebook he had looked at on the plane from Geneva. This was Sekhmet, goddess of war, renowned for violence and strength.

She sprawled on the operating table, and purred as the warrior was cut open from throat to pubis. The crocodile-head with his assistants opened the man up like a book. Rib-bones creaked. The warrior lay with open eyes, staring at nothing. Sekhmet purred more deeply.

Jars and glasses of medicaments were brought up, together with rolls of linen and live snakes to be milked of their venom. An embalming process was taking place, all performed with routine care by those involved.

North had little time to regard this fearsome sight, for he was pulled over to a great pair of scales, in which Anubis evinced intense interest. He left North standing in order better to inspect a weighing ceremony which had evidently been awaiting his arrival.

Small men with wolf- and dog-heads, encased in green linen tunics, were fussing over the scales. Towering above them was the god in charge – Thoth, the scribe, the ibis-headed one, his eyes blackly calculating above his long yellow beak. Thoth wore a thick yellow wig, crowned by a crescent moon, from which light poured.

Thoth and Anubis conferred. The former's voice was light and hesitant, while Anubis's was guttural, growling and fast.

As they talked, the amanuenses brought over to the scales the soul of the dead warrior, contained in a small red vase. It was to be placed on one of the bronze pans of the scales, while a feather from a wild goose was to be placed on the other.

This was the ceremony of judgement. Thus was the warrior to be judged, according to whether his life had been good or evil. The scales would decide whether he would be allowed to attain the bliss of the summer stars, or go to the infernal regions, the Abyss.

All this North understood. It was being acted out in front of him. And in the vast chamber other warriors waited, strangers now to the world above and due for embalming and judgement. Their faces were grey and bloody. They stood on their dead feet, submissive to the law of the underworld.

North was not submissive. He was a citizen of the United States. He had no wish to undergo these alarming processes.

Anubis had his back to him, examining the scales.

North turned to run.

He made a dash for the nearest door.

A sound like a cymbal-clash clanged in his head. He was aware of the red-clad Sekhmet leaping down from the operating table and bounding in his direction with all the energy of a lioness.

But it was Isis who struck. Isis, the beautiful and terrible, mother and destroyer.

It seemed she merely raised a hand in North's direction. He saw the movement from the back of his head. Her luminance increased.

He was grovelling on a grassy bank. She was standing on him, smiling, swinging a great sword.

He was trying to swim the Nile. She was bearing down upon him, riding a crocodile.

He was flying on white wings. She was astride an eagle, firing golden arrows at him.

He lay on his back on the stone floor, paralysed. Isis had already turned away. Two minions were scooping him up and carrying him towards the operating table, from which the body of the warrior, now swathed in linen bandages, was being removed. He could not think. A tiny moon burned in his skull. He could see it, could distinctly see hieroglyphics neatly turned in columns on his skull's inner walls, though their meaning was lost on him.

As he wandered under the neat columns, padding softly up innumerable stairs, he was also aware that the great dark form of

Anubis loomed above him, as if to tear him apart. It appeared to him no contradiction that he was at once climbing the many steps inside his skull, glancing into its apartments, and also lying on the operating table. A scalpel shone in the glare of Isis.

'First, something for you to drink,' said Anubis.

He thrust at North a misty beaker in which reposed an inch or two of a dark liquid. Unable to resist, North took it and swallowed. It was a bitter medicine, tasting of wood smoke and herbs.

He was wearing a lion mask and dancing. The papyrus reeds danced also. The music is shrill, with flutes and stringed instruments. The whole village dances about me. This year – plenty – feasting, fat cattle.

He was rushing in his chariot, desert hot about him. Ahead, the waterhole. The excitement of the chase. Dogs by my wheels, yipping as they sight the antelope. Arrows fly, the sun bleeds. But with nets we capture one antelope alive. I hold it, its eyes wild with terror. He embraced it, kissed its foamy mouth.

He was in the flood, fleeing here and there, a fish. The annual inundation. Sparkling shallows, then mud. Bigger fish ahead.

Then being a different fish, tame. I swim round in a vase on the high priest's table. Every day, sounds of worship. The great, the echoing temple. I can foretell eclipses.

Trudging the muddy field, my ox dragging the plough before me. Flies, the hollow curve of my stomach. He is the near-naked farmer. Up before dawn each day. The snake crouching in the ashes of the stove.

It's me, Hathor, the she-ox, named after the goddess so that I may be strong and work all day. Soon, soon, food and shade and the stench of the household. My shoulders creak. Do I command the sun? It follows where I go.

He longs for marshes again. He is the tame goose. Here comes my owner to feed me, except – as he sticks his neck from the basket, he sees the knife in the owner's hand, bright as a sliver of evening sun.

He fights and struggles under his hallucinations. For a moment he is the husband of Isis, bearing her down on a golden shawl. Flashing lips, the secret parts of a goddess, blinding to mortals. Tastes of syrup, overwhelming embraces, a wigwam of hair. Joy, joy, and upward slide, source of merriment and all lived life. A million births born from their union. Genius, triumph, the stars in a great sweet hurricane blowing. The glitter of the dagger.

And all the time the little dark people were hurrying up and down the stairs of his brain, unloading everything, bearing it away. The whole castle denuded, defenceless, empty. The closure of windows, the excluding of light.

Someone with a falcon head was helping him up from the table, another warrior was taking his place. His mind still swam from the dose of anaesthetic Anubis had administered. He was hollow, frail.

It was impossible to take notice of what was happening.

Now it seemed as if he was again in a boat. It had a high curved prow like the beak of a bird, and made good speed over the water. The water was perhaps the Nile, or perhaps that other dark river which flows somewhere far below the Nile.

Anubis told him that his soul had failed the test. He was not destined for the summer stars. That was the judgement.

'What then?' North asked.

'You go to the Abyss.'

'Is the Abyss very bad? Tell me.'

Anubis nodded his jackal head.

'It is where the damned go.'

He was still confused by the potion he had been made to drink. It seemed he could hear the creak of oars, rrrurrrk, rrrurrrk, rrrurrrk, or perhaps it was his backbone as he strove to gain a sitting position.

'My soul was too heavy with sin?' he asked.

The jackal-headed god made no response, perhaps because none was needed, perhaps because they were pulling rapidly into a quayside.

His sense of sound was distorted. What he thought at first was the noise of a waterfall proved to be the music of a harp, played by a blind harpist sitting with her back to the ship's mast. She continued to play without interruption as they drew in against the quay.

'Out you get,' said Anubis. 'And take these with you.'

North was looking about him in bewilderment. The light was peculiar, transfixing buildings as if they were semi-transparent; but it seemed to him, unless he imagined it, that he was back at the Sheraton hotel. It loomed above them. He could see the corner balcony of the room he shared with Winny.

He took the objects Anubis gave him almost absent-mindedly.

'Ra's sunboat will soon achieve the eastern sky,' said the god. Perhaps it was a form of farewell, though the fur-covered face in no way changed its solemn expression. He motioned to his rowers and the boat began to pull back into the river.

Still numb, Oscar North looked down at the objects he had been given.

A small red glass vase, in which his soul fluttered.

A pottery coffer, capped by a lid in the form of a cat's head, heavy to hold because it contained his preserved intestines, which he would certainly need in the Abyss.

And a return ticket to Geneva.

Already, the boat was entering the mists which concealed the mid-channel. In the stern, a dark figure with a jackal-head was guiding the boat by means of the large steering oar. He was not of the world of men and women, although his traffic was with them.

His barque in its stealthy retreat cast no reflection on the flood, and no shadow into the depths below its keel.

And the voice of the harpist came faintly to North where he stood:

'Even though you are in the realm of ghosts
Imprisoned by what you most believe
Yet you will see the sun to shine in the sky
And the moon to remind you of the shining truth . . . '

ALPHABET OF AMELIORATING HOPE

Angelic voices speak of a utopia which will soon come about once the secret research in Wisden, Ohio, is completed.

Basically, existence of a 'circumstance-chain' in human relationships will be established, proving causality between mental activity and the external physical world.

'**C**ircumstance-chains' are operative in all human lives; for instance, the child deprived of love develops into a being who finds difficulty in establishing loving relationships in adulthood.

Directly the research is complete, we shall view the world anew.

Example: terms like 'loser' or 'the guy who has all the luck' will be seen as labels for those who are bound, favourably or otherwise, by circumstance-chains.

For clarity, this revolutionary new aspect of the human condition will be termed '*transpsychic reality*'; a new sanity will prevail on earth.

Going mad will no longer be necessary.
Horror will vanish, fear will never strike.
Intellect will never more be scorned.
Joy will visit rich and poor alike.
Keeping faith in love and life will be an easier thing.
Love will not be just a theme that people sing.

Madge Winterbourne was the hero in Wisden, Ohio; she had originated the anti-catastrophe hypothesis.

No one who met her doubted she was the modern equivalent of a seer or saint.

Or an Einstein of the female sex.

Plans were hatched to release details of transpsychic reality to the whole world on the same day, the first of a new century.

Qualitative tests on volunteers in Wisden suggest that once people understand the pattern of their lives, they can be taught to take command of them.

Reality will then change; those who are malicious will see the root causes of the misery provoking their malice, and be able to expunge it.

Some criminals and power-seekers may prove more difficult to readjust, may indeed form a core of rebellion against the new utopia.

Transpsychic reality will see them gradually phased out.

Utopia, once on the move, will prove as irresistible as a glacier.

Very soon, a golden age – long dreamed of in the hearts and minds of men and women – will be established, which the animal kingdom will share with humans.

Wonder will grow like the cedar.
Xenophobia will die without voice.
You too will prevail, dear reader.
Zygotes themselves will rejoice.

BOSTON PUBLIC LIBRARY
3 9999 02375 160 3